Readers love
Rowan
McAllister's

Elemental Harmony:
Book One

Air and Earth

"I was really blown away by the amount of detail that was put into this story, this world, and these characters McAllister has created."

—MM Good Book Reviews

"I really liked this book and recommend it."

—Love Bytes

"I was really intrigued by the world-building and enjoyed the characters and their romance very much and am looking forward to the next book eagerly!"

—The Kimi-chan Experience

http://www.dreamspinnerpress.com

By ROWAN MCALLISTER

Cherries on Top
Cuddling (Dreamspinner Anthology)
A Devil's Own Luck • Never a Road Without a Turning
Feels Like Home
Grand Adventures (Dreamspinner Anthology)
Green the Whole Year 'Round
Hot Mess
Lost in the Outcome
My Only Sunshine
A Promise of Tomorrow
Riding Double (Dreamspinner Anthology)

ELEMENTAL HARMONY
Air and Earth
Water and Fire

Published by DREAMSPINNER PRESS
http://www.dreamspinnerpress.com

WATER AND FIRE

Rowan McAllister

Published by

DREAMSPINNER PRESS

5032 Capital Circle SW, Suite 2, PMB# 279, Tallahassee, FL 32305-7886 USA
http://www.dreamspinnerpress.com/

Water and Fire
© 2015 Rowan McAllister.

Cover Art
© 2015 Maria Fanning.
Cover content is for illustrative purposes only and any person depicted on the cover is a model.

ISBN: 978-1-63476-038-6
Digital ISBN: 978-1-63476-039-3
Library of Congress Control Number: 2014922085
First Edition March 2015

Printed in the United States of America
(∞)
This paper meets the requirements of
ANSI/NISO Z39.48-1992 (Permanence of Paper).

To Wildwood Grove, lifelong friends, and fond memories.

PROLOGUE

"I FOUND him."

The fury that had been building in him for weeks over Bob's incompetence and excuses vanished at those few sweet words, and he released his death grip on the phone even as his heart sped in anticipation.

"You're certain?"

"Yes. It's him," Bob whispered excitedly. "I couldn't get too close, in case he recognized me, but I didn't have to. Even without the Jeep, I'd know that evil anywhere. It's him! I did it, Father. I found him!"

Forcing his voice to remain steady and calm, he leaned forward in his leather office chair and grabbed a pen and notepad from his desk. "Where are you?"

"Nantucket. That's why it took so long. But I found him now, Father. I *found* him… and he's not gonna get away again. I followed him to where he's staying. I can get him. I can show you I'm worthy. I am a true soldier of God, no matter my mistakes. I'm ready to be welcomed back into the fold. God led me to him. He must have."

"Enough," he barked, and Bob's pointless rambling stopped. He glanced through his half-open office door, but thankfully Mrs. Ford, the church secretary, wasn't at her desk. Throttling down his temper and his impatience, he lowered his voice. "Listen to me. You are to do nothing until I get there. Do you understand?"

"But, Father, I can do it this time. I swear! I know I messed up before. But this one's alone now. He won't catch me by surprise. You don't have to come all the way out here. I can prove I'm worthy of your forgiveness, of God's forgiveness. Please!"

"Enough, Bob," he said, more kindly this time, despite his almost overwhelming urge to reach through the phone and squeeze the man's flabby neck until his fat face turned a satisfying shade of blue.

Bob was flawed and fragile. Those traits that made him a dutiful and obedient member of the flock also made him unstable and unpredictable when Bob was outside his control. The situation called for the carrot now, not the stick.

"Your perseverance at this task has proven your remorse. Whether you are truly deserving of God's forgiveness and the forgiveness of the rest of the flock will become apparent soon enough. But you *must* do as you're told and have faith that I know what is best. You will watch. That is all, until I can free myself from my obligations here and join you. Do nothing else. Do you understand?"

He heard a shaky indrawn breath on the other end of the line, then Bob's pathetic mewl.

"Yes, Father."

"Good. Find someplace to stay. Make sure to stay out of sight as much as possible. The police are still looking for you. Remember that. You haven't told anyone else about this as we agreed?"

"No, Father."

"Good, Bob. Very good. Keep it that way. There is no need to upset the rest of the flock before we have to. We need to protect them from this evil, to keep them safe."

"Yes, Father."

Satisfied Bob would be a good little sheep for the time it took to get his affairs in order, he leaned back in his chair and smiled. "I will let you know when to expect me. Until then, get some rest, get yourself cleaned up, and try to stay calm. We don't need you drawing attention to yourself. I'll be there soon."

CHAPTER 1

AIDEN TUCKED his hands inside the sleeves of his oversized hoodie and hugged himself as another burst of laughter was carried to him on the wind coming off the ocean. The breeze was cool, signaling the end of summer, but it wasn't the chill that made him shiver and seek the comfort of his own embrace. Less than thirty yards away from the little dune he huddled behind, a beach party raged. Loud music, plenty of beer, a bonfire, and thirty or so hot young men and women laughing, dancing, talking, and fooling around—all the things normal people his age did on a Friday night—and Aiden couldn't be a part of it.

He'd been okay when he'd spotted the first of the group carrying coolers and blankets down the beach. He'd been in the kitchen listlessly pondering the pile of delivery menus in anticipation of another night alone on the couch, streaming something on his parents' monstrous TV, when movement up the beach had caught his attention. The summer crowds had thinned so he hadn't seen much activity after dark lately. He'd been strong for the last month and a half. He'd stayed inside, done his penance, and kept a safe distance while thousands enjoyed the sun and sand around him. He'd thought he'd already weathered the worst of it, but he was pretty confident he could handle one more night of fending off the pangs of loneliness and envy while people made merry nearby. He was actually feeling pretty proud of himself, right up until sunset when they lit the bonfire.

Another burst of laughter carried over the dune, and he closed his eyes and huddled down against the softness of the sand as the thunder of waves on the shore competed with the music. He should never have allowed himself that first step out his back door. He should have gone back inside and cranked up the stereo or the TV—anything to block out the sounds from the party—but for the last hour, his body seemed to have a mind of its own. Now here he was a pile of misery in the sand.

In a way, this was penance too. What could hurt worse than being so close to a party and not joining in? He could rationalize it that way. This was simply more of the punishment he'd earned. But the truth was he didn't have it in him to leave now that he was there. So he lurked in the shadows like some campy villain in a melodrama, fighting an internal war, until a volleyball flew over the side of the dune, narrowly missing his head.

"You dumbass. What the hell was that? Shit. Where'd it go? You know I'm making you go get it next time."

The voice came closer with each slightly slurred word, and a few seconds later a shadow appeared above him, backlit by the bonfire.

"Oh, hey man. Sorry about that. Can you toss me the ball?"

Aiden reached behind him, grabbed it, and stood up. He lobbed it back to the guy hoping that would be the end of it—and hoping it wouldn't. But instead of leaving, the guy propped the ball on his hip and said, "How come you're not over with everyone else?"

Aiden shrugged tense shoulders and looked away. "Not my party."

"Well it *is* my party, and I say everyone's invited," the guy replied with a chuckle.

When his buddies started yelling for him, the guy turned to glance over his shoulder, and in the light from the bonfire, Aiden got a good look at a handsome profile, the gleam of perfect white teeth, and the outline of a truly beautiful set of pecs beneath a tight, faded T-shirt. Blood rushed south, and Aiden's resolve to maintain his distance began to crumble.

God, he was so horny. A month and a half was a lifetime in abstinence years.

He hunched his shoulders and looked anywhere but at the guy. He was not on the island to party. He was not there to have a good time… or to pick up hot, sun-bleached dirty blonds with gorgeous tanned legs and bright, welcoming, slightly inebriated smiles.

"Come on."

Aiden wished he could say he held out longer than he actually did, but his resolve shattered like safety glass after a single hit from a car hammer.

One night couldn't hurt.

He didn't want to be rude.

He could go down, maybe have a beer, and then go back to his fortress of solitude and suffering. Not even Adam would expect him to spend his *entire* life alone, no matter what he'd done. He had enough control to manage a party without destroying anything.

"Come on," the guy cajoled. "Come say hi to everyone. I don't think I've seen you before. You live around here?"

The guy's free arm, the one not holding the volleyball, lifted in welcome, and Aiden couldn't take it anymore. If he didn't have some human contact, he was going to go completely over the edge.

"Yeah. My folks' place is just up there," Aiden replied, pointing behind him at his parents' rather unremarkable little Cape Cod as he climbed the dune.

The guy's smile widened. He draped an arm around Aiden's shoulder, leaning a little clumsily on him as he led him back toward the party. "Oh, awesome. That place's been empty a long time. It's why we take the parties down here. My folks own a place farther up the beach, but down here's always been more private… if you know what I mean. I'm Con, by the way."

The guy's scent, a combination of clean sweat, woodsmoke, beer, and expensive cologne, filled Aiden's nostrils, making it even harder for Aiden to remember why he wasn't supposed to be doing this. "Con?" he asked a little dazedly.

"Conrad Theodore Billings Jr.," one of Con's friends supplied, affecting a horrible British accent and accentuating the title with a cocked eyebrow, pursed lips, and a royal wave. The friend's smile flashed brilliant white against the dark brown of his skin as Con chucked the volleyball at him, but Aiden hardly saw the gleaming pearly whites. His eyes were riveted on the friend's beautifully muscled bare torso as the firelight played across it.

"Just Con," Con said, and Aiden swallowed and dragged his eyes away from one bit of eye candy to land on another.

"I'm Aiden."

To give his hands something to do other than make the "gimme" gesture, he pulled the hood back on his sweatshirt and unzipped it. Despite the fact that this was not what he was on the island for, he couldn't help the small burst of pleasure he felt at the spark of interest that ignited in Con's eyes. As the warmth of it bloomed in his gut, he couldn't stop himself from searching the crowd for more approving glances from men and women alike, and he wasn't disappointed. While he accepted the beer he was offered and smiled his thanks, he preened under the attention, reveling in that rush of energy. It was just like being on stage back at school. If his entire life hadn't fallen apart a month and a half ago, he would have been well into the fall semester by now.

Con eventually went back to kicking and tossing around the volleyball with his buddies, leaving Aiden to chat up a couple of girls who immediately swooped in to take his place, but out of the corner of his eye, he caught Con watching him from time to time. With every glance, every bit of attention, every dance and flicker of the bonfire nearby, Aiden felt stronger, brighter, more like himself.

He'd missed this so much. Not only had he stayed away from people as much as he could, he hadn't even lit a candle or even a match since he'd been on the island. Every day, standing in front of his bathroom mirror, he'd watched his complexion turn grayer and more sallow as the little tan he'd managed over the summer faded and any and all joy was denied him. Every day his cheeks became hollowed, and his eyes dulled to a flat murky green. But now, after only a few precious minutes of attention and being so close to that oh-so-beautiful bonfire, he was back. He was the life of the party. He was admired. He was desired. He didn't even need the beer to get drunk.

As the bonfire leapt higher and danced beside him, groups of two or three at a time came and introduced themselves, and then stayed to listen to him tell stories. He could only remember a few of their names, but it didn't matter. He wasn't looking to make friends. He just needed a break. His conscience prickled weakly once or twice, but he silenced it with assurances he'd go back to his cave as soon as the party was over.

Just let me have this one night, and I'll be good. I promise.

By the time Con and his buddies came back to put more wood on the fire, Aiden had quite an audience, both men and women, hanging on his every word. So when a pretty little blonde, bursting out of a bikini top and tight white cutoffs despite the chilly breeze, wrapped her tanned arms around Con's neck and kissed him, Aiden didn't even bat an eyelash. Con was either in the closet or played for both teams. Either way Aiden didn't care. He was surrounded by plenty of other hot guys... and he wasn't supposed to be looking anyway, no matter how horny he was.

After the girl pulled away, Con looked over and caught Aiden watching. Aiden didn't bother to pretend he wasn't, and Con grimaced. He opened his mouth to say something, but the music suddenly cut off, and everyone turned to stare at a man in his bathrobe, standing just inside the ring of light from the bonfire.

"Party's over people," the man yelled loud enough to be heard over the crashing waves and the few complaints and conversations that hadn't stopped. "You don't have to go home, but you can't stay here."

The guy was older than the rest of the crowd, maybe in his late thirties, his thick black hair silvered at his temples. He was average in height and build, but his features had an exotic cast Aiden couldn't quite place... and couldn't tear his eyes away from. While everyone else started to mill about and grumble, Aiden stayed frozen where he was, his audience forgotten. He wasn't sure how long he would have stayed that way if Con hadn't stepped between them, blocking Aiden's line of sight.

"Who the hell are you to tell us we have to go?" Con demanded.

Irritated with Con, Aiden stepped to the side to keep the newcomer in view.

"I'm the one who owns this property," the man replied as he folded his arms across his chest. "I've been patient. I've let you play around down here all summer, and I haven't complained. But enough's enough. Summer's over, it's one o'clock in the morning, and I'm trying to sleep. Find somewhere else to—Hey. Hey! Watch out! You're going to burn yourself."

When the man rushed forward, Aiden's attention shifted from where they had fixated on the man's lips to his eyes. They were wide with alarm and staring right at him. Con turned and yanked Aiden sideways, away from the bonfire.

"Jesus, man. Are you okay?" Con asked.

The sleeve Con wasn't gripping was singed, as was that side of Aiden's shorts, and his flip-flop had melted along the edge. Aiden flushed hotly as he shrugged off Con's hand. He wasn't burned. He couldn't be. But everyone was looking at him now, and not in the happy ego-stroking way they had been earlier.

"I'm fine," he stammered as he locked gazes with the bluest eyes he'd ever seen.

For a breathless moment, Aiden could do nothing but stare back at the newcomer, but then a log popped loudly, scattering cinders across the sand, and the man's attention shifted to something in the fire.

"What the hell?"

The man gaped at whatever it was before casting about until his gaze landed on the pile of wood sitting next to the bonfire. He pointed at the pile and turned furious eyes back to Con. "How dare you! You had no right. That was private property!"

Aiden squinted at the pile of wood. The broken pieces were all fairly regular, obviously boards at one time, though faded and cracked. If he looked closely, he could see specks of white paint clinging to a few of them, but they didn't look like they belonged to anything precious.

"You had no right," the man repeated, choking on the last word, and Aiden's heart squeezed. He heard more than rage. He heard pain, and as the waves crashed loudly into the silence that followed, Aiden's own pain surfaced, and suddenly his joy from the party seemed shallow and pointless.

After a few seconds where everyone stood frozen, the man blew out a breath, squared his shoulders, and lifted his chin. "I want you gone, all of you. If you don't leave, I'm calling the cops. Stay off my property. Don't ever come back."

With that, he spun and charged back up the beach toward a tiny Cape Cod, the one right next door to Aiden's.

"What an asshole," Con grumbled, and several people agreed as they began collecting their belongings. "Aiden, are you okay? You were really close to that fire. Are you sure you didn't get burned?"

Aiden absently waved off Con's concern, still caught up in the man with the blue, blue eyes. He turned back to the bonfire to find what it was that had caught the man's attention, and buried in the center of the fire, burning along with the driftwood, beer cartons, and other trash people had tossed in, was a board similar to those in the pile, only this one had two sets of initials carved inside a heart.

Without a moment's hesitation, Aiden reached into the fire and pulled it out.

"Shit! What're you doing? Are you crazy?" Con yelled, clutching at his arm again.

Aiden dropped the wood and kicked damp sand over it to smother it. Embarrassed that he'd been stupid enough to do that in front of people, he sheepishly held up his undamaged hand and showed it to Con. "No harm done. I was quick. I didn't hold it long enough to burn me."

Con stared at Aiden's hand in disbelief. He even grabbed it and checked both sides. "Jesus, man. You scared me. Had me wondering how many beers you'd had." He laughed uncomfortably as he slowly let go of Aiden's hand.

Realizing he still held his half-finished beer, Aiden upended it on the board for good measure. Then he threw a completely cocky—and completely false—smile at Con. "It's a party trick. It takes more than a couple of beers to get me drunk. I'm not that cheap a date."

The little blonde chick chose that moment to return and wrap an arm around Con's waist. "What're we gonna do now, baby?"

Con started guiltily and his smile faltered, but he squeezed her back as he said, "Looks like this one's a bust. My folks'll flip if I get another fine. It's not like they can't afford it or anything, but whatever."

Con lifted his head and raised his voice. "Come on everybody. Let's give the asshole his beach back."

Everyone who hadn't already left started grabbing their stuff and stumbling up the beach while Aiden hung back by the fire. His reprieve from solitude had been short-lived, but he couldn't dredge up much regret. His mind was too preoccupied with Mr. Blue Eyes.

"Hey man," Con said, bursting in on his reverie. The little blonde was noticeably absent. "Sorry about this. Maybe we can try another time."

"Who was that guy?"

"Beats the shit out of me. Never seen him before. My family only comes down for the summer, and I swear I always thought *both* these places were empty."

Aiden nodded absently before glancing down at the bit of blackened wood at his feet. He didn't know why he cared. The whole mess was none of his business, but that pain stuck with him.

"Hey man, I gotta go."

When Aiden glanced up, Con gave him an apologetic smile and gestured toward the blonde, who was impatiently waving at him.

"No problem. Thanks for the invite."

Con stepped closer and cleared his throat. "Well, I know you're down here now, so I'll hit you up sometime maybe. Here, give me your phone."

Aiden handed it over, and Con typed on it for a bit before handing it back. A few seconds later, a ringtone came from Con's pocket.

"I got your number now. I'll text you."

Aiden didn't really expect him to, but he didn't care either way.

"Sure. Don't worry about the fire. I'll put it out."

Con clapped him awkwardly on the shoulder. "Thanks, man."

As Con went to join his girlfriend, Aiden chuckled, momentarily distracted.

Definitely still in the closet, whether he bats for both teams or not.

After they disappeared up the beach with the rest of the partiers, Aiden reached down and picked up the board at his feet. The wood was still warm to the touch as he traced the initials with his finger.

MM + FP

He frowned and glanced up toward his neighbor's house. The lights were still on through the french doors leading to the back deck. Obviously the man hadn't gone back to bed, no matter what he'd yelled earlier.

Aiden absently reached out toward the fire again to knock the last of the wood down and absorb what heat he could to help put it out, when the hairs on the back of his neck rose, and he jerked his hand back. Nervously he searched the darkened beach around him, but he didn't see anyone. He was never this stupid and careless. What was the matter with him? Was he trying to scream "freak show here" to the whole of Nantucket?

Shaking his head, Aiden set the board safely to the side and dug through the pile of lumber until he found a piece of driftwood. With a pang of regret, he knocked the fire down, spread out the coals, and kicked sand over it until it was reasonably covered.

As the last flickering flames disappeared, he shivered in the darkness. That feeling of being watched was still there, and the thought of going home to his empty house when his emotions were this keyed up was almost unbearable. He had to do something, so he picked up the carved board again and headed over the dunes toward his mysterious neighbor's back door.

After opening the gate and letting himself into the man's backyard, he paused at the base of the steps leading to the deck. Maybe he should've let it go. None of this was his fault or his business. But the memory of the pain in those beautiful blue eyes haunted him. If the guy knew this one small piece wasn't completely destroyed, it might make him feel a little better, right? That was a good thing to do, the *right* thing to do. He could use all the good karma points he could get right about now, and a smile from those lips wouldn't be a bad image to fall asleep to, either.

CHAPTER 2

"SON OF a bitch!"

Tears sprang to his eyes, and Murphy grabbed his foot and hopped to the couch. He dropped onto the cushions and squeezed his big toe as he hissed in pain. It served him right, banging around his house like a lunatic because some punk kids were having a party on his beach. He had no idea what had possessed him to go charging down there and order them off his land when he could've called the sheriff's office and let the cops deal with it. If he had, he wouldn't have known about the bench being destroyed until the morning, and he might have been safe, warm, and comfortable in his bed right now instead of clutching his throbbing toe.

You hated that bench, anyway. Felix's voice sounded in his head.

"I didn't hate it," Murphy grumbled aloud. "We learned the handyman gene skipped both of us when we built that thing. It was a good memory, even if the bench was a disaster."

When some of the white-hot pain had receded, Murphy opened his palm to examine his toe in the light from the small lamp next the couch. It looked a little red and swollen, but he hadn't stubbed it hard enough to make it bleed. He dropped his head back on the cushions and took a deep, cleansing breath as he flexed it. The bench was gone now, broken up for firewood, no use flipping out about it and doing himself any more bodily injury stomping around his house like a crazy person.

In the quiet of his living room, Murphy strained his ears, but the only noise that reached him now was the crashing of the surf, the sound as soothing as always. The music hadn't started back up again. If the kids were still down there, at least they were being quiet.

As his anger dissipated, Murphy was left with the same hollow ache in his chest he always had when memories of Felix were forced so vividly to the surface. He'd jogged past that bench practically every morning for years. He barely even noticed it anymore. But he would notice its absence now.

One more absence he'd have to get used to.

Tonight was going to be another sleepless night. He could tell already, so instead of wasting time tossing and turning in his empty bed, he might as well get some work done. He ended up sleeping on the couch in his home office half the time anyway. To the point where he sometimes wondered why he bothered to keep their old king-sized bed at all.

He flexed his sore toe a few more times as the last of the pain faded to a dull ache, and then climbed to his feet. Taking a moment to smile sadly at the picture of him and Felix on the mantel, he let out a long sigh and started for his kitchen. If he was going to stay up, he needed some tea.

He'd just set the kettle on the stove when someone knocked on the french doors leading to his deck. His earlier temper flared to life with surprising speed, letting him know he wasn't as over the incident as he'd tried to convince himself, and he stomped to the door and flung it open.

Standing in the dim light cast by the small lamp next to his couch was the pretty redhead he'd seen nearly set himself on fire on the beach.

Wonderful, a drunken, spoiled frat boy to cap off my night.

"What do you want?"

He practically shouted the words, and the young man flinched back for only a brief second before his pretty jaw tightened and his pointed chin lifted stubbornly.

But instead of speaking right away, the kid took a breath, and his jaw muscle visibly relaxed as he let it out again.

"I just came to give you this," he said quietly after another breath.

The kid held out a charred piece of wood, and it took Murphy a second to see the carved initials. Over and above the stab of grief, Murphy's anger surged anew as the smell of beer and smoke wafted over him, and he scowled at the kid.

"What the hell am I supposed to do with that?"

"I thought—"

"What?" Murphy cut him off. He so wasn't in the mood. "You thought that would make it all right? You destroyed my property, something *personal*. You didn't give a rat's ass when you were tearing the thing apart. And now you bring me *this*, this half-burned stick. And what? You expect me to be grateful?"

Even if Murphy had intended to say more, he wouldn't have been able to. A sudden blast of anger rolled over him, nearly knocking him off his feet with its intensity. It sucked the oxygen from his lungs even as he was hit with a gust of hot air out of nowhere.

"Fuck you!" the kid shouted. "I didn't have anything to do with that. I didn't break your goddamned bench! It wasn't even my party!"

The kid threw the board on the deck and lifted blazing green eyes to Murphy's.

"I was just trying to help. But if you don't want it, then screw you!"

Murphy was struck dumb. All he could do was watch as the redhead spun on his heel and stomped down the steps, past the neatly potted plants Felix had insisted on buying, and then slammed the gate in the white picket fence closed behind him. Instead of heading out to the beach or around to the street, the kid cut across the dunes, and after a few more seconds passed, Murphy heard a door slam and saw a light come on in the house next door. He'd noticed the lights on in that house over the past month or so, for the first time in years, but he'd never actually seen or met his neighbor.

Apparently now he had.

The intensity of the emotion surge that had pummeled his senses faded as soon as the kid put some distance between them, and Murphy slumped against the doorframe and sucked in a breath.

What the hell was that?

A chilly gust off the ocean dispelled the last of the lingering heat, and Murphy shivered and wrapped his robe a little tighter. Before going back inside, he bent and picked up the piece of charred wood. It was still warm, and despite the soot and faint tang of beer, he clutched it to his chest as he closed the door.

The whistle on the kettle eventually startled him out of his daze, and he set the board on the breakfast bar before moving to shut off the burner.

After washing his hands, he pulled out a tea bag and poured the hot water on autopilot. When his tea was ready, he took it to the couch in front of the fireplace, along with the board, and set both on the coffee table.

His own emotions were all over the place. He wouldn't be able to think, let alone put any kind of label on what he'd just experienced, if he didn't calm down. Drawing his legs up in a half-lotus pose, he closed his eyes and concentrated on centering himself. With deep even breaths, he sought and found the core of him, visualizing the calm pool inside that reflected the world but remained undisturbed by it. His shield was the mirror surface of that pool. It was supposed to protect him.

When he was calm enough, he searched that mirror with his inner eye, looking for cracks or ripples, but he found none. Puzzled, he swam back to the surface of his consciousness and expelled a long breath. He dragged a hand down his face, and then picked up his mug of tea out of habit but stopped with it hovering in front of his mouth as he frowned.

He couldn't understand it. His shields were fine. He'd stomped his way into a party full of drunk children and hadn't felt a single one of those spoiled rotten little rich kids' emotions.

That's not exactly true. Is it, Murph?

Murphy couldn't remember exactly when his conscience had taken on Felix's voice, but it comforted him even as it pointed out things he didn't necessarily want to admit.

He *had* felt the redhead at the party. Not as strongly, but he'd felt him. Curiosity and surprise had brushed against his consciousness even as Murphy had yelled at the little shits on his beach. That was why he'd noticed how close the redhead had been to the fire. He'd managed to ignore the sensation then, but there was no way he could've ignored the bullhorn the kid had used to broadcast his feelings on Murphy's deck, and like the buzzing of a fly, now that he'd noticed it, he could still feel the guy, faint but there, even with the considerable distance between them.

If he strained, the buzzing at the edge of his consciousness resolved itself into hurt and anger, and even as Murphy puzzled over it and marveled at its intensity, his guilt began to nag at him. He'd been unfair. The guy had been telling the truth. He hadn't had anything to do with what happened to the bench. Murphy would have known if he was lying. And even with all that anger and outrage blaring at him from his deck, Murphy had felt the hurt. He just hadn't been willing to look past his own pain and anger. The young man had been trying to do the right thing. He'd saved what he could, probably risking getting burned in the process, and brought it to Murphy out of kindness… and Murphy had shit all over him.

He groaned, set his cup back down, and dragged both hands across his face this time. When had he become the cranky old hermit at the end of the road? He wasn't that guy.

Old grief, new guilt, and some residual anger rasped and crackled inside him, poking him with sharp pointy edges. His emotions hadn't been stirred up like this in such a long time. For the last several years, dull melancholy had been his most constant companion.

For a second he was tempted to call Howard, his sponsor, for a sympathetic ear, but it was after one in the morning, and Murphy was a big boy. He'd been in AA for over seven years now. He didn't need to call Howard in the middle of the night because he was a little upset. He wasn't going to fall off the wagon. For one thing, there wasn't a drop of booze in the house. For another, he wasn't actually craving a drink any more than usual. The beer smell on the board made him nauseated more than anything. He just felt like shit, and that was hardly an excuse to wake Howard up.

Instead, he turned on the TV for some distraction, sipped his tea, and made a promise to go next door and apologize like a grownup at a decent hour tomorrow. That should hopefully take care of some of the guilt, and if the rest of the turmoil didn't settle after that, then he might call Howard for a chat.

HE WOKE on the couch as the sun broke above the ocean. He was tired and he had a crick in his neck, but he wouldn't let that stop him from his morning run any more today than after every other night he hadn't slept. In fact a run would probably do him more good than anything else.

Dragging through his morning ritual, he pulled on his jogging shorts, his sneakers, and a T-shirt and stepped out into the moist chill air. As goose bumps peppered his skin, he closed his eyes and soaked in the sound of the waves, allowing them to soothe and energize him. With a slight smile on his face, he stepped off the deck and started for the gate, but halfway across his backyard, he stopped when he noticed how wilted all the potted plants looked.

When did that happen?

Gardening wasn't exactly his thing, but he'd never had trouble keeping the few plants Felix bought alive. He hadn't noticed anything wrong with them yesterday, but maybe he'd missed it.

After making a mental note to check them out after his run, he jogged to the gate but stopped again when he saw a large discolored section of paint around the latch. Some of the paint actually cracked and peeled off when he touched it.

What the hell?

After glancing around to make sure no other damage had been done to his property, and not finding any, Murphy pushed through the gate and jogged down to the water line. He knew the kids were pissed off at him for ruining their party, particularly the redhead next door, but he hadn't expected actual vandalism.

What did they do, piss in my potted plants?

He did a whole body shake, hoping to loosen his suddenly tense muscles. His run was supposed to be the most relaxing part of his day. After a little stretching, he pushed his irritation aside and took off. He let the sound of the waves and salt spray wash over him, putting him in the zone, as his heart pumped in time with his steps. He always jogged as close to the water as he could, which meant his shoes were usually damp by the time he got home, but he was happiest there. In the summer he swam as much as possible, but in the winter he had to be content with only his runs because even the gentle, loving embrace of his ocean wasn't proof against hypothermia.

He jogged his usual distance and then turned around. When he was within sight of his house again, he slowed to a walk to cool down, and once he wasn't in the zone anymore, the mystery of his damaged property came flooding back. He was in the middle of trying to decide if he should call the sheriff about it when he spotted a pile of clothes in a sand dune off to his right. Scowling, Murphy started toward it. As if the damage to his property, the remnants of the fire, cigarette butts, and bottle caps left on his beach weren't enough.

Those spoiled brats better not have just dumped the rest of their trash in a pile behind the dunes.

Except as he got closer, the pile resolved itself into a single set of clothes, clothes that were still occupied. Murphy recognized the flame red hair immediately, and his stomach flipped in concern. When he jogged nearer he was relieved to see the guy's chest rise and fall. He was just asleep.

"Hey. Are you okay?"

The sun was still warm enough during the day to hang out in T-shirts and shorts, but the nights were too cold to sleep on the beach without even a blanket.

Starting to get a little worried, he crouched down next to the guy and tried again.

"Hello? Are you okay?"

The guy grumbled and opened sleepy green eyes. When he saw Murphy, his eyes widened and he bolted upright. "Yeah. I'm okay. I was just sleeping."

Murphy couldn't help but poke at him a little. "Sleeping or sleeping it off?"

The guy frowned at him—more of a pout really—and Murphy felt the kid's emotions begin to intensify, buffeting his shields.

"I wasn't drunk."

Murphy held up his hands. He didn't want to get blasted again. "Sorry. Just, last I saw you, you were going inside, and then this morning I find you out here. It's a little cold for camping on the beach, isn't it?"

The kid shrugged and looked away. "I couldn't sleep, and the cold doesn't bother me."

Murphy got a sense of hesitation, as if the guy was leaving some things out, but that was all. He couldn't read minds, only feelings. And though he felt blessed by that fact most of the time, sometimes he really wished he could.

Clearing his throat awkwardly, Murphy said, "Well, as long as you're okay, then. I'm sorry I woke you."

The young man glanced at him sideways as the wave of emotion Murphy sensed began to ebb. "It's okay."

Since the guy didn't seem in any hurry to move, Murphy sighed and dropped his butt in the sand. His knees were starting to ache from crouching, and he still had an apology to make. He only hoped his muscles didn't cramp up so much that he couldn't get back up again after he'd said what he wanted to say.

"Look. About last night… I'm sorry I yelled at you. It wasn't your fault, and I was wrong to take my anger out on you."

"Yeah?"

Slight tremors of hope enveloped Murphy, and he didn't try to shield himself from them. He wasn't even sure he could with this kid. If the average person radiated emotion like a hundred watt bulb, this guy was a nuclear power plant. Murphy prayed he wasn't in the same time zone if the guy ever melted down or decided to use his gift as the weapon it could be.

Keeping that unsettling thought to himself, Murphy smiled reassuringly.

"Yeah. You tried to do something nice for me, probably coming close to burning yourself again in the process, and I was pretty rude in return. I'm sorry."

The kid smiled then, and Murphy's breath stuttered as a wash of pleasure blanketed him. He cleared his throat and shot to his feet. Extending his hand, he said, "If you don't mind starting over, I'm Murphy Mizuuchi. Welcome to the neighborhood."

The kid quirked a half smile, stood up, and shook his hand. "Aiden Flanagan. Nice to meet you."

If Murphy thought the guy was a powerful projector before, it was nothing compared to being in physical contact with him. Overwhelmed by the intensity of it, Murphy put everything he had into his shields and dropped Aiden's hand like he'd been burned.

Appearing a little shaken himself, Aiden rubbed his hands together and licked his lips. "So, uh, two last names, huh?"

Now that they were no longer touching, the roar of Aiden's energy subsided to a more manageable level, and Murphy was able to find his equilibrium. He relaxed into familiar territory. He even smiled as his heartbeat settled into a more normal rhythm. "I'm half Japanese, half Irish—both parents very proud of their ancestries and determined to pass it on in some way. My dad was just lucky convention was on his side or my mom might have put up more of a fight over the last name… or, God forbid, made me hyphenate."

"I like it," Aiden said as his smile warmed, and he gave Murphy the once-over. "It fits that hint of the exotic about you."

Murphy froze with his mouth hanging open.

Oh good Lord, is he flirting with me?

Aiden looked at him innocently enough, but Murphy could feel the stirrings of attraction coming from him, an attraction that wasn't exactly one-sided. Aiden was undeniably gorgeous, with his tousled flame red hair, sharp features, and sexy green eyes. Add young and fit on top of all that, and who wouldn't want him? But Murphy was not looking for a tumble with the very pretty boy next door, or anything more serious either.

He put a little more distance between them and cleared his throat again. "Anyway, I'm sorry again for last night. And thank you for trying to save what was left of the bench. I appreciate it. Maybe I'll see you around."

He might have retreated a little faster than was absolutely necessary. Howard would've definitely called it running away, and Felix's laughter rang loudly in his head.

Since when had a pretty young thing been able to send him scurrying into his house?

Apparently, since now, Felix mocked.

CHAPTER 3

MURPHY HID in his house the rest of the day—not that that was much different from any other day. Other than a few AA meetings, lunches with his sponsee—when he had one—the occasional dinner with his sponsor, and a couple trips a year to Boston to meet with his editor, Alexa, or his family, Murphy didn't exactly get out much. He had his routine and his comfortable little house, and he got along just fine within the confines of it.

Surprisingly, though, despite the distractions of the night before and that morning, he did actually manage to get some work done while he was hiding. He even finished this month's "Murphy's Law," his syndicated advice column, and e-mailed it to Alexa *before* she started to freak about the deadline. Though her response of "Who are you and what have you done with Murphy?" made him wonder if perhaps he should have waited another couple of days to send it, so he wasn't setting a bad precedent.

Never in a million years would he understand why his column remained as popular as it was, but people all across the country still sent him letters every week, and the magazines still printed his attempts to answer them, so he wasn't complaining. The money from it didn't exactly pay the bills, but it stretched the royalties he still received from the one bestseller he and Felix had written together and the interest from the investments Felix had made for them when the money rolled in from it. Murphy could have lived comfortably on that alone, but then what would he have done with himself? Rattle around in the house they bought together like he was now? Begin another pathetic attempt at a follow-up novel without Felix?

He glanced over at the stack of discarded legal pads filled with scribbled notes for that novel. If he weren't such a neat freak, the dust would be about an inch thick from the last time he'd touched them. With a sigh, Murphy looked away, shut down his computer, and made his way to the kitchen for some tea. As he stood over the stove waiting for the water to boil, the board—what was left of that stupid bench—kept calling to him from the living room, waiting for some kind of closure. It and his neighbor had plagued him off and on all day, no matter how many times he'd pushed them away.

What the hell am I supposed to do with a half-charred board with our initials carved into it?—a half-charred board that smells like beer?

Should he put it on the mantel, add it to the other remnants of their life together, next to the picture of the two of them on the boat Felix bought the first time one of his investments paid off… the boat Murphy's few friends took out more than he did?

He glared at the blackened piece of wood. The bench had been fine where it was. The wind and rain had broken it down a little more each year, until it was barely recognizable as a bench anymore, but it hadn't been hurting anyone out there. Now every day its absence would remind him that the world had moved on. He didn't need another reminder of that. He wanted things to stay as they were.

Without bothering to fix his tea, he shut off the burner and stomped over to the coffee table, grabbed the board, and headed out to the beach. The sun was setting by the time he reached the water, painting the sky in oranges and pinks, but he was blind to its beauty tonight. Goosebumps rose on his skin as the cool water lapped playfully at his feet, and he tried to let the sea soothe him as he clutched the board tightly in his fist and closed his eyes against a wave of grief.

It hit him like this sometimes. He'd be fine for weeks, *months*, a little melancholy and lonely, but mostly okay. Then something would happen, and he'd be reminded of what he'd lost, reminded that the rest of his life wouldn't have Felix in it. He clenched his jaw and breathed through the pain. He couldn't spend forever grieving. He had to move on, otherwise what was the point of continuing to breathe?

With his eyes still closed, Murphy sank his consciousness into the waves as they rocked into shore and out again. He stepped farther into the surf until it curled around his calves. It chilled his skin, and he shivered. He couldn't stay out there long, but he let the water soothe him, cradle him that little bit.

He drew in a lungful of damp, salty air, pulled his arm back, and hurled the board as far as he could into the ocean, like he'd done with Felix's ashes five years before.

"Take care of it please."

He knew the currents around the island as well as he knew his own body. He knew exactly where to throw the board so the ocean would take it out to sea rather than bring it back to shore. But he still used his connection to the water to give the board a little push for good measure.

Once it was on its way, the vise around his chest eased, and he forced his shoulders to relax, but the pins and needles in his toes and calves had faded to numbness by now, so he turned and walked back to shore. The surface of the sand was still a little warm from the sun—warmer than the water at least—and he dug his toes in with a sigh as feeling slowly returned. He was about ready to jog back to his house to change into drier pants and pull on some socks when a surge of anguish from outside smacked into him, sending him reeling where he stood.

Guilt, loneliness, and despair crashed over him in waves as he struggled to strengthen his shields and shake them off. When he was centered enough to think, he had no doubt where it was coming from. He'd only ever met one person who could project with that much strength. And despite the effort it took to wade through it, Murphy was drawn to it like a moth to flame. He couldn't help himself. Even as logic and good sense told him to not get involved, he turned away from the promise of warmth and comfort and headed toward his neighbor's house.

He didn't have to go far. He found Aiden curled up behind the same dune he'd been sleeping in that morning, huddled with his legs hugged tightly to his chest and his forehead pressed to his knees. Misery rolled off him in waves.

"Are you okay?"

It was a stupid question, but he had to start somewhere.

Aiden jolted and quickly rubbed his forearm across his eyes. With a barely audible sniff, he said, "Yeah. I'm fine."

Even if Murphy weren't an empath, and Aiden wasn't broadcasting his emotions with a loudspeaker, he'd have to be completely blind or an idiot to believe that.

"I don't mean to pry, but you don't sound fine."

In the deepening darkness, Murphy saw Aiden's jaw clench as another surge of pain mingled with need poured off him. This wasn't a physical need but an emotional one, a longing for comfort, and Murphy began to wonder what he was getting himself into even as he moved a little closer and sat down.

"You don't have to tell me if you don't want to. But I'll sit with you awhile, if you don't mind."

Aiden's jaw clenched again, and his lip trembled as he nodded.

In the silence that stretched between them, Murphy closed his eyes and settled into a relaxed, semi-meditative state as he listened to the waves hit the shore. The tension in the air lifted as Aiden's emotions faded and the rhythm of the surf infused Murphy with its strength. Even if he hadn't heard Aiden's sigh, he would have known the moment the worst of the storm inside him subsided to a dull throb. When he opened his eyes, he found Aiden watching him, but Aiden quickly averted his gaze.

"I… I did something a couple of months ago… something terrible."

Murphy kept his face passive in an expression he hoped was encouraging, and Aiden let out a shuddering breath.

With his fists still clenched around his knees, Aiden continued in a whisper, barely loud enough to be heard over the wind and the surf, almost as if he were talking to himself. "I didn't mean to. It was an accident. But that doesn't make what happened any better…. What I did hurt someone I cared about. And if he knows it was my fault, he'll never forgive me."

"Have you tried talking to him about it, tried to tell him it was an accident?"

Aiden shook his head. "Even before it happened, we had a fight, and he told me he didn't want to see me or talk to me anymore."

Aiden wasn't exactly giving him much to work with, but as a recovering alcoholic, Murphy definitely knew all about trying to live with regret and longing for absolution. He'd celebrated seven years of sobriety in May, and there were still plenty of wrongs he wasn't sure he could ever make right. But the storm of emotion stirring in Aiden was just waiting for a chance to explode outward again, so he wasn't going to get into any of that now. He was there to soothe, not make things worse and get blasted again.

It was time for a distraction.

"I know you said the cold doesn't bother you, but I'm a little chilly. I was going to go inside and have a cup of tea. Would you like to join me?"

Relief and gratitude flowed over him, warm and soothing, and Murphy knew Aiden's answer before he nodded. They walked back to his house in silence while Murphy struggled not to react to that drugging flow of energy. By the french doors, Aiden took off his shoes, and they both brushed sand off their legs and feet before stepping into his living room.

"Make yourself at home while I put the kettle on and get some dry pants."

Murphy went to the kitchen while Aiden wandered toward the couch. As Murphy got the water heating again, he watched Aiden move around his living room. First Aiden ran a hand over the khaki chenille throw Murphy draped over the back of his cream sofa. Then he wiggled his toes in the flokati rug in front of the fireplace, peered between the panes of the vintage windows that served as Murphy's coffee table— where Murphy kept his sea glass collection—and then moved on to run a finger over the driftwood and shells perched on every flat surface about the room. Aiden was obviously a very sensual young man, and Murphy had to drag his mind and his gaze away by sheer force of will from the direction that realization took them.

Oh come on, Murph. Live a little.

Silently telling Felix to hush, Murphy pretty much ran back to his bedroom. After washing the soot from the board off his hands and dumping his damp pants into the hamper in his bathroom, he was torn between pulling on a nice pair of jeans or his sweatpants. He stood in the middle of his room with both in his hands until he caught a glimpse of himself in the mirror on the door and rolled his eyes. He was a thirty-seven-year-old widower. He hadn't exactly let his body go to fat, but he was graying at the temples, and he had more laugh lines at the corners of his eyes every time he checked. What the hell did it matter what he wore?

Wear the jeans. Your ass always looked great in those.

"Shut up, Felix. You're not helping."

Aiden would not be looking at his ass.

He was interested this morning. You felt it. You know you did.

"Wishful thinking. Besides, he's what, ten years younger than me? Probably more like fifteen if I'm being brutally honest? Why am I even having this conversation?"

With an exasperated huff, Murphy deliberately put the jeans down and pulled on the sweatpants. He tugged on a pair of thick socks and didn't even bother looking in the mirror as he made his way out of the room and down the hall to the kitchen.

"What kind of tea do you want?" he asked as he took the whistling kettle off the burner. "I have black, chamomile, green, and a few other herbals." He pulled a couple of mugs from the cabinet as he tried to calm his nerves so his voice didn't continue to sound so strangled.

"Whatever you're having is fine."

Aiden sounded a little distracted too, and when Murphy glanced over the breakfast bar, he found Aiden standing in front of the mantel looking at the picture of him and Felix. Murphy cringed inwardly but didn't comment on it. He didn't think he could go there right now, and besides, they were supposed to be talking about Aiden, not him. He poured the water and set the teabags to steep while he tamped down on his nerves. They were making his shields a little shaky, and Aiden's mingled curiosity and disappointment were leaking past despite Aiden not being in any particular distress at the moment.

As he took a moment to shore up his shields, Murphy was reminded of why he'd invited Aiden in. He was simply trying to help a fellow human being in need, paying it forward. He wasn't there to invade Aiden's privacy or get too deeply involved in his life.

To be fair, Aiden didn't exactly make that easy. When someone was shouting at him, it was hard not to listen. But Aiden was obviously in pain, and Murphy needed a clear head if he was going to be any help at all. And he needed to help. It simply wasn't in him to ignore another living thing in pain.

Doesn't hurt that Aiden's hot as hell either. And the way those shorts hug his ass is just—

He blocked out Felix's voice before it could finish that sentence.

"Here you go," he said as he set the tea tray on the coffee table. He'd picked soothing chamomile for both of them. He only hoped it helped. "There's honey and sugar if you want."

Aiden accepted the cup with a smile, scooped a large spoonful of honey into it, and collapsed onto the couch. As Aiden's pleasure lapped at the edges of his shields, Murphy cleared his throat and picked up his own mug. Not wanting to be too obvious about keeping some distance between them, he opted for the other end of the couch rather than the armchair a few feet away. He might regret it later, but he was a polite host, and he didn't want Aiden to feel like he was in a therapy session. Murphy didn't have the training or the desire to be anyone's therapist.

After taking a long sip, Aiden settled a little deeper into the cushions and visibly relaxed.

"Thank you. This is really nice of you."

Murphy blew on his tea, but it was still too hot to drink, so he simply cupped it in his palms, allowing it to warm his hands. "I owe you at least that much after being so shitty to you last night."

"It's okay. You already said you were sorry. All's forgiven."

Aiden gave him another small smile, and Murphy returned it with a chuckle. "Just like that?"

"Why not?" Aiden shrugged. "If you didn't notice, I have a bit of temper myself sometimes. I'd be a bit of a hypocrite if I held yours against you, wouldn't I?"

"That's very mature of you."

Aiden's laugh held a bitter, self-mocking edge. "You're probably the only person on the planet who ever used that word to describe me."

Murphy was balanced precariously on the edge of wanting to dig deeper and knowing he shouldn't get any more involved than whatever was causing Aiden's current distress. After keeping enough distance between himself and the rest of the world for so long to maintain his sanity, it would be all too easy to be dragged under again by someone like Aiden, someone so passionate, with so much fire and emotion boiling beneath the surface. He was as tempting as he was terrifying—both very good reasons Murphy should have run in the opposite direction.

"Look, Aiden. We just met. And I obviously don't know you that well, or the details of whatever happened to you... what you did. But I usually have pretty good intuition about people, and I don't get the feeling you're a bad person. You're obviously torn up about what happened, so you can't be all bad, right?"

He smiled to show he was teasing, and Aiden gave him a half smile back.

After reminding himself yet again how young and vulnerable Aiden was, Murphy took a breath and said, "Maybe if you told me what happened, I might be able to help you figure out what to do."

Aiden's jaw tightened, and he shook his head even as Murphy felt the warmth coming from him withdraw. "I can't."

Tamping down on a surge of unwarranted disappointment, he set his cup back on the tray and folded his hands in his lap. "Okay. Is there someone else you can talk to, someone you trust?"

Aiden shook his head again. "Adam's the only one I might've been able to talk to, and he's the one I hurt."

"Adam is...?"

"My ex."

"What about your family?"

Aiden stiffened and Murphy sighed. Aiden's emotions were getting stronger again, louder as he got more upset. Instinct made Murphy want to wrap Aiden up and hold him until the pain went away, but that kind of comfort wasn't his to give, and he wanted to offer it a little too much for his own comfort.

Dirty old man.

At least this time he and Felix were on the same page, even if Felix's voice was full of laughter.

"I wish I could say something that might help, but I'm not sure I can. Maybe you should try to call this guy, Adam. I know you said he didn't want to talk to you, but it's been a little while, right? Maybe he's changed his mind. Maybe he's even worried about you."

It was a shot in the dark, and Murphy obviously missed the mark. Aiden set his mug down and jumped to his feet. "He's not. He has someone else now, someone better." Visibly struggling against the rising tide inside him, Aiden wrapped his arms around himself. "I'm sorry. I shouldn't be dumping this on you. I better go. Thanks for the tea."

With a quick wave, Aiden rushed out the french doors. They banged closed on a gust of wind, and Murphy was left feeling like he'd failed.

Why was this always easier when he was answering letters for strangers?

Do you really want me to answer that?

He groaned and buried his face in a throw pillow. If Felix were actually here instead of just a voice in Murphy's head, they might've been able to help Aiden together, make him feel safe enough to unburden himself without inviting a level of intimacy Murphy wasn't prepared to offer. But Felix wasn't, and Murphy was left to muddle through on his own.

You were always such a soft touch, Murph. It's why I loved you.

He groaned into the pillow. He should leave Aiden to work through his issues on his own, but he knew he wouldn't be able to. Some addictions were harder to beat than others. Aiden wouldn't stop projecting, and his emotions would be like a siren song, haunting Murphy until he tried again. Of all the places in the world, the fates had to drop a projector of Aiden's magnitude on Murphy's doorstep. Was that just cruelty, or was he supposed to find some meaning or lesson in it?

He needed to talk to someone who wasn't involved. Maybe he should have called Howard after all. Howard had been the hardass Murphy needed after Felix died, the kick in the pants that kept him going. Howard might have a better suggestion than tea and sympathy, one that didn't involve Murphy getting too close. Of course, Howard would probably tell him it's none of his business, and if Aiden wanted his help, he'd ask for it. That would be the smart way to look at it. Murphy just wasn't sure he'd be able to manage smart.

CHAPTER 4

AIDEN THREW himself onto his mattress and moaned into his pillows. No one could see him. He could be as much of a drama queen as he wanted, and no one would judge. He pounded the mattress with his fists and kicked his feet until he was panting for breath and the sheets started to get a little too warm, like fresh from the dryer warm, releasing the scent from the fabric softener into the air.

"Oh my God. Oh my God. Oh. My. *Gawd*!"

He flopped onto his back and stared up at the darkened ceiling as the wind off the ocean lifted his curtains through the open windows of his bedroom and dispersed the smell of toasted cotton and flowers.

Could he be any more mortified?

Bad enough he'd been caught bawling his eyes out on the beach by his superhot, supersophisticated neighbor, but then he'd run out on said hottie like a twelve-year-old girl instead of accepting the help he'd been offered. Murphy had been so good, so compassionate, so mature and together. Aiden had been close to dumping all over the guy, every bit of pain and hurt and fear and guilt inside him.

And what would Murphy have said once he heard the truth? Even if Aiden left out the part about him being a walking time bomb, what would Murphy think of him if he knew what a spazz he was?

He'd probably be too classy to say anything. He'd just run in the opposite direction as fast as he could, or dismiss Aiden as some stupid kid and go all paternal. Aiden wouldn't blame him.

As the sheets cooled beneath him, Aiden took comfort in one thought. At least as long as he wallowed in self-recrimination and self-pity, he didn't get mad. He only truly lost control when he was mad. In the month and a half he'd been there, he'd already singed a bit of carpet in the great room, and a couple of the couch cushions were a little crispy now too. Hence why he'd slept out on the beach last night after Murphy yelled at him. He couldn't afford to lose it any more than he already had. If his parents got another call from the security company about the fire alarm going off, he might not be able to stop them from sending him to another "facility" for a "rest."

He wasn't going to the nuthouse again. He wasn't nuts. He might be a little crazy over-the-top, but he wasn't *crazy* crazy. And cooped up in a hospital or some posh little rest home with dozens of stressed-out and unpredictable people was the last place he should be. He'd had a hard enough time not burning down the last hospital they'd sent him to when he was twelve, and his gift—or curse—wasn't nearly as strong then as it was now.

He had to get his shit together. He had to get control of this. He was getting stronger and that was a bad thing, *really* bad.

Though he didn't need the warmth, he grabbed the blanket from the foot of his bed and wrapped himself in it. In his cocoon, he tried to avoid reliving the last embarrassing hours of his life and concentrated on happy things like bunnies and rainbows and last year's production of *The Music Man* that had had everyone on campus talking about him for weeks after its final show.

Needless to say he didn't get much sleep. At least he didn't have to go back out to the beach, but he tossed and turned most of the night. By morning he felt like the walking dead, but that wasn't necessarily a bad thing. He couldn't do much damage if he was exhausted.

He hoped.

In a daze, he stumbled into the kitchen, where he realized he was out of coffee and nearly cried. He couldn't curl up in a ball of misery and stream stupid movies on Netflix until his eyes bled if he didn't have coffee. He had to go out. His refrigerator was empty anyway, and he could only take so much delivery before he could never look a pizza box or Chinese carry-out container in the face again.

On a brighter note, Crystal was probably working at the coffee shop today. If anyone could help him think about something other than the absolute wreck of his existence and what an idiot he must've looked like to his sexy neighbor, it would be her. Besides, after his little taste of social interaction last night, he was kind of jonesing for another fix, worse than he had been before.

He took a shower but forced himself to ignore his reflection in the bathroom and bedroom mirrors. He didn't want to know, and his vanity was only one of the dozens of faults he was trying to fix. Besides, Crystal didn't care if he was pretty. Or at least if she did care, she'd never acted like it. He thought maybe she might be a lesbian, but the new and improved Aiden was willing to admit just because she never showed any interest in him didn't mean she was a lesbian. She could simply not like gingers, or even just not him.

It was possible.

He wasn't to everyone's taste. He wasn't *that* vain.

As he stepped out the front door and climbed into his cherry red Jeep, he studiously avoided looking longingly toward Murphy's house. That ache for the comfort Murphy offered was still firmly lodged in his chest, but he had a lot of work to do before he deserved it, even if Murphy was willing to offer again.

Avoiding temptation, he put his foot to the floor and tore out of his driveway, though he slowed to a more reasonable pace by the end of the street before he crashed into someone's Benz and really gave his parents something to bitch about. The parking area in front of the coffee shop was nearly empty when he pulled in. It was late enough in the day for the morning rush to be gone, at least what there was of it, now that the summer crowds had thinned. Paulie, the skinny guy with bad teeth who usually worked Crystal's shifts, was behind the counter when he stepped inside.

"Hey man. Haven't seen you for a while. You want your usual?"

"Thanks."

Paulie had given him the cold shoulder Aiden's first couple of weeks on the island, until he figured out Aiden was gay and not going to ruin his romantic hopes for Crystal. To Aiden at least, Crystal seemed even more disinterested in Paulie than she was in Aiden, but he wasn't going to be the one to crush Paulie's little heart.

"She's out back on her break," Paulie said as he handed over Aiden's caramel latte.

"Thanks, man."

He wandered around to the back of the building and found Crystal perched on the wood railing by the delivery entrance and smoking a cigarette. As soon as the carcinogen-laden smoke hit him, Aiden scrunched up his face, but he knew better than to say anything about the cancer stick. He just propped himself against the wall nearby and took a sip of his caffeine and sugar in liquid form. They'd already had the "smoking is bad for you" conversation, and Crystal had told him where to shove his advice. It was one of the reasons they'd become fast friends.

"How goes it?" he asked between sips.

She blew out a stream of smoke and shrugged. "It goes."

As a general rule, Crystal was pretty unflappable, the other reason they'd become friends. He liked unflappable, since he was usually the one doing all the flapping. She smelled of patchouli and cigarettes, and she wore enough hemp on her wrists and around her neck to tie down a cruise ship. With her thick, frizzy blond dreads threaded with cowry shells, her tank tops, and her layered skirts, she looked like she belonged on a beach in the Bahamas more than Nantucket. But what did he know? The last time his parents had brought him here he'd been maybe ten at the most, and hiding out for the last month and a half hadn't exactly given him much insight into Nantucket culture. She could be their poster child, for all he knew. Though he highly doubted it.

"How about you?" she asked between puffs.

"The same. Maybe a little worse."

"Still pining for lost love?"

He'd told her about Adam, not some of the freakier details of his colossal fuck-up, but enough for her to understand that it was all his fault, and he deserved to be miserable. She didn't try to make him feel better, but talking to her usually did anyway, whether he deserved it or not.

"Have you heard of a guy named Murphy Mizuuchi?" he asked oh-so-casually.

Her gaze sharpened, the corner of her mouth curved up, and she cocked an eyebrow. He could feel the blush creeping up his cheeks. He hadn't meant to blurt the question out like that. He wasn't even sure where it came from.

"Why do you want to know?"

He shrugged like it didn't matter, but he could tell she wasn't buying it. Obviously he'd wasted the last several years of his life, *and* his parents' money, on those acting classes.

"He's my next door neighbor. I'm just curious."

"Uh-huh."

She smirked at him and Aiden pouted. "Really."

She took another puff off her cancer stick and pursed her lips. When Aiden was right about to break down and beg or stomp his foot in a huff, she laughed. "Fine. He's a year-rounder, been here for years, I guess. I'm not sure how long. Keeps to himself mostly. I asked around a little when I first started working here."

Now it was her turn to blush, and Aiden grinned. "Oh really?"

Obviously his earlier supposition had been incorrect.

"Shut up. He's cute, all right? I admit it."

"He's more than cute."

She snorted. "Well, you might have better luck than me. He apparently bats for your team, not mine."

"Yeah. I figured that one out on my own," he said, remembering the picture on Murphy's mantel and the sizzle that climbed up his arm the first time they shook hands—the sizzle that had been familiar and strange at the same time, kind of like what he'd felt with Adam, but not.

And look how that turned out.

"Oh really?"

Crystal echoing his words right back at him made him laugh in spite of the memories. "I was having kind of a rough night, and he invited me in for tea."

He had her full attention now as she spun around and faced him on her perch. "Do tell."

"Stop. He was just being nice, too nice. But I fucked it up, like always."

She sat there puffing away, with her eyebrows raised until he gave in. It didn't take long. "Fine. I lost it in front of him, and I'm sure now he thinks I'm some pathetic loser drama queen, okay? Happy? Now will you please share some dirt on my seriously hot neighbor before I expire of mortification?"

She grinned and opened her mouth, but Paulie chose that moment to poke his head out the back door.

"Hey, I get a break sometime too, you know."

"Yeah. Yeah. I'm coming back in a minute."

She made shooing motions with her hands, and Paulie frowned but went back inside anyway.

"You know, he only lets you get away with that because he's in love with you."

Crystal smiled and snubbed out her cigarette. "I know."

"You're terrible."

"I know that too."

"So come on, spill. Tell me about Murphy."

"For someone who's supposed to be doing penance and mourning a failed relationship, you're awfully interested in the guy next door."

"Crystal!"

"Fine. Goddess bless! You need to stay away from the caffeine, mister. Anyway, all I know is he's some big author or something. Cowrote a bestseller years ago, but after his partner died, he hasn't written another novel. Old Mr. Sherman from the barber shop told me he writes an advice column now… you know, like Dear Abby or something. He comes in once every couple of weeks. I think to get his mail, like his Dear Murphy letters. He orders a Chai latte to go every time, and I don't see him again for another couple weeks. That's about all I got."

"How did his partner die?"

"I don't know. Nobody said anything dramatic like murder or a car accident… nothing that would've made the news. Maybe he got sick."

Aiden thought about that stupid board with the initials on it, and his heart hurt. How awful that must've been for Murphy to see it tossed in the fire like that, with the garbage and the driftwood.

"Hey. You okay?"

He glanced up from his cup and found Crystal watching him with a frown.

"Yeah. Just feeling bad for him, I guess."

"I think you have enough things to feel bad about without adding any more. Don't you?"

He grimaced. "Don't remind me."

"It's my job, remember? Look, I gotta go back in. Obviously poor Paulie can't handle it on his own for long."

"I'll come in with you. I'm not ready to go home yet anyway."

She shrugged and hopped off the railing, and he followed her through the back door into the café area. He bought a muffin to go with his coffee and grabbed a table by the counter to hang out while Crystal and Paulie helped a sudden influx of customers.

Two guys and a girl grabbed one of the tables farther back. Aiden thought he recognized one of the guys from Con's party, but he wasn't sure. Shortly after that a man took one of the tables closer to Aiden's, tucked in a corner, but the rest of the crowd got their coffees and left.

As he sat waiting for Crystal to finish with the last few people in line, he had the odd sensation the guy sitting alone was watching him, but when he turned to look, the guy's face was buried in a book. A little bored and looking for a distraction, Aiden checked the guy out. He had dark hair and a lean build. Before he'd sat down, Aiden had noticed how tall he was, like *really* tall, well over Aiden's five ten and a half. He wasn't bad to look at, if Aiden had been in the market. But Aiden wasn't, and the guy was older anyway. Adam had been the oldest guy Aiden had ever dated. And though, after meeting Murphy, Aiden had to admit he appeared to be on kind of an older guy kick at the moment, this one couldn't hold a candle to Murphy. Aiden still enjoyed the attention, though he never could seem to catch the guy looking.

"That guy is totally checking you out," Crystal whispered as she pretended to wipe crumbs off his table.

Aiden shrugged. The fact that he couldn't catch the guy was borderline creepy, but he wasn't going to sweat it. If the guy was shy, so what?

"You know who he is?" he asked, curious more out of boredom than anything else.

She shook her head. "Never seen him before."

"Huh. Whatever. I'm not in the market anyway, so it's not like it matters. I think I'll go, though. Don't want him to get the wrong idea."

With a grin and a wink for Crystal, he stood up and tossed his trash. When he came back and gave her a hug and an enthusiastic peck on the cheek, she smirked at him and shook her head. "Be good."

"Always.… Hey, do you think I should get a thank-you gift for him… Murphy, I mean. You know, since he was so nice to me?"

She rolled her eyes. "Oh sure, that's not an excuse to see your hot neighbor again. You're just being polite and showing your gratitude… and this fits into your whole seclusion-slash-hair-shirt-wearing monastic solitude gig how?"

"It's a thank-you gift. I'm not jumping his bones or anything. I feel bad for acting like an ass."

"Uh-huh."

When Aiden stuck out his tongue, she laughed.

"Come on, what should I get him?"

She shrugged. "I don't know. Get him a bottle of wine. He seems like the fancy bottle of wine type, don't you think? Something sophisticated and pricey."

Aiden hugged her again.

"Good idea. Thanks!"

He sauntered out the glass doors with renewed purpose. This wasn't what he'd come to the island for, but building up more good karma points couldn't hurt either, right?

His earlier mortification, Crystal's teasing, and the creepy older guy still watching him forgotten, Aiden headed for the market practically whistling. He had to go to the grocery store anyway for food and coffee beans, so it wasn't like he was making a special trip. Besides, he'd already drowned his sorrows with what little wine was left in his parents' house his first week anyway, not that it had done much good. Now he had the perfect excuse to restock.

At the market, he first picked up a few things to refill his refrigerator. He didn't cook, so everything was simple and microwave or oven friendly. It probably wasn't the best food for him, but he'd eaten worse at school. Then he grabbed the most expensive bottle of red he could find, plus a couple others. He had no idea what kind Murphy might like, but expensive hopefully meant good. That was his parents' attitude anyway, and while he had a feeling Murphy was more old money classy than the Flanagan family, expensive rarely meant bad.

At the checkout, Aiden handed over his credit card and prayed it wouldn't be declined. His parents hadn't cut him off yet, but they were pitching a hissy about him not going back to school and not making any plans beyond hiding away on Nantucket. He wouldn't be able to put them off forever, but he hadn't quite figured out what else he could do yet either.

Luckily the amount cleared, and Aiden breathed a sigh of relief. He should probably make a list and stock up while the going was good, but he rarely thought that far ahead, and he was anxious to get home.

Out in the parking lot, Aiden lifted the bags into his Jeep, grinning as he carefully wedged the wine bottle behind the passenger seat. He was about to climb in when that weird creepy feeling of being watched came over him again, like it had on the beach. He scanned the parking lot and the surrounding area, but he still didn't see anything.

Ever since all that scary shit that went down in Ohio—with the gun-toting crazy guy, Bob, who was bafflingly obsessed with Adam's new boyfriend—Aiden wigged out and got the heebie-jeebies sometimes, for no reason. He still had nightmares about exploding guns and exploding trees, but he could understand those. That didn't explain why he got creeped out walking around in broad daylight, hundreds of miles away from all that crap.

As he tried to shake the feeling, his mind went to the guy in the coffee shop, and he shivered.

Oh my God! A guy can't even check me out anymore without me getting freaked. What is wrong with me?

Next he'd be suspecting Con of asking him to the party for some dastardly plot instead of probably hoping Aiden would blow him behind a dune.

Fed up with himself, Aiden shook off the odd feeling and hopped in his Jeep. He needed to find a gift bag or a ribbon or something... and maybe a thank-you card too. He did *not* need to suspect thieves and ne'er-do-wells lurked around every corner.

After another shower and an extended session with his hair products and the small wardrobe he'd managed to accumulate since his mad dash to the East Coast, Aiden was as ready to head over to Murphy's as he was ever going to be. He'd tried to tell himself not to care. Murphy had seen him all puffy and pathetic already, and this was only supposed to be an apology, not a come on. But it didn't work. His vanity won that battle. He was nervous. He needed to primp when he was nervous, and his bravado would only take him so far if he knew he looked like shit.

Wine bottle in hand, he crossed the yard, climbed Murphy's front steps, and rang the bell.

"Aiden, hey."

Murphy looked surprised but not displeased to see him when he answered the door. That was a good start.

"Hey, Murphy, I—"

After all his years of fucking up, Aiden should have had apologizing down pat by now. He should have been an expert. But apparently he needed a refresher.

Murphy just stood there, his expression open and concerned, and Aiden shivered inside. The strange energy was back, the pull that made Aiden want to be so much closer, to forget about the wine, the apology, and all of his wrongs and jump the man right there on his porch, or cry all over him, or both. Aiden fought it like he fought every other crazy part of himself.

He took a fortifying breath and tried again. "It's my turn to say I'm sorry… about last night, running out on you like that when you were being so nice to me. I feel really stupid about it now. I'm sorry." He held the wine bottle out to Murphy, now wondering if the big gold bow he'd put on it was too much. "I got you this as a kind of thank-you-slash-I'm-sorry-for-being-a-freak present."

Murphy smiled gently at him but made no move to take the bottle, and Aiden's stomach sank a little.

"You didn't have to do that."

"I wanted to."

But Murphy still didn't reach for it, and Aiden was starting to feel a little ridiculous dangling it in the air between them.

"I'm sorry, Aiden. That's very thoughtful of you, but I… I don't drink."

"Like, at all?" Aiden asked stupidly as he lowered his arm.

Murphy shook his head. "Sorry. I'm actually in recovery."

Aiden's brain was a little slow to catch up, and Murphy sighed. "I'm an alcoholic."

"Oh! Shit. God, I'm sorry."

If he'd had a board, he would've smacked himself in the head with it. As if last night hadn't been bad enough, Aiden seriously wished he could crawl under a rock and die, and his face had to be as red as his hair.

"Don't worry about it, really. It's no big deal. I appreciate the thought. And you don't have to apologize for offering me a gift *or* for last night. I just wish I could have been more help."

After tucking the wine bottle mostly out of sight under his arm, Aiden shifted uncomfortably and tried to will himself to chill out, to be cool and calm like Murphy was. Intentionally ignoring all the reasons he shouldn't do this, Aiden pulled the shreds of his confidence together and tried one more time to fix this disaster.

"Will you let me take you to dinner instead?"

Aiden held his breath as Murphy blinked at him in what he hoped was surprise.

"I, uh…."

Please say yes. Please say yes.

Murphy seemed to struggle a bit, and Aiden braced himself for another blow to his ego. But then Murphy blew out a breath and gave him a gentle smile. "Okay, sure. That would be nice."

Aiden would've whooped for joy, but he had a feeling something like that wouldn't impress a guy like Murphy. In fact, Murphy looked a little dazed as it was, and Aiden decided to push on through before Murphy could change his mind.

"So, do you want to just go now, or do you want me to give you a little time to change?"

Murphy looked down at his faded UMass sweatshirt and lounge pants like he hadn't seen them before.

"Uh… yeah, I think, uh, give me a half hour. I'll come over, though. You don't have to pick me up at my door."

"Okay, cool. See you soon."

Aiden beat a hasty retreat, leaving a somewhat bemused-looking Murphy on his front step.

Did he just do what he thought he did? Did he just ask Murphy out on a date?

No, of course not. This isn't a date. I'm not dating. I'm thanking him for being so fucking awesome… and hot, and kind, and….

I need to get a grip. I'm not even fooling myself.

As he stashed the wine bottle in the back of the pantry—for later consumption if he fucked up again tonight—his phone buzzed, telling him he had a text.

Hey man. It's Con. Party tonight on the beach by my place. You in?

He considered ignoring it but then changed his mind. He was supposed to be working on becoming a better person. Just because he had something better to do, and he had no interest at all in finding out what exactly Con wanted from him, didn't mean he had to be rude about it.

Thnx, man, but I got plans. Maybe next time.

Bummer. Yeah, next time.

He wouldn't be going next time either. He shouldn't have gone the first time. He also shouldn't be going on this date with Murphy, but he'd get back to beating himself up and figuring out what to do tomorrow.

He promised.

MURPHY KNOCKED on his door almost exactly a half hour later. He'd dressed in a pair of jeans and a navy blue cotton sweater that made the color of his eyes even more intense, and Aiden had to check himself before he gushed anything too embarrassing, especially since those jeans fit Murphy's ass and legs to perfection.

This is not a date.

Murphy had dressed nicely, but not too nicely. What did that mean? It wasn't supposed to mean anything, yet Aiden was sweating bullets anyway. He hadn't been this nervous since his first date more than a decade ago.

As they walked down the driveway and climbed into his Jeep, Aiden drew on every acting class he'd ever had so he wouldn't look as nervous as he felt.

When Murphy was buckled in, Aiden asked, "So where do you want to go?"

"I'm not picky. Anywhere's fine. You choose."

Well, that was completely unhelpful.

He decided on an Italian place he'd tried one of the few nights he'd actually left the house because he was bouncing off the walls and afraid he'd burn it down if he stayed any longer. The restaurant was a quaint little bistro, not too expensive, but not cheap either. In the middle of the week, somewhat off-season, it shouldn't be too hard to get a table.

Murphy was quiet for most of the drive, making Aiden nuts, but after Aiden reminded himself to chill and not be such a spazz about this not-date, Murphy's calm reserve started to have the opposite effect. There was something incredibly soothing and serene about the man. Self-contained was the word he was looking for. Aiden wished a little of that would rub off on him. He could use a little containment.

Who was he kidding? He could use a *lot* of containment.

When they reached the restaurant, he hopped out of the driver's side and hurried around to get Murphy's door, but Murphy was already out of the Jeep before he got there. He pouted a little. He couldn't play the gentleman if Murphy didn't cooperate. Forcing a smile to cover his nerves, he gestured for Murphy to precede him, and they went inside.

Once they were seated, Aiden surreptitiously tucked the wine menu away before opening his dinner menu, but apparently Murphy had eyes in the top of his head.

"You can have wine if you want, you know," Murphy said, without looking up from his own menu.

"No. I'm good."

Murphy set his menu aside and gave Aiden a gentle smile. "I don't mind. I've been sober seven years now, so it doesn't bother me when people drink around me anymore. I don't want you to feel like you can't just because I don't."

Aiden could feel himself flushing. "I don't drink much anyway. Never have. I don't know. I guess my metabolism must be high or something because it always hits me hard right away, but then a half hour later the buzz is gone. Hardly seems worth it most of the time. I am a bit of a caffeine junkie, although that burns off pretty quick too, I'm afraid."

Shit, should I have said junky?

"Relax, Aiden. It's pretty hard to offend me," Murphy said, as if he'd read Aiden's mind. "I'm only responsible for me. You can drink whatever you want."

But Aiden ordered water with his lasagna, and Murphy didn't make any more comments about it. When the waiter left after taking their orders,

Aiden decided to take the conversation to something a little less personal. Small talk he could do.

"So how long have you lived here?"

"Eleven years, I think. It hardly seems that long, but I guess it has been. You just got here a month or so ago, though, right?"

"Yeah. My folks bought the place a long time ago, and we came here when I was a kid, but it's been forever since I've been back."

"I'd ask how you're liking living on the island so far but—"

He stopped and grimaced, and Aiden flushed a little more and decided to take a surprising amount of interest in his water glass. He really didn't want to go there. Well, he did, but he didn't. It wasn't the kind of thing that was going to exactly impress Murphy. He had a sudden feeling his usual playing to his audience, flirting, and teasing weren't the right way to go either, but he wanted to keep Murphy talking. He wanted to know all there was to know about the man, but subtlety had never been his strong point.

Murphy started to laugh, the low rumble cutting in on Aiden's thoughts and doing funny things to his insides. He forgot whatever it was he wanted to ask in favor of melting a little as he gazed raptly at Murphy's warm smile and deep blue eyes, now crinkled at the corners with his laughter.

"We're a pair, aren't we?"

"Huh?"

He cringed the second the syllable was out of his mouth, but Murphy chuckled again and shook his head. "I have a feeling we're both struggling with the same thing here."

"What?"

"I have questions about the other night, personal questions I'm not sure I have a right to ask. And something tells me you have questions you want to ask me too, but you're not sure if you should."

Was the man psychic, or was Aiden really that obvious?

"How'd you guess?"

Murphy shrugged. "You seemed a little… conflicted, I guess. I'm assuming that's why, although I could be wrong. Besides, most people are curious when they hear I'm in recovery. It's not something you hear every day, I suppose."

"Well, yeah, that too."

"That too?"

"I'm curious about other things as well. I may have heard a few things around and…." He needed to shut up now.

"Around?" Murphy's smile said clearly he knew Aiden had been checking up on him, but he didn't seem to mind. "And what did you hear?"

Blushing again, Aiden took another drink of his water before saying, "You're a writer, a bestseller even."

Murphy nodded as he sat back in his chair. "That was a long time ago. I'm afraid I haven't done anything big in years."

"But you have an advice column, right?"

"That hardly counts as big," Murphy said with a chuckle.

"That's more than a lot of people do. You're printed in magazines." He wasn't sure why he felt the need to defend Murphy from himself, but he did.

"I guess you could say that."

"So that's *cool*." In the low lighting of the restaurant and with Murphy's caramel coloring, it was a little hard to tell, but Aiden thought Murphy might be blushing.

"I like helping people in my little way, I guess."

"Well, there you go. That's big."

Murphy chuckled. "You're good for my ego."

Aiden couldn't help the grin that split his face. "I certainly hope so."

He hadn't meant for that to come out quite so flirty. He'd stopped himself from waggling his eyebrows but only barely. Murphy straightened in his chair, looking uncomfortable, and Aiden cringed inwardly, his brief lapse into overconfidence gone.

Luckily, the waiter brought their meals and the silence wasn't quite so painful as they dug in. Aiden made a few comments on the food, and Murphy gave a few stilted replies, but he didn't seem as serene and composed as before. He looked agitated, and that was the opposite of what Aiden had been going for. He felt like he should apologize, but he wasn't sure how without making it worse.

After the waiter took their plates, Aiden encouraged Murphy to order dessert, but Murphy didn't take him up on it, and before Aiden knew it, he'd paid the check, and they were on their way back out to his Jeep.

Logically he knew he shouldn't be upset. This hadn't been a date, so he hadn't completely screwed up any chances with Murphy because there weren't supposed to be any chances to begin with. But logic and Aiden had never been boon companions, so he spent the drive back kicking himself while Murphy stared quietly out the window.

He knew he'd fuck it up. He'd known it before they even went out. He should have done better. He knew he *could* do better. A mature, together Aiden was in there somewhere. He just had to keep his head in the game and be the person he wanted to be. He needed to fix this.

When they pulled in to Aiden's driveway, Aiden hopped out as quickly as he could. The cool rush of evening air hitting his face made him realize how warm the air had gotten inside the Jeep, and he took a calming breath to settle his jangling nerves before the leak got any worse. He didn't get to the passenger side in time to open Murphy's door, but he did close it for him. Murphy tried to say a polite good night, but Aiden couldn't let it end like that. He insisted on walking Murphy to his door to give him time to think of something to say, and Murphy didn't fight him on it.

When they reached his front steps, Murphy cleared his throat and smiled stiffly. "Well, thank you for a lovely dinner, Aiden. You didn't have to do it, but I appreciated it."

"I'm glad you said yes." Drawing on what bravado he had left, Aiden closed the distance between them. "You know, the night doesn't have to be over. I mean, I could come in, and we could try that conversation over tea again, if you wanted to, that is."

He held his breath while Murphy searched his face with those incredible blue eyes, and Aiden knew the answer before Murphy even opened his mouth.

"I'm a little tired tonight. Maybe another time, okay?"

His tone was so gentle and full of regret Aiden didn't crash into the depths of despair like he usually would have. The new Aiden was more mature than that. He shoved his disappointment aside enough so he could reply. He intended to say "I'm gonna hold you to that" or something similarly cool and flip, but that isn't what came out of his mouth.

"Can I kiss you good night?"

Murphy froze for a few heartbeats, enough time for Aiden's heart to squeeze. Then, wonder of wonders, Murphy's expression softened and he smiled.

"Okay."

Before Murphy could change his mind, Aiden cupped his cheeks. His fingertips barely grazed the silver at Murphy's temples and that strange electric connection traveled up his arms. It soothed him, giving him the courage to step confidently into Murphy's space. He didn't want to ruin the moment by pushing his luck, so he put as much feeling as he possibly could into a simple, gentle meeting of lips. He couldn't resist teasing his tongue the tiniest bit across Murphy's upper lip. And sucking on Murphy's lower lip ever-so-gently, tugging on it as he withdrew, wasn't going too far, was it? Before he gave in to any more temptation, he forced himself to let go and step away.

"Good night, then."

His voice sounded thready and breathless, not quite the cool and collected he was hoping for, but he could only manage so much when nearly every fiber of his being wanted to jump Murphy and drag him to the nearest bed.

Murphy stared at him with wide blue eyes, his lips still temptingly parted. Aiden was very close to forgetting the meaning of the word "restraint" until Murphy cleared his throat, and then cleared it again, before he said, "Good night."

Aiden forced himself to turn around and walk back to his parents' house with as much composure as possible. He had a date with a long cold shower and his left hand—and maybe his right hand after that—but Murphy didn't need to know that.

CHAPTER 5

Murphy closed the door and promptly slid to the floor behind it.

Holy hell.

I mean damn, just… damn!

A boy that age, whatever age Aiden actually was, should not be able to rock Murphy's world with just a kiss. He was on fire from his hair to his toenails.

What the hell had he gotten himself into?

You didn't get yourself into anything. Although, you probably could've gotten in there, if you hadn't been such a coward.

"Not now, Felix," Murphy groaned. "And I'm not being a coward. I'm trying to be a sensible, *responsible* adult."

All work and no play, my dear.

"We did plenty of playing for way too long, in case you forgot that part. We nearly wrecked our lives playing."

You don't have to be trashed to have a good time, and you know it. Live a little, honey, before it's too late.

He really needed to get out more. These conversations in his head were getting a little over-the-top. At least his hard-on was subsiding. If Aiden had stood any closer, he would have felt how much Murphy didn't want to say good night. And now he was arguing with the memory of his dead lover about whether or not to fuck the boy next door.

Murphy groaned again and climbed to his feet. After dumping his wallet and keys on the foyer table, he kicked off his shoes and went to fix himself a cup of tea. He curled up on his couch and tried to immerse himself in the gentle tinkling of the fountain in the corner of the room as it melded with Delerium's music from his sound system. But after fretting uselessly for another twenty minutes, he finally gave up and decided to ask for help. He dialed Howard's cell, but it went straight to voice mail.

"Hey, Howard, I was just checking in. It's been a little while, so I thought we should try to make another lunch date soon. Give me a call when you can."

Disappointed, he hit End but didn't immediately put his phone away. It occurred to him that he might need the kind of advice Howard couldn't give, advice of the more esoteric variety, given what he'd sensed of Aiden's ability. Feeling a little silly but unsettled enough to admit he might be in over his head and beyond his limited knowledge of the psychic, he scrolled through his contacts until he found the right name, and then hit Send.

"Hello, sweet boy."

Her quiet, slightly wavering contralto immediately helped him relax. He even chuckled.

"Hi Lola. You don't sound surprised to hear from me."

"I had a feeling you might be calling me," she replied in that way she had.

Lola was his first sponsor in the program and only the second person he ever told about his abilities—the first being Felix, of course, though he hadn't had names for what he was until after meeting Lola. A pagan high priestess, long retired from active leadership in her coven, she'd pretty much told him she knew all about him before he even had a chance to open his mouth. She was the one who taught him grounding and how to design his meditation to best suit his gifts, how to use what he had instead of letting it use him.

He'd kept his ability to sense emotions and his affinity with all things water to himself for so long. Growing up half Japanese, half Irish and gay, he'd figured he didn't need anything else to set him apart, and as it got stronger he'd taken the wrong path, self-medicating with alcohol instead of seeking the right way to deal. Lola had turned all of that around, once he'd finally made the decision to ask for help.

After Felix died, he'd changed sponsors because Howard was a widower too and understood a lot of what Murphy was going through. But

Lola would always hold a special place in his heart, and she'd promised to be there for him whenever he might need her again.

If anyone might understand his predicament now, it would be her. Although he doubted she'd understand his hang-ups about Aiden's youth and vulnerability. She tended to be a lot less uptight about certain social no-no's than Murphy was.

"Did your witchy intuition tell you *why* I might be calling?"

She laughed. "Something to do with your gifts and a dark cloud I sense hovering over the island."

Her words made him tense a little as he remembered a strange queasy foreboding he'd had when he was outside the restaurant with Aiden, but he brushed it off now as he'd done then. Bad vibes were just something he'd learned to deal with because of his empathy. The shields blocked most of it, so all he usually got were hints of negative and positive emotions. They hampered his ability to sense real trouble, but it was preferable to the alternative of being overwhelmed whenever he was out in public. Besides, Lola liked to stir things up with her vague portents. His feelings could be completely unrelated.

"Well, I don't know about the dark cloud, but I am having a little trouble with my gift...." He took a steadying breath and dived in. "And my new next-door neighbor."

"Oh?"

The way she drew that one word out, Murphy knew he'd be blushing before the end of this conversation. Hell, he was blushing already. He took a breath and gave her a brief synopsis of how they'd met and his concerns over Aiden's emotional turmoil and the strength of his psychic ability.

"He's the strongest projector I've ever met. I *can't* block him out. I've tried."

"And you're thinking there's something wrong with your shields?"

"I don't know. I don't think so. I'm not sensing anyone else more than usual. He's the only one I can't seem to block...." He sighed. Time to be honest with himself as well as with her. "And I guess there's a part of me that doesn't want to."

"Tempting, is he?"

"God, yes. He's beautiful. He has so much energy about him, so much passion. It flows off him in waves. I don't think I've ever had that much energy in my life, even as a kid. When he kissed me it was… indescribable.”

“So he kissed you?”

“Yes. He asked to kiss me good night, and I said yes before my brain caught up. Just being near him is intoxicating.” Halfway through their date, Murphy hadn’t been able to deny that was what it was any longer. He still wasn’t sure how he felt about that, but he couldn’t pretend it was anything else, not without a much larger pool of denial than the one he drew from. Despite the flush of embarrassment creeping up his cheeks, Murphy shared the rest of the details of their date, knowing he should get it over with or he’d just be wasting time making her pry them out of him.

“Apparently I have less willpower than I thought,” he finished.

“Then why fight it? Obviously this young man knows what he wants.”

Groaning and chuckling at the same time, he shook his head. “How did I know you’d say that? Lola, I don’t need another little devil on my shoulder. It’s the angel that’s already outnumbered.”

“And what would the angel say?” She chuckled throatily. “You’re going to have to help me here since that’s not usually my department.”

“It would say he’s too young, and vulnerable, and hurting. His gift is out of control. He’s projecting all over the place, and he’s dealing with some heavy guilt and pain. He’s fragile.”

“Then maybe you’re exactly what he needs right now—*all of you*, not just Murphy the martyr. Perhaps Fate put you in his path for a reason. Fate dropped him right next door, right?”

“You’re right about one thing. You make a terrible angel.” He sighed and rubbed his forehead. “Looking past the fact that I don’t know if I’m ready to date again. I don’t want to take advantage. I mean you have to admit it’s a little unfair knowing his every emotion whether he wants me to or not. Maybe Fate just put me here to help him, and that doesn’t include sleeping with him.”

“Were you taking advantage of Felix?”

“That was different. Felix was older than me, more mature. He wasn’t falling apart when we met.”

She harrumphed. “I’ll give you the older part, but I think the two of you were about equal on the maturity… and the falling apart. But what

I'm saying is being an empath makes you *more* careful of others, not less, my heart. You're one of the most caring, nurturing people I know. If you were hurting him by letting him into your heart, you'd know. Why wouldn't that be a good thing for him?"

"Because maybe he doesn't need a lover. Maybe he just needs a friend."

"They can be the same thing. I never will understand why people feel the need to separate the two, like they're two completely different emotions. Besides, you're an adult. He's an adult. With your gifts, he'd not likely find a more generous lover *and* friend. Of course maybe you're just using all this as an excuse not to put your heart out there again."

That hit a little close to home. Lola always swore she wasn't an empath, but despite his gifts, he was never quite sure if that was true. He couldn't read her. She was the one who'd taught him shielding, and hers was thicker than the Hoover Dam.

He had his suspicions, though.

"I just want to do the right thing."

She clucked her tongue. "Well, let's think about that, shall we? Exactly who knocked on whose door? And who asked whom to dinner?"

"Aiden," he mumbled reluctantly.

"And who asked whom to come inside, and when rejected asked for a kiss instead?"

"Aiden."

"So other than that one night you asked him in for tea, who's made most of the moves so far?"

She really didn't need an answer to that one.

It was her turn to sigh. "My heart, I hate to say it, but it doesn't sound like you're the one driving, if you catch my meaning. Maybe you should stop worrying for once in your life and just let him get on with it."

Murphy could hear the smile in her voice, and he couldn't help but return it. When he still couldn't come up with anything to say to that, she said, "Remember, the Fates know what they're doing. They bring people into your life for a reason. You surrendered to your higher power in the program. Why not try giving it a shot in your love life?"

"And if one of us gets hurt?"

"That's life, honey. Not all the psychic powers in the world can stop us from experiencing a little pain from time to time. What matters is what you do after. Though I will say, whatever you decide, it sounds like you need to teach that boy how to shield. If you won't do it yourself, you need to get him to someone else who will."

"Yeah. I was thinking the same thing." He wished she were there with him so he could give her a hug. "Thanks, Lola. It's been too long since we talked. I won't let it be this long again."

"You had some things to work through. You still do. But maybe this Aiden will finally light a fire under your britches so you get to it instead of cooling your heels on the bench."

He laughed. "Yes, ma'am. We should get together soon for lunch. I'd love to see you, to thank you in person… and just to see you."

"Don't worry. We'll be seeing each other soon. I'm sure of it."

And with that cryptic prediction, she ended the call.

He felt a little better as he set his phone on the coffee table and picked up his lukewarm tea again. He still wasn't completely convinced. He was a worrier. It's what he did. He couldn't dump everything into the hands of fate. He was responsible for the decisions he made, and he'd have to live with the consequences. But she did have a point. Aiden was the one making the moves. Murphy had to admit he was more than a little flattered with the intensity of Aiden's attentions, though from what he could sense, Aiden was never anything *but* intense. Which led to a completely different kind of worry. Could he handle that kind of intensity? Was he up to it?

He had put himself on the bench. He hadn't even tried to date since Felix died. And he could already tell Aiden wasn't the kind to sit back and let him dangle his toes in the shallows. Any kind of relationship with him would mean jumping in the deep end, head first.

He set his mug down, drew his legs underneath him, and attempted to meditate. When that didn't work, he took a long bath, but it wasn't long before feelings not his own crept into his consciousness and being naked in the bathtub was no longer relaxing. The distance between their houses helped, but he was tuned in to Aiden now, and the connection was getting stronger. Try as he might, he couldn't help but sense what was going on next door, what Aiden spent most of the night doing, and it made for an exceedingly uncomfortable and sleepless night for Murphy.

In the morning he woke hard and sweating despite the chill. After a lengthy self-pleasuring session in the shower to take care of his morning wood, Murphy was feeling a little less grumpy and a little more clearheaded. He assumed Aiden must have finally masturbated himself into exhaustion around two o'clock in the morning because Murphy didn't feel any more spikes in emotion after that point. Still not completely resigned to allowing whatever had started between them to progress, he *was* sure of one thing. Whether they got together or not, if Aiden was going to continue to live next door, Murphy needed to give him some lessons on shielding before Murphy lost his sanity.

In the interests of retaining what little he had left, he decided to go into town for his morning tea. Aiden didn't appear to be awake yet, but a little distance to clear his head still sounded like a good idea. He stopped at the post office first for his usual installment of "Dear Murphy" letters. While he got hundreds more via e-mail these days, a few stolid souls still put forth the effort to pen him real paper letters. He had a soft spot for those and tended to publish more of them than the ones he received in e-mail.

Today wasn't his usual day, and Phoebe at the post office was surprised to see him. The level of her shock and confusion and the number of times she checked her calendar to make sure she had the day right gave Murphy pause. Had he really become such a creature of habit?

My love, you've been walking around like a zombie for five years. It's time.

Murphy almost didn't want to go to his usual coffee shop, afraid he'd see the same look on their faces. But he'd have to drive miles out of his way to go to the next closest and this one made a pretty fantastic chai latte. After stowing the box of letters in the back of his blue Mini Cooper, Murphy headed for the café but stopped and groaned when he recognized Aiden's red Jeep parked outside. He'd managed to not think about Aiden for approximately ten minutes. He was about to turn around and just go home when he spotted Aiden talking to someone inside, a very tall, handsome someone with thick dark brown hair, who was standing way too close to Aiden for Murphy's comfort.

Murphy didn't like the guy on sight, but that probably had something to do with the spike of jealousy that shot through him when the guy put his hand on Aiden's upper arm and leaned closer to him. Murphy felt a growl building in the back of his throat, and it startled him. They weren't even dating yet. They'd been on one sort of date, but that didn't give him the right to be jealous.

Murphy deliberately looked away to gain some composure, but then his eyes landed on a man standing in the alley between two buildings watching him. He felt a sudden sick wave wash over him, and his chest tightened. After taking a closer look at the little man, Murphy couldn't be sure if the guy was looking at him or past him. He swung around again in time to see Aiden leaving the café with the tall man still holding his arm, and his gut clenched. Something was wrong. But he couldn't sense any fear from Aiden. Actually he couldn't sense much of anything from him, even when he tried.

Alarm bells started ringing in his head.

He was trying to decide if he should risk letting his shields down to get a better read when Aiden stumbled. The man's hand on Aiden's arm seemed to be supporting him now, and Murphy couldn't take it anymore. He gave in to instinct, rushed over to them, and put his hand under Aiden's other elbow.

For a split second Murphy felt something pulling on him, like the tide rolling back, but it faded as the other man stepped back.

Aiden's skin was sallow and pale, and his eyes were bloodshot when he looked at Murphy. "Murphy?"

Murphy felt a surge of relief and pleasure from Aiden, and despite his earlier desire to get away from it, Murphy was ecstatic that he could feel him again.

"Murphy, I don't feel very well," Aiden said unnecessarily.

Any idiot could see that.

"He was okay in the café, and then he started feeling a little lightheaded, so I thought some fresh air might help," the man said, his brown eyes radiating nothing but concern.

"Thanks," Murphy said somewhat begrudgingly, "I'll take care of him."

The man hesitated for only a beat before taking another step back. "If you're sure…. It was a pleasure meeting you, Aiden. I hope it's nothing serious, and we can continue our talk some other time."

Not if I have anything to say about it.

Even as the man walked away, Murphy glared at his back until Aiden shifted a little and swallowed thickly. Murphy helped him to the curb and sat next to him as some of Aiden's color returned.

"When you're feeling up to it, I'll drive you home," Murphy offered quietly.

Aiden didn't even try to argue. He simply nodded, slumped against Murphy's side, and rested his head on Murphy's shoulder. Murphy's heart melted.

He wrapped an arm around Aiden's waist and waited in silence until Aiden shifted and blew out a breath.

"Are you feeling better? Should I take you to the hospital instead?"

"No. No. I'm feeling better. Home would be good, though."

"Can you tell me what happened?"

"I don't know. One minute I was getting my coffee and talking to that guy, Richard something, the next I felt dizzy and exhausted, like I just wanted to curl up on the floor and pass out. It was weird. I never get sick, like *ever*."

"Are you okay to stand now? My car's right over there."

When Aiden nodded, Murphy helped him to his feet and kept a hand on his arm as they crossed the street to his car. Once Aiden was safely in the passenger seat, he went around to the driver's side. Before he climbed in, he glanced over at the alley, but the strange little man was gone. To say the morning had turned out a lot weirder than he expected was a vast understatement. But as he drove them back, helped Aiden into his house, and tucked him into bed, he wasn't exactly complaining either.

Felix had always told him he was a worse Jewish mother than Felix's mother, sisters, and grandmothers combined, but Aiden didn't seem to mind in the least. He soaked up every bit of attention, radiating pleasure and contentment as Murphy fussed over him until his eyelids drooped closed and he started snoring softly.

After programming his number into Aiden's phone and leaving it by his bed, Murphy touched Aiden's cheek, one last time because he couldn't help himself. Then he crept out of the house and back to his own. He'd check on Aiden again later, though he seemed to be recovering quickly from whatever it was.

Over the next few hours, Murphy tried to work, but he mostly fretted. Aiden had sent him a text thanking him and saying he was feeling better, but something else was bothering him about the morning. He couldn't quite put his finger on it. The creepy homeless-looking guy was a little weird, but often people with psychological problems set off warning bells with his gift, though they were harmless for the most part.

Murphy was still a little puzzled by his reaction to the other guy, Richard, but he supposed it was excusable. He'd been jealous, plain and simple, probably for the first time in more than a decade. This whatever it was with Aiden was new, and he might be a little raw with all the new feelings and sensations he'd been having lately. He was considering putting himself out there again after a five-year hiatus from anything beyond the bare minimum of human interaction, and maybe he was a little off-balance because of it… or a lot off-balance, all perfectly excusable.

When he realized he'd skipped his morning run in his hurry to escape his neighbor, Murphy finally gave up on trying to work and got changed into his jogging gear. A little physical exercise might help him shake off some of the unrest and give him some much-needed calm. As he stepped out his back door and peered up at the sky, he smiled. Thick black clouds rolling in from the west would deter any but the most desperate beach goers, so he shouldn't have too many people to dodge even in the middle of the afternoon. If it weren't for the chill in the air, he almost looked forward to getting drenched in a downpour.

The rain held off until he made it back to his house, though Murphy was still looking forward to a long hot shower to chase away the chill from jogging in the spray. Except halfway through his shower he not only knew the moment Aiden woke for the second time, but also that Aiden was feeling *a lot* better. Whatever had masked his emotions earlier was long gone, and Murphy had to brace himself against the tile as sensations crashed over him.

Shields. I have to get that boy some shields.

With every pulse of pleasure Aiden radiated, weakened by distance though it was, Murphy felt an answering pulse in his own body. He was halfway hard before he even stumbled out of the shower. Before he could get his pants zipped, he was fully hard and panting. Thank the gods this connection to Aiden hadn't become this strong before now or he would have spent the last month and a half in a constant state of arousal every time Aiden chose to jack off. His body throbbed in time with Aiden's desire, and he had to close his eyes and lean against the wall in his bedroom.

He had to make a choice. He could take care of himself and continue to wrestle with the morality of what he wanted, or he could give in and accept what fate was offering him, what Aiden was offering. Given that most of the blood had left his brain by that point, option number two was looking like a sure thing.

Shit.

This wasn't like him at all. He was supposed to be the calm collected one. He was old enough to have better control, not to let his dick do all his thinking.

As the rain started pounding on his roof, Murphy charged out his french doors and raced out his gate. His heart thudded in time with the rain on his head and shoulders and the surf against the shore as he pounded on Aiden's back door. Then Aiden appeared, holding the door open and motioning him inside.

"Murphy? God, you're soaked. Come in. Come in. Let me get you a towel."

Murphy didn't let Aiden take more than a step before he grabbed Aiden's arm and pulled him close. While Aiden stared at him with wide, startled eyes, Murphy cupped Aiden's cheeks and kissed him hard. Aiden's lips opened instantly allowing him access, and Murphy sank deeper into the kiss, plunging his tongue inside to battle with Aiden's. Like last time, that tingling energy spread like wildfire. Aiden's skin was scorching against Murphy's chilled hands and lips.

Before he could get too carried away, he pulled back and searched Aiden's face.

"Do you want this? I mean, really want this?"

"Are you kidding? Hell yeah, I want it."

Aiden dove back in before Murphy could say anything else, sealing their lips together as he started tearing at Murphy's belt. Murphy chuckled even as he tried to help. He kicked off his boat shoes and stepped out of his pants. He dragged his shirt over his head while Aiden did the same. Then Aiden wrapped Murphy in his arms again, skin against skin, Aiden's pale ivory next to the darker beige Murphy inherited from his father.

They were only in boxers now, and Murphy could feel the heat and hardness of Aiden's erection through both layers of fabric as Aiden ground into his hip. It took three tries, but Murphy was finally able to break free of Aiden's eager hands and kisses enough to drag him back to the bedroom. Their first time together was not going to be on the living room floor. He had plans, all kinds of things he'd dreamed up last night. It was hard to remember exactly what they were with his entire body on fire and Aiden's need buffeting him like the storm outside, but Murphy wanted more than a quickie on the floor. This gorgeous young man wanted him, and Murphy was going to make every moment as memorable as possible.

Once they were in the bedroom, Aiden allowed Murphy to push him down onto the bed. He grinned and reached out with welcoming arms as Murphy sank down on top of him. Aiden's pleasure and want enfolded him even as his arms locked around Murphy's shoulders. Murphy didn't even try to block him out this time. He let Aiden's emotions wash over him as the heat coming off Aiden's body made Murphy's blood pump feverishly beneath his skin.

He kissed Aiden again and again, tasting him, memorizing his soft lips as his hands memorized the dips and valleys of Aiden's frame. He learned what made Aiden's pleasure surge, what made him shiver. When Aiden was reduced to moaning and writhing against him, clawing at Murphy's skin, Murphy decided now was the time to show Aiden just how good sex with an empath could be. He might not be confident in all aspects of his life, but in the bedroom he definitely knew what he was doing.

He broke free of Aiden's arms enough to begin working his way down Aiden's body. He kissed and nipped at the spot on Aiden's neck that made Aiden jerk and tremble. Then he slid farther down. He suckled Aiden's nipples, spending quality time with each one while Aiden moaned and clutched at him, fisting a hand in Murphy's hair and the other in the sheets.

As he slid lower still, Aiden drew his knees up and spread his thighs. Murphy gripped the waistband of Aiden's boxers and dragged them down his hips and off with a little awkward wriggling and a helping hand from Aiden. His cock bobbed free, arching beautifully toward his navel, but Murphy resisted the tempting beads of moisture on his crown. Instead, he held Aiden's cock out of the way with gentle pressure and teased Aiden's navel and the heaving hard flat expanse of Aiden's belly with his tongue. When Aiden's breathless pleas turned desperate, Murphy finally gave in and buried his face in the copper thatch at the base of Aiden's cock. He tongued the base and tightened his grip on the shaft, and Aiden let out a mewling noise as his hips bucked.

Smiling, Murphy explored Aiden's most private and sensitive spots. He nuzzled and suckled Aiden's balls. He teased and tormented with his lips, tongue, and fingers, registering every nuance of Aiden's reactions until he knew what buttons Aiden liked pushed the most. When he finally drew Aiden's cock deep into his mouth, Aiden let out a moan that reverberated through his entire body and along their psychic connection. Murphy's cock throbbed in his shorts, and he ground it against the bed for relief, even as he pushed Aiden's cock to the back of his throat.

He sucked, licked, and pumped, bringing Aiden to the edge over and over until he was teetering on the edge right along with him. When he finally took Aiden over the edge, Aiden screamed his pleasure almost loud enough to rattle the windows, unloaded into Murphy's mouth, and then promptly passed out.

Murphy gently withdrew from Aiden's spent cock and wiped his face on a corner of the sheet. He slid out from between Aiden's thighs and settled next to him. With his chin propped on his hand, he studied Aiden's slack features with a smug grin and tenderly brushed his fingers through Aiden's sweat-soaked dark red curls before he grimaced and palmed his aching erection.

He considered whether or not to take care of it himself, but luckily he didn't have to wait long before Aiden opened his eyes, blinked a little blearily at him, and then flushed in embarrassment.

"Shit. I'm sorry. I've never done that before… passed out I mean."

Murphy's smug grin returned. He was feeling pretty proud of himself. After being out of the game for five years, apparently he still had it.

Aiden glanced down at the tent in Murphy's shorts, and his eyes sparked.

"Saving that for anything particular?" Aiden asked as he reached over, covered the hand Murphy had over his cock, and squeezed.

Murphy moaned and pumped his hips into that grip.

"Delayed gratification?"

Aiden rolled on his side and scooted closer to Murphy. When his lips were only inches away from Murphy's, he whispered, "Oh. And here I thought you wanted to fuck me with it."

Murphy shuddered as a pulse of lust ran through him.

"That's very tempting…."

Murphy left the sentence unfinished, and Aiden pulled back.

"But?"

Thanks to his coloring, Aiden probably couldn't see him flush any darker in the dim light. "I'm actually more of a bottom than a top."

Aiden's grin was a wicked thing to behold. "Oh yeah?"

He squeezed Murphy's dick again, and Murphy's hips jerked.

"Yeah." He shrugged with as much nonchalance as he could manage. "I'd say nine times out of ten."

Murphy barely got the sentence out before Aiden let go of his cock and pounced. Murphy was on his back staring up at a very happy, very ready Aiden before he knew it. Aiden kissed him hard. After making short work of Murphy's boxers, Aiden grabbed Murphy's wrists and pinned them to the mattress as he ground his now fully recovered erection into Murphy's hip.

When Aiden let Murphy come up for air at last, he put his mouth close to Murphy's ear and whispered, "You're in luck, then, because I actually prefer the top."

Aiden bit his earlobe and then the muscle on the side of Murphy's neck, and Murphy's cock pulsed as a bead of precome slid down it. Murphy shivered in a sudden chill when Aiden pulled away and lunged for his nightstand. Aiden kept the temperature in his house remarkably low. They'd probably have to talk about that at some point.

"Fuck! No condoms. Shit. Shit. Shit."

Murphy would have laughed if he weren't so disappointed, but then Aiden shot out of the bed in a dead run for the door. "I'll be back."

Murphy shivered again and grabbed the sheet, but thankfully Aiden was back less than a minute later. He burst through the door clutching a strip of condoms triumphantly in his fist.

"My backpack from school was still in the garage," he said with a grin.

Murphy wasn't sure if he should be relieved or upset that Aiden kept condoms in his book bag, but Aiden didn't give him much time to think about it. He dove for Murphy, tackling him across the mattress, and Murphy laughed. He couldn't help it. He felt like he was twenty years old again, in his parents' basement, so desperately horny he couldn't see straight.

Aiden slid down the bed and crawled between Murphy's thighs. He kissed and nuzzled Murphy's cock settling in to torture him probably every bit as much as Murphy had done, but Murphy made him stop.

"I'm not gonna last," he managed, and Aiden seemed happy to take the hint.

Murphy snatched the lube off Aiden's nightstand and handed it to him. Aiden slicked his fingers and slid them back to Murphy's opening.

As Aiden breached him slowly and gently, Murphy let out a shuddering breath.

"It's been a while," he whispered, and Aiden gentled his fingers even more.

Murphy enjoyed the care and attention, but when he thought he couldn't take any more without popping, he tugged on Aiden's shoulders, and Aiden came up over him. Murphy lifted his legs to Aiden's shoulders, cupped Aiden's cheek, and drew him down for a kiss. Their mouths stayed connected as Aiden pushed ever so gently inside him, and they moaned into each other's mouths.

Aiden's cock was as hot as the rest of him, branding Murphy inside while Aiden's hands did the same over the rest of his skin. Murphy concentrated on the physical sensation of being filled by Aiden, stroked by him, as Aiden's pleasure and desire washed over him again, mingling with his own.

For being so young, Aiden was a goddamned miracle in bed, a machine. He fucked Murphy slow and deep for a *very* long time. Obviously taking care of Aiden first had been a brilliant idea on Murphy's part because this second round lasted a hell of a lot longer than he ever expected it to. This time Murphy was the one who screamed. He was on the verge of passing out too until he heard Aiden murmur groggily, "One out of ten."

"Huh?" Murphy was struggling to get his brain to work.

"You said nine times out of ten. I'm just keeping count."

Murphy snorted, and then he really did collapse into blissful unconsciousness.

CHAPTER 6

As the sun rose over the ocean, Aiden watched Murphy sleep with a profound sense of joy and welling excitement. Murphy was beautiful, kind, hot as fuck in bed, and gave the best blowjob Aiden had ever had in his entire fairly active sexual career. As if that weren't enough for Aiden to fall head over heels for him, there was that strange connection between them.

He felt a little twinge at that, remembering Adam and the penance he should be doing. He was a horrible person, weak-willed and selfish, but staying holed up in his parents' beach house hadn't gotten him anywhere, so maybe this was okay.

Murphy murmured in his sleep and snuggled a little closer to him, and Aiden's heart squeezed as he brushed his fingertips down Murphy's cheek.

Oh dear Lord, he's a snuggler too. How could I possibly not fall in love with him?

He closed his eyes so he could form a cohesive thought that didn't involve rainbows and unicorns and glass slippers. The old Aiden would have been picking out matching rings by now, even if only in his head. He wouldn't have been able to help himself. That was the way he was made. He always threw his whole heart at everything, even though he knew that wasn't the way normal people acted. He'd meant it when he'd told Adam he loved him, and he'd mean it now if he thought Murphy would want to hear it this soon. But the new Aiden had promised to turn over a new leaf. The new Aiden was going to stay calm and collected.

Murphy was classy and mature. Murphy was stable and gentle. Aiden would have to prove he could be all of those things, or Murphy would end up running away from him like everybody else in his life. There was a motivating factor if there ever was one.

Patience was another virtue he was sorely lacking, but he was going to find some somewhere. Maybe he should try to channel a little of Adam. Adam had always been the king of stoicism and patience until Aiden had pushed him too far. But thinking about Adam inevitably brought him around to the memories of the disaster he'd left in his wake, and he withdrew a little from Murphy.

I'm not going to fuck it up again. I'm not going to be crazy drama queen Aiden. I'm going to keep it together and be the kind of person a guy like Murphy would want, like he deserves.

Aiden could feel himself beginning to vibrate with pent-up energy. He wanted to get started with his great personality renovation right now, especially now that he had a clear direction to go in. He needed to think of a way to show Murphy he was mature relationship material without being obvious that that was what he was doing. It really wasn't fair that most people came by this sort of thing so naturally, and Aiden had to work so hard at it, always afraid he'd do something stupid and blow it, forget to think before every word, every action.

Needing comfort, Aiden moved closer to Murphy again and let Murphy's aura, that strange, calming energy between them, soothe him. Only by the time Aiden finally felt his heartbeat slow, Murphy's eyes were open and his gentle smile was shadowed by something that kicked Aiden's heart painfully.

"Wow, it's morning already. I, uh, should probably go," Murphy croaked a little groggily.

Why?

Aiden wanted so badly to ask, but he was the new Aiden, not the old one. This was only their first night together. It might count as their second date, but that was it. They didn't have to be attached at the hip. Mature adults had their own lives, their own interests. He didn't want to look desperate or pathetic… any more than he already had. Scary, clingy, and codependent was not what he was going for.

"Can I make you some breakfast or some tea before you go?"

Murphy gave him that heart wrenchingly gentle smile again and kissed him tenderly.

"Thank you, but I'm fine."

While Murphy collected his discarded clothes and pulled them on, Aiden forced himself to remain in bed. They would have more nights like this. He only had to play it cool, keep his head and his emotions in check, and everything would be fine.

"Aiden, is everything okay?"

Murphy was watching him with concern written all over his face, and Aiden cursed himself. Murphy's ability to read him despite his best efforts to mask his feelings was uncanny. He needed to try harder. He'd been a theater major for how many years, and he couldn't manage even that much of a poker face?

"Sure. Why wouldn't I be?"

He smiled as innocently as he could, but Murphy's eyebrows were still drawn into a deep V. He sat on the bed next to Aiden and gave him another kiss.

"Do you want to go get your Jeep now, before I start work?"

"Naw, it can wait. I'll probably just hang around and chill for a while, make sure no more dizzy spells. We can get it later."

"Okay. I'll call you tonight."

"No problem."

After another gentle kiss, Murphy left, and by sheer force of will, Aiden kept himself in the bed until he heard the door open and close.

Too keyed up to sleep, despite the early hour, Aiden immediately hopped out of bed and went to the kitchen to get some coffee brewing. He was a mess—emotionally, intellectually, even psychically—an utter disaster. But he was going to fix it. He had motivation now. What he did to Adam and how terrible he felt about that should have been enough. He recognized that. But it hadn't been. He hadn't tried hard enough to fix himself. He'd hidden away.

Did that make him a bad person?

Probably.

But he'd be better. He had to be, or he was going to spend the rest of his life fucking up one relationship after another or hiding out in a cave. The shrinks didn't understand. The ones he'd been sent to had all kinds of diagnoses for him, but none of them believed the truth. They wanted to keep him drugged up all the time, numb. But that stuff hit him so hard and then burned away so quickly, that the doses they'd had to give him made him a fucking zombie. How was he ever supposed to get better if he was a zombie? He could control it. He'd managed pretty well for years until that disaster with Adam. He could get there again. Somehow. He just had to figure it out.

By about three o'clock in the afternoon, Aiden was driving *himself* crazy. He wanted to see Murphy, but he had to resist the urge to call him. He wanted to come up with something brilliant that would solve all of his problems, but he hadn't had one of his surges of inspiration in months, not since the fire.

Going a little stir-crazy in the house, he decided to step out on the beach before something caught fire. A few intrepid beach goers had spread out blankets this far down, soaking up the last of the late summer sun now that yesterday's storms had passed, and Aiden smiled. He turned his face to the sky too and let the warmth flow through him. He was in the sand. He wasn't in danger of burning anything. Everything always seemed better, less hopeless when the sun was shining down on him, filling him.

When his cell beeped, his heart leapt in his chest, and he practically tore his pocket getting the thing out.

Hey. How's it going?

Disappointed, Aiden tried to dredge up enough enthusiasm not to insult the guy, but Con was most definitely not who he'd been hoping for.

Good. You?

Good. Saw your Jeep at the coffee shop. The girl said you were sick yesterday. You okay?

He had a voice mail and a couple of missed calls from Crystal he'd been too distracted to return. Now he felt shitty, both for not returning her calls and for how disappointed he'd been to see Con's name on the screen. He was a shitty friend.

Yeah. I'm okay now. Maybe something I ate. I don't know. Thanks for checking.

No probs. Would've come by, but the girl said you already had someone looking out for you. She mentioned a couple guys actually.

Con was fishing, but Aiden wasn't interested in taking the bait. He wasn't looking to hook up, either in the closet or out of it, and he couldn't think of any other reason why Con would want to know. Maybe Aiden was being harsh, but Con hadn't exactly struck him as the altruistic type, or as having a shortage of friends.

Yeah. My neighbor brought me home. Gonna rest some more. But I'm good.

Okay. Good. Guess I'll talk to you later.

Later. Thanks for checking.

As brush-offs went, he didn't think he was too harsh. He doubted he'd hear much more from the guy once he realized Aiden wasn't interested. But he hadn't been mean or careless. Old Aiden might have strung him along because he craved the attention or maybe even blown him out of boredom—at least if he didn't have a boyfriend at the time.

See. I'm showing improvement already.

Now all he had to do was keep himself from going completely crazy until Murphy called him tonight.

And if Murphy doesn't call?

He was not going to freak, not one little bit. That was old Aiden.

Determined to spend his time more productively, Aiden went back inside and started Googling meditation techniques again. He'd spent days reading up on it his first couple of weeks on the island. But so much of it had been just text on the screen. Vague words like center and core, root and pelvic floor hadn't meant anything to him. He wasn't stupid. He got the definitions, but they didn't fit who he was. He couldn't *feel* the words.

Did he even have a center? What was he, a Gobstopper or a Tootsie Pop?

He also hadn't been able to see the point in sitting still that long. He breathed all the time as it was. He didn't need to sit on his ass to do that. He had to have been doing something wrong, but he hadn't been able to figure out what it was. He was going to try harder this time. He was going to figure this out. He was going to be the Zenest of the Zen, and then he wouldn't be a spazz anymore, and then Murphy would fall for him as hard as Aiden was falling, and the world would be sunshine and roses. He could do it.

He grinned up at the sun, clapped his hands together, and spun around. He was stoked. He was all brightness and positive energy as the french doors banged closed behind him, and he marched over to his laptop.

He spent an hour rereading some of the sites he'd bookmarked before, hoping to find something he'd missed, but everything was still just as vague and esoteric, and his little happy balloon started to spring a leak. Discouraged but not defeated, he went to his bedroom. Trying his best to ignore the rumpled bedding and smell of sex that lingered in the air, he grabbed the one meditation tool that he'd already had limited success with.

Back in the great room, bright sunlight poured through the wall of windows that showed off the house's million-dollar ocean view, and he plunked himself down in a ray of it. He lit the incense he'd grabbed, set the stick in the holder on the coffee table, and sat cross-legged in front of it. He liked the glowing coal at the end of the stick and the swirling smoke enough to at least keep still for a little while. He couldn't do it for hours yet, but from what he could tell, this was the closest he got to what they all called a "meditative state." Closing his eyes and staring at the backs of his eyelids for an hour just hadn't cut it. He needed something to look at.

He'd also tried staring at a flickering candle flame too, thinking that could keep his interest, but he should have known an open flame was a bad idea. The candle had melted into a puddle of wax all over the table in less than a minute, and he certainly hadn't felt any calmer afterward. The incense tended to burn faster too if he spent too much time watching the coal, so he concentrated more on the smoke tendrils instead. They had a lazy, calming effect he hoped would be enough.

As the sweet, spicy smoke surrounded him—exotic yet reminiscent of many a college dorm room he'd visited—Aiden let his shoulders relax and forced his thoughts away from Murphy. He could be stoked about a new relationship without obsessing over it. He'd show Murphy he could be calm. He could be mature. He could be passionate, but his emotions didn't have to rule him, didn't have to be all over the place like crazed flying monkeys. Murphy was going to get the new and improved Aiden and—

Shit. I'm still thinking about Murphy. Obviously I'm not doing this right.

Aiden glared at the smoke tendrils as if they were the only thing left on the planet. Anyone peering through the windows would think he belonged in a straightjacket the way he must have looked. To keep focused, he played a game in his head, trying to decipher the curling smoke, read some sort of message spelled out in it, but he didn't have much luck. After what felt like forever, though probably was only fifteen minutes, he groaned in frustration and was about to grab himself a bottle of water when movement outside the window caught his attention. He saw the briefest flicker of a shadow between the houses, but then it was gone.

A bird maybe?

Then he saw Murphy step out onto the back deck of his house, and Aiden forgot all about the shadow in lieu of something much more riveting. If Murphy was outside, it would be okay to wave hello, especially if Aiden just happened to be outside too, right? That wouldn't be too needy.

His incense forgotten, Aiden grabbed his bottle of water and headed out the french doors to his own back deck. He casually strolled to the fence between their two properties, making a big show of examining the landscaping his parents had to pay a fortune for, especially for a place they almost never visited. When he thought he'd played it cool long enough, Aiden glanced over at Murphy through the trellis covered in trumpet vine that he *wasn't* hiding behind and promptly felt like an idiot for bothering with the show because Murphy wasn't even looking in his direction. He was on the phone with someone, staring out at the ocean.

He shouldn't eavesdrop. The phone call wasn't any of his business. But apparently "new" Aiden hadn't quite gotten the message, because he didn't budge from where he stood. The wind was only a gentle breeze today, so Murphy's voice carried well enough Aiden didn't have to strain.

"Is that better? Sometimes reception's a little wonky in the house…. Yeah, it's no big deal. I know you're busy. I just had some things on my mind the last couple of days but nothing major. We can talk about it next time we get together, nothing to worry about."

Nothing major?

Aiden frowned and pouted a little. What did he mean "nothing major"? And what was that bullshit about the next time they get together?

"Tonight?" Aiden looked up in time to see Murphy glance in his direction. Luckily he didn't see Aiden skulking behind the trellis. "No, I can make it. I'll be there. Dinner before or after? Okay, that works for me. Just give me a couple hours, and I'll meet you…. And, Howard? Thanks."

Murphy pulled the phone away from his ear and went back inside, leaving Aiden practically boiling over with questions and worries. Half of him wanted to march over there that second and demand Murphy tell him what he'd meant and who he was going to see, but the other half knew how stupid and crazy that would be, particularly when he was this worked up.

Aiden closed his eyes and took some deep breaths. He could do this. He could stay calm and be reasonable. Murphy was a great guy. Of course he'd have other friends, and he'd want to spend time with them like any other normal person. Aiden was the freak who had to hide away hundreds of the miles from the friends he'd made at college because he couldn't be trusted around normal people.

Releasing the grip he had on the trellis, Aiden forced himself to turn around and go back inside, purposefully ignoring the cracked and yellowed handprint he'd left behind in the white paint. He fought his crazy all through a shower, a change of clothes, and lunch. But barely five minutes after he heard Murphy drive away, he couldn't take the silence in the house anymore, and he called a taxi and headed into town.

He visited with Crystal for a little while, but no matter how much she teased, he wasn't in the mood to talk about Murphy, and eventually he waved good-bye and wandered around the shops, killing time. He was tempted to take the ferry to the mainland for a real distraction but figured it would only be a waste. He wasn't going to be able to stop thinking about Murphy, no matter how hard he tried, at least not until he'd had a chance to talk to him. His best bet was to go home, maybe take a nap, and hope Murphy didn't stay out too late or wait too long before he made that call he'd promised.

He opened the door to his Jeep and was about to climb in when a hand on his shoulder made him jump.

"Sorry. I didn't mean to startle you," Richard said. He smiled brightly at Aiden. "I just saw you from across the street and thought I'd check on you after yesterday."

Aiden gave him a smile in return but didn't let go of the Jeep door. "I'm feeling better. Thanks for the help."

"No problem. Hey, do you want to get a cup of coffee and maybe finish our conversation from yesterday?"

New Aiden didn't want to be rude, but he didn't feel like chatting. After their lengthy discussion the day before, ranging from Aiden's school experience to his favorite songs, he didn't think Richard was hitting on him anymore, or wanted anything other than friendly conversation, but he wasn't in the mood. He should have welcomed the distraction, but he was feeling drained again all of a sudden, and he just wanted to go home and lie down.

"Thanks for the offer, but I have some stuff to do at home. Maybe I'll see you at the café another time."

Richard's bland smile didn't falter, but he also hadn't let go of Aiden's shoulder yet either. "Are you sure? A cup of coffee wouldn't take long. I'm buying."

Beginning to get a little uncomfortable, Aiden shrugged off his hand and stepped closer to his Jeep. "Thanks. But I really need to get going. I'll take a rain check though."

Aiden climbed into his Jeep and closed the door. Richard made no move to stop him. The man simply shrugged and said, "Sure. Maybe next time, then. I'll see ya around."

As Aiden pulled away, Richard waved, and he started to feel a little silly for getting so uncomfortable. Aiden was a hugger, a touchy-feely kind of guy. He was the last person who should get weird about someone invading his personal space. He'd like to blame Murphy for his current emotional issues, but that roller coaster was all his and had been for a very long time.

Just another ride on the Aiden Flanagan crazy train. All aboard.

Taking a breath to dispel his funk, he turned his Jeep toward home.

CHAPTER 7

Howard was waiting for him outside the center. Murphy was running a little late, so they only had time for a hug before going inside. They settled in the back as the rest of the group filed in, and Murphy felt his shoulders relax for the first time all day. There was nothing like a little normalcy and routine, a shot of the familiar, to settle him down after the kaleidoscope of emotions he'd been going through since last night.

As the regulars he'd known for years filled the seats around him, Murphy waved, chatted, and shook hands, happy to be among friends. It was an open meeting tonight, and he smiled welcomingly to the few newcomers he didn't recognize, but the smile froze on his face when the man from the coffee shop, Richard, came through the doors. At probably close to six-foot-four, he loomed over the people in front of him, and for some reason Murphy couldn't shake the image of a vulture or bird of prey that popped into his head, though Richard's smile was bright, his expression open and seemingly harmless.

"You okay?" Howard asked, and Murphy realized he was scowling.

Shaking off the tension, he shrugged. "Yeah."

"Someone you know?" Howard asked, nodding toward the corner where Richard now appeared to be holding court with many of the younger members.

"Not really. I met him yesterday but only briefly."

"The way you're looking at him, I would have thought he shot your dog or something."

Murphy chuckled and forced himself to look away. "Sorry. Something about him bugs me. I don't know exactly why. It might have something to do with what I wanted to talk to you about, but we can discuss it over dinner, after the meeting."

Howard pursed his lips and nodded, unconcerned and unflappable as usual.

After the preamble, the meeting statement, and the "How it works" reading, Brenda, their secretary, started the discussion portion with her own story, and then opened the floor to anyone else who wanted to share. When Richard popped to his feet, Murphy wasn't surprised.

He knew he was being uncharitable and completely unsupportive of his fellow AA member, but he couldn't help his frown of disapproval at the way the man drank in the attention of everyone around him. From a purely logical standpoint, Richard wasn't doing anything thousands of other members hadn't done before, but Murphy never claimed to be purely logical or perfect. He continued to scowl as Richard shared his story of hitting rock bottom after years of addiction and gushed about the outpouring of love and support he'd received during his decade in the program. He couldn't shake the feeling something was off about the man. No one else seemed to notice, at least as far as Murphy could tell from the enraptured expressions of the people around him. Even Howard seemed mesmerized until Richard took his seat again and someone picked up the discussion.

After the meeting Murphy headed outside while everyone else milled around and chatted. Once he was out in the fresh air, he felt a lot better and shook off any lingering unease about Richard. He was being stupid. Richard was just a guy, someone in the program like Murphy and most of his friends. Just because Murphy was apparently a jealous freak didn't make Richard a bad person.

"You ready?" Howard said coming up behind him.

"Yeah. I'm hungry."

He followed Howard to the restaurant, a Thai place they both loved. When they were seated at a small table in the back and the server had brought Murphy a steaming cup of jasmine tea, he settled into his seat with a deep, contented sigh.

"I needed this. The meeting, you, the tea. Thanks for calling me back today. Otherwise I might have skipped altogether and spent the night rattling around my house fighting with myself."

Howard raised a bushy graying eyebrow and pursed his full lips as he studied Murphy from behind his thick black-framed glasses that had gone out of style sometime in the eighties.

"Are you going to tell me what's going on now?"

Howard never beat around the bush. It was one of the things Murphy loved about the man. Simply being across the table from him made Murphy start to feel silly for all of his angst over the last few days. Echoes of previous conversations they'd had ran through his head.

Are you dying? Is your house falling down? Is the IRS coming to take everything you got? Are you going to go hungry? Then what's the big deal?

He tried to hide a smile behind his teacup. "Nothing much. Or nothing to worry about anyway."

"Now you're smiling," Howard said with a smirk of his own.

"I always smile. When do I not smile?"

"Yeah, but this is different." Howard leaned a little closer and squinted at him. "This is more like a grin. You're happy, excited. But before, in the meeting and on the phone this afternoon, you sounded a little stressed."

After another couple of seconds of intense study, during which Murphy squirmed in his seat, Howard sat back in his chair and snorted. "You got laid."

"Howard!"

"I knew it," he crowed.

The couple at the table closest turned to look at them, and Murphy could feel himself flush.

"Shush. You don't *know* anything."

"Uh-huh," Howard grunted and rolled his eyes. "Don't believe the hype. Just because I'm a sixty-year-old straight guy who's been out of the game for more than a decade, doesn't mean I'm completely clueless. I was married to Barb for twenty-five years before she passed, and she taught me a thing or two. Besides, I know you. You haven't smiled like this in the five years since we met."

Holding his hands up in surrender, and in the hopes that Howard would keep his voice down, Murphy capitulated. "Okay, okay. Yeah. I did. We did… what you said."

Howard gave him a look that clearly said he what thought of Murphy's pathetic confession, and Murphy groaned. He sounded like a sixteen-year-old confessing to his dad.

"Look. I can't talk about it yet, and I'm sure you don't want the details anyway. It's new, brand-new, like last night kinda new, so I'm still working on how I feel about it."

The server brought their orders before Howard could say anything, and Murphy happily dove into his duck in green curry to give himself time for his cheeks to cool and to figure out how much he wanted to share.

Howard had been his rock, his anchor after Felix died. But Howard didn't know all of Murphy's secrets. Howard was a little too rooted in the mundane to be comfortable with some of the strangeness of Murphy's life. He hadn't really needed to know it all to be a fantastic sponsor when Murphy needed him.

"You know," Howard said around a mouthful of fried rice, "you called me before last night, though, so this can't be that new."

"The sex is new. I met him a couple days ago, and let's just say he made an impression."

"Oh really?"

"Don't look at me like that. Look, I called because I wanted to talk to someone who was levelheaded, since I know I'm not sometimes."

When Howard chuckled in full agreement, Murphy was the one to roll his eyes. "He's younger, okay? I wasn't sure if it was a good idea to get involved, and I needed to talk it out a little. That's all."

"Why didn't you leave a message, then? You know you need to leave a message if you want me to call you back."

"I know. When you didn't pick up, I decided to call Lola instead of bothering you."

Howard's eyebrows shot up and his mouth quirked. "I thought you said you wanted levelheaded."

"Funny."

With a quiet chuckle, Howard set his fork down and steepled his fingers. When he lifted his gaze to meet Murphy's again, his expression had sobered. "This isn't another one of your strays is it?"

"No, no, not at all."

Murphy's reply came out a little more defensive than he'd planned, and Howard didn't seem too convinced.

With a sigh, Murphy set his fork down too. "Look, I'll admit that Aiden might have a few issues he's working through. But I really am attracted to him… *very* attracted. And not just in a Florence Nightingale kinda way. I know that's what you're thinking."

When Howard continued to stay silent, Murphy shifted uncomfortably in his seat. The man had a way of making him squirm without saying a word.

"I know he's not a lost puppy or a kitten. He's a person with a hell of a lot to offer. I think he's just going through a rough patch right now, and I want to help him."

Howard held up his hands. "Okay. You're a grown man, Murph. You can make your own decisions, and mostly you make good ones. You've just got a soft heart, and I wanted to make sure you'd thought about those possibilities too… and it looks like you have. So that's good."

Feeling a little embarrassed about how defensive he'd gotten when he was the one who'd called for advice, he gave Howard an apologetic smile.

"Thanks. You're right too. I wouldn't have tried to call you if I hadn't had reservations. I mean, I haven't dated in something like ten years, not since Felix and I moved in together. This is moving a little faster than I'm ready for maybe. I don't know."

Howard nodded sagely. "You have to have a solid foundation before you can build on it. It may be trite, but it's also true. If you feel like it's moving fast, then maybe you should slow things down, especially if this guy, Aiden, has some issues he's working through and his foundation's a little rocky. Anyway, what's the rush? Date for a while. If he's got things he's working through, give him some space to do that. You know as well as anyone, a man has to fix his own messes. No one out there can do it for him."

Murphy sucked in a long breath and blew it out. "Yeah. If it's healthy and right, it'll keep. That makes sense. Some space and going slow is probably the best thing to do. I can do slow. I'll admit part of me doesn't want to. When I'm around him, I just… but no, you're right. Slow is not a bad thing."

Over Murphy's second pot of jasmine tea, they chatted about other things for a while. Feeling guilty for all the time they'd spent talking about his issues, Murphy made sure to give Howard equal time. Howard was still his sponsor, but they were more friends now than anything else, so their meetings didn't have to only be about supporting him anymore. Over mango and sticky rice, Murphy got to hear all about the group Howard had joined for the active and over fifty. He hadn't found anyone special yet, but he had a few ladies he was keeping his eye on. Knowing Howard was getting back out there too made Murphy smile and eased a little of the tumult in his own mind. Maybe it was time for both of them.

"Thanks for tonight," Murphy said as they were walking to their cars. "It was wonderful to see you as always, Howard."

Howard shook his hand and clapped him on the back. "Anytime. And don't stress too much about the new relationship. You've been alone a long time. You deserve to enjoy yourself again. We both do… only as long as you *are* enjoying yourself. If it turns into something more like some of your early rescue missions, you need to take a step back… and you need to call me so I can kick your ass."

On impulse, Murphy gave him a hug. Howard was never much of a hugger, but he endured whenever Murphy felt the need. "I will. I'm going to take it slow, give us both some space, and see what happens from there. I'll talk to you soon, and I'll keep up with my meetings."

"You do that. That sponsee of yours, Grady, he left for California over a year ago, didn't he?"

"Yes."

"It might be time to find you a new one soon. Keep you out of trouble."

They usually gave Murphy the new and vulnerable ones, or the ones that needed coddling, not the ones that needed a kick in the pants. Murphy could do the ass kicking, but it wasn't his first inclination. He was a tea and sympathy kind of guy, and he was okay with that.

"Give me a little time to settle things in my personal life, now that I'm actually thinking of having one again, and you're on."

On the drive home, Murphy ran through their conversation and firmed his resolve to take things slow with Aiden. He was out of practice at the whole dating thing, and Howard was right. They didn't need to jump into a full-on committed, in each other's pockets relationship right away. Aiden was hurting and vulnerable, and Murphy would be doing him a disservice if he tried to be everything Aiden needed right now, tried to fix all that ailed him. Just because Murphy could feel everything Aiden felt didn't mean he had a right to try and fix it. Aiden hadn't even asked him to. They'd had sex, not exchanged vows.

As he paced his living room, he ran through what he was going to say to Aiden a few dozen times, with a few dozen variations. He'd promised to call Aiden tonight, but there was no way he was going to have this conversation over the phone. He'd just check in, make a date for them to talk later, and then say good night. After wrapping up in his thick gray cable-knit cardigan, he stepped out on his back porch and dialed Aiden's cell.

"Hey! I was starting to think I wasn't going to hear from you."

Aiden's voice sounded a little tight, his cheerful tone too forced, but Murphy resisted the impulse to call attention to it and firmly ignored any vibrations along his other senses.

"I'm sorry it's so late. I had dinner with a friend, and it went longer than I expected. How are you feeling?"

"I'm okay."

Again he wasn't going to open any cans of worms tonight. He'd know if Aiden was in any real distress, so reading too much into his tone wasn't necessary.

"Good. I'm glad you're feeling better."

"Are you home now?"

"Yes. I got in a little bit ago."

"Can I come over?"

Murphy froze. He hadn't anticipated this, and he should have. But he'd made up his mind to move slow, and that's what he was going to do, no matter how tempted he was.

"Not tonight, Aiden. I'm pretty tired. I think I should just go to sleep."

"I could still keep you company while you sleep."

His tone was teasing and a little seductive, but there was still that odd note to it that Murphy wasn't ready to deal with. He couldn't come up with any reason they shouldn't without starting the conversation he was trying to save for a better time, so all he said was "I don't think so. Not tonight, okay?"

When that was met with dead silence, Murphy's chest tightened.

"Aiden, are you there?"

There was another small silence before Aiden said, "I'm here. I just... I wanted to see you. I thought, after last night, you'd want to see me too."

Aiden was still trying for light and flirty, but now he was failing miserably. When the barest hint of emotional pain brushed along the edge of his shields, Murphy's resolve weakened. But he needed to stay strong. He couldn't cave every time Aiden got a little upset. He was going to have to open that can of worms on the phone.

"I do want to see you, Aiden. I just think maybe we jumped into this a little too fast. You know, too much too soon? I think maybe we should slow down a little, spend some time—"

"Don't!" Aiden's shout cut him off. "Don't say it. I can't... not again."

The emotion surge that hit Murphy this time was much stronger. The strength of it at that distance left him breathless. He scrambled to think of something to fix it.

"Aiden, I'm not saying—"

"Just stop, okay?" Aiden said more quietly. The quaver in his voice tore Murphy's heart even more than his words. "I got it. I know the drill. I just... I wanted it so bad. I knew I shouldn't have. I'm not ready yet, not good enough, but I thought we could.... Fuck it! You're right. This is stupid. I won't bother you anymore."

Aiden hung up, and Murphy simply stared at his phone for a few seconds wondering what the hell just happened. But when the wave of pain grew stronger, followed by a wave of anger and despair, Murphy was moving before he knew it.

He hit the gate at the same time the back doors of Aiden's house flew open, and Aiden came running out toward the beach. Murphy raced after him and caught up to him as Aiden slumped to the ground in his spot behind the dune. Murphy was sure it had to be a trick of the moonlight, but he could swear Aiden's eyes flashed a brilliant green in the darkness as he glared up at him.

"Fuck, Murphy! Go away, okay?"

Despite the chill on the ocean breeze, a gust of warm air washed over him. And that along with the waves of emotion buffeting him made Murphy sway on his feet.

"What did I say? I don't understand," he managed to get out despite the dizziness.

"Just go. Please!"

Murphy took a deep breath and fought through the storm.

"I can't. I can't leave you like this. At least tell me what I said."

Aiden wrapped his arms around himself and rocked in the sand. After a few deep shuddering breaths of his own, he said, "It's not your fault. I know it's all me. Just like you said. I'm too much... too much trouble, too much drama, too much, too fast."

That feeling of heat intensified around them, pulsing as if keeping time with Aiden's rocking. Murphy could swear he heard hissing and crackling from the grasses nearby, but he couldn't take his eyes off Aiden.

"Aiden—"

"No. I know. I'm too intense, too much of a drama queen, too broken, too high maintenance, too... *everything!*"

The sleeve of Aiden's sweatshirt burst into flame as he shouted that last word. The sudden burst of light dazzled Murphy's eyes, but that didn't slow his reaction.

"Aiden!"

Without thinking, Murphy lunged for him to put out the fire, but Aiden threw up a hand to stop him.

"Don't! Go away, Murphy. I don't want to hurt you."

The fire went out almost as suddenly as it started, and once the shock of what he'd just witnessed wore off, Murphy moved forward again.

"Stop. Please, Murphy. It would kill me if I hurt you," Aiden begged.

His eyes glistened in the light from the houses, and Murphy couldn't have stopped himself even if he'd wanted to.

"You won't," Murphy said with certainty.

"You can't know that," he cried, curling in on himself a little more.

"Yes, I can."

"How?"

"It doesn't matter right now. Just trust me."

Aiden's anger had faded with the fire. It no longer buffeted Murphy's shields. But now it was replaced by anguish, and all Murphy cared about was another human being in pain, Aiden in pain, someone who meant a great deal to him already, despite every logical reason he shouldn't.

He drew on the waves crashing behind them and the wind heavy with saltwater to give him strength as he closed the last distance between them and pulled Aiden into his arms.

"You won't hurt me. It's okay. Everything's okay. You just need to calm down a little."

Aiden let out a long shuddering breath and buried his face in Murphy's neck. "I'm trying. I'm always trying," he whispered against Murphy's skin.

"I know."

Murphy squeezed Aiden tight to his chest and petted his back and hair until Aiden let out one last shuddering breath and the storm inside him subsided. In the now peaceful darkness, Murphy sighed too.

"You know," he whispered against Aiden's hair. "For the record, I never said you were too much. That may be what you heard, but it isn't what I said."

Aiden sniffled and nodded.

"I'm sorry, Murphy," Aiden mumbled against his skin.

"It's okay. But I think we've done enough for one night. Come on. Come inside and I'll—"

"Make me some tea?" Aiden finished with a watery laugh, and Murphy smiled.

"Yes. I'll make you some tea."

Once they reached Murphy's living room, Aiden curled up on his couch while Murphy boiled the water and brewed the tea. The familiar activity was calming when his thoughts and feelings wanted to go in every direction at once. He'd witnessed something incredible, amazing, and he wasn't sure what to make of it. He was beginning to realize he'd probably only sensed a small part of what Aiden could actually do. Aiden was much more than a projector in the same way that Murphy was more than an empath.

He filled the tray with the two mugs of tea and a jar of honey and carried it to the couch.

"So are you going to tell me what happened out there?" he asked casually as he handed over Aiden's mug, then grabbed his own and sat on the couch.

Aiden ducked his head and grimaced. He stared resolutely at the mug in his hands as he asked, "Which part? The I-freaked-out-and-made-an-idiot-of-myself-as-usual part… or the… *other* thing?"

With a laugh, Murphy settled back against the arm of the couch facing Aiden and took a sip of his tea before he said, "I wouldn't have put it quite that way. But why don't we start with what made you so upset in the first place and go from there? Obviously, I touched a nerve, though I didn't mean to."

Aiden winced and wouldn't look at him. "I'm sorry, Murphy. I'm sorry I flipped out on you."

Murphy could have told Aiden not to bother with the apologies. The remorse and embarrassment pouring off him spoke for themselves. But he wasn't quite ready to delve into his own revelations yet, so he stayed silent, waiting.

"I'm an idiot," Aiden began. "Last night with you was so awesome, and you're so wonderful. And I promised myself I wasn't going to blow it this time. I wasn't going to be crazy and needy and annoying. I was going to give you your space and let you set the pace. But then I heard you on the phone this afternoon, and you left, and I started worrying that maybe you were already dating someone… and this morning you went home so early, and…. God, I sound like a fucking freak. I'm sorry. I just… like you a lot, and I want you to like me too. But I think I'm going to shut up now before I screw things up even more."

If there were a guidebook to Murphy's heart, he would have sworn Aiden was reading directly from chapter one. He set his mug on the coffee table and scooted across the couch. When he was close enough, he took Aiden's mug, set it on the table as well, and then cupped his cheek.

"You didn't screw anything up. I'm flattered you feel so strongly. I guess I should also be flattered you think I have such a rousing social life that I might juggle two lovers at once, instead of seeing me for the dried-up hermit I've been for the past five years. But I promise, if I were seeing someone else, I'd tell you. I'm a one man at a time kind of guy, though, so that's not going to happen."

Aiden closed his eyes and rubbed his cheek into Murphy's palm, the fine copper stubble along his jaw making Murphy's skin tingle.

"I know I freaked for no reason. I just heard that word… and you didn't want to see me tonight, and I lost it."

"What word are we talking about so I don't use it again?"

"You know, T-O-O. As in too much of a pain in the ass to be worth it."

Murphy bent and gave Aiden a light peck on the lips. "I wasn't saying *you* were too much. You got that, right? I only meant what was happening between us was a bit fast for me, and not just on your part, but mine too." Murphy withdrew his hand from Aiden's cheek, wrapped it around Aiden's hands instead, and sat back a little. "You have to understand. I'm picking back up after a five-year hiatus here. I know they say it's like riding a bike. But this is going from training wheels to entering the Tour de France in the space of a couple days. And I'm trying to do the right thing and not rush it."

"I'm sorry."

With a growl of frustration, Murphy gave Aiden's hands a shake. "Don't be sorry. I'm trying to tell you, it's not just you. Do you think I don't want to just dive right in with you and mainline whatever it is that's happening between us? Of course I do. I could get so addicted to you so fast… your passion, your spark. I've been coasting for years in this fog of my own making, and then you show up bright as the sun, and miracle of miracles you want me too. My ego is about to burst out of me and do a jig while the rest of my brain is scared shitless. You can't tell me this isn't scary for you."

"Not the you and me part. Not when it's right."

"You really are fearless, aren't you?"

Aiden laughed bitterly. "I'm afraid of a lot of things. I'm afraid I'll hurt someone again. I'm afraid this horrible feeling, this guilt, will never go away. I'm afraid I'll never be who I want to be, and I'll be alone forever. But saying yes to whatever is happening between us isn't something I'm afraid of."

Aiden's eyes had gone wide and soft. Murphy could feel the energy pouring off him, blanketing Murphy in hope and want. But before he could get carried away by it, he let go of Aiden's hands and put some more distance between them. He took a steadying breath, fighting his own emotions and his body's reaction.

"We need to talk. We need to do a lot of talking *before* we jump in with both feet… at least I need that. Is that okay?"

Nodding eagerly, Aiden scooted closer, buffeting Murphy with happy vibes. "Yes. Anything you want."

"It's not all about me, you know. What you want is important too."

"I just want to be with you, any way I can. I feel so much better when I'm near you. You have no idea."

Murphy was beginning to get an inkling, but he decided he would ponder that at another time.

"Look. We *should* talk, but frankly right now I'm exhausted. I think we should wait until I've gotten some rest."

Aiden sighed and nodded. "I guess I should go, then, huh?"

Honestly, Murphy didn't want Aiden to go any more than Aiden wanted to leave, so he decided to give in for tonight. He wouldn't be able to sleep if Aiden went home anyway.

"No. You were right. I wouldn't mind the company. Please stay… if you want to."

Aiden's reaction lit up the room. He didn't have to say a word, and Murphy couldn't help himself. He stood and pulled Aiden off the couch and kissed him gently on the lips. When they drew apart, Murphy took Aiden's hand and led him to the bedroom.

As he stepped into the room he and Felix had shared for five years and turned on the light, he felt a brief twinge of something—guilt maybe?—but he was too tired to deal with it now. He shoved the feeling aside as he moved to his side of the bed and pulled the covers back.

When he tugged off his shirt, kicked off his damp socks, and stepped out of his pants, Aiden took the hint and got himself undressed too. Aiden hit the light switch and moved to the opposite side of the bed, and they slid under the blankets together without a word. Murphy stretched out with a relieved sigh. The bed was king-size so there was quite an empty expanse between them, and even through his exhaustion, Murphy could feel Aiden hesitating on the other side of it. In the darkness he rolled toward Aiden and lifted his arms, and Aiden was in them in less than a second, warm and happy, making Murphy wish he had the energy to do more. But his eyelids were already drooping, and he could barely say good night without yawning halfway through it.

Tomorrow. They'd deal with everything tomorrow.

CHAPTER 8

WHEN AIDEN woke in the middle of the night, it took him a few seconds to remember where he was. The bed was huge and unfamiliar… and empty. Frowning, he sat up and scanned the room until he spotted Murphy curled up on a window seat. He was still only in his boxers, staring out at the ocean, shivering in a shaft of moonlight.

"Hey," Aiden called out softly. "Everything okay?"

Murphy turned, but his face was in shadow, so Aiden couldn't read his expression.

"Yeah. I think so."

"You don't sound so sure. And you look like you're freezing. Come here. Come back to bed."

Aiden lifted his arms and beckoned, half afraid Murphy would turn him down. But he wasn't going to jump to conclusions this time. Murphy had invited him to stay. That had to mean something. And whatever had him up and fretting in the middle of the night might not have anything to do with Aiden.

He continued to repeat that to himself until Murphy uncurled from the window seat, closed the distance between them, and allowed himself to be pulled back into bed. The sigh Murphy let out as Aiden wrapped him tightly in his arms went a long way to soothing his nerves and gave him the confidence to ask, "Do you want to talk about it?"

"I don't know."

Unsure of what to do with that, Aiden squeezed Murphy tighter and kissed his temple. "Okay."

Eventually Murphy stopped shivering and relaxed completely in Aiden's arms. At least the fire inside him was good for something. Murphy seemed to be soaking up every bit of warmth Aiden had to give, and that was a very good feeling.

"You're the first lover I've had since my partner died, the first person I've had in my bedroom. I just have some feelings I need to work through because of that, I guess," Murphy murmured quietly against his chest.

Aiden swallowed and squeezed Murphy tighter.

"You said it's been five years?"

"Yes."

"I don't mind if you want to talk about it… about him, if it helps."

Murphy propped himself on his elbows above Aiden. His face was shadowed, but Aiden could hear the gentle smile in his voice.

"Thank you. You have a good heart, Aiden Flanagan. Don't let anyone ever tell you different."

Aiden chuckled around the tightness in his throat. "I'll remind you, you said that next time you're pissed at me."

"I haven't been pissed at you yet. That first night doesn't count. It wasn't you I was angry with."

"Don't worry. You will be at some point. I can pretty much guarantee it."

Murphy didn't respond to that. He just petted Aiden's cheek with gentle fingers. As much as Aiden was enjoying the petting, he didn't like knowing Murphy was sad.

"Are you sure you don't want to talk about anything?"

With another sigh, Murphy sank back down and rested his head on Aiden's chest. "I will, sometime. I promise. But not tonight. I need to figure out what it is I'm feeling before I can talk about it…. I am glad you're here, though. Don't think I'm not, okay?"

Even when something was really bothering Murphy, he still took the time to reassure. The sad part was, Aiden needed that reassurance. He didn't want to. He wanted to be the strong one for Murphy, like Murphy had been for him. But he wasn't there yet, and Murphy knew it somehow.

The realization was a little shaming, but Aiden couldn't seem to hide anything from the man. He was usually better at acting than this.

"I'm glad I'm here too."

Thankfully, the next time Aiden woke, Murphy was still cuddled up next to him. Not waking up alone meant more to him than he thought it should, but at least Murphy seemed to be on the same page, judging by the sleepy smile he gave Aiden when he opened his amazing blue eyes.

"Good morning," Aiden said around a yawn.

"Good morning. Would you like some breakfast?"

"You cooking?"

"I can manage something… although, I don't have any coffee. I'm sorry. I don't drink the stuff."

Aiden kept his groan of disappointment to himself. He could run next door if he got desperate.

"That's okay. I'll have whatever you're having."

Murphy regarded him with a knowing smile on his face, but all he said was "Okay, good. Breakfast it is."

Still mostly hard from spending the night with Murphy wrapped around him, Aiden had kind of been hoping for morning sex, but he kept his mouth shut on that too. He was going to let Murphy set the pace between them from now on if it killed him. Then Murphy climbed out of bed and stretched right in front of him, and Aiden was almost positive it *would* kill him. His cock twitched, and he dropped a hand below the sheet to give it a rub as he watched Murphy's tight ass flex inside his shorts.

Murphy moved to his closet and reached for the robe that hung on a hook on the door but froze halfway and glanced back over his shoulder. Aiden tried to smile innocently, but Murphy wasn't buying it. His gaze dropped to where Aiden massaged his dick beneath the covers, and Aiden licked his lips almost involuntarily.

"You know. It really isn't fair teasing me when I'm trying to do the right thing and make us a nice breakfast so we can talk."

"What? I didn't say anything."

Murphy rolled his eyes. "You didn't have to."

Aiden sat up in bed and huffed in mock outrage. "You can't blame me if you're thinking the same things I am. I didn't say a word. That's all on you."

Murphy came back to the bed and crawled across the mattress until he straddled Aiden's hips. Not exactly displeased with this turn of events, Aiden dropped back onto his pillow as Murphy braced his palms on either side of Aiden's head and glared down at him with mock severity.

"What?" Aiden asked, trying not to look too triumphant.

With a groan, Murphy closed his eyes and pressed his forehead to Aiden's.

"You don't even know you're doing it, do you?" he murmured cryptically.

Aiden would have asked what he meant if Murphy weren't so close and didn't smell so damned good—like sea salt but also spicy sweet like tea or incense. He wanted to lick every inch of him, taste that salt, and bask in his throaty moans of pleasure. His cock throbbed and his body pulsed with heat at the images those thoughts conjured, but Murphy was the one who gasped.

"Fuck, Aiden. You're killin' me."

Having no idea what Murphy meant by that, Aiden would have protested again that he hadn't done anything, but Murphy captured his lips and started sucking and nibbling, and Aiden lost any verbal capacity he might have had. With an inarticulate growl, Aiden shoved his hands down the back of Murphy's boxers and squeezed his firm, taut ass while he arched off the mattress and ground his cock against Murphy's.

Murphy propped himself on one arm and used his other hand to drag his boxers down, freeing his cock. It sprang back against his navel, and Aiden licked his lips, remembering his earlier fantasy. Using his grip on Murphy's ass, Aiden shimmied down between Murphy's legs, pushing the sheet and blanket out of the way as he went, until he could lick that plump red crown. With another groan, Murphy spread his legs wider and dropped down on his elbows, cocooning Aiden as Aiden drew more of Murphy's cock into his mouth. Before the other night, Aiden had always been rather proud of his cock-sucking abilities, at least until Murphy blew the top off his head. Aiden wasn't sure he'd ever be able to achieve that kind of greatness, but he sure as hell was going to give it his best shot.

While he sucked and pumped Murphy's cock, drawing it deep into his mouth, Aiden released one hand from Murphy's ass and cupped and rolled his balls. Literally warming to his task, he deep-throated Murphy while he teased the fingers of his other hand down Murphy's crack.

"Oh God," Murphy moaned above him.

Murphy's thighs trembled on either side of him, and Aiden smiled as he drew off Murphy's crown with a sucking kiss before stuffing it back in his mouth again. He worked Murphy's body with both hands and his mouth, teasing and tormenting until Murphy ground out a breathless "Stop."

"I'm going to come if you don't," Murphy gasped after lifting his face away from the pillow he'd been moaning obscenities into.

"And the problem with that is?" Aiden asked between panting breaths.

He kissed and nuzzled along Murphy's hip while Murphy tried to formulate a reply. But when nothing appeared to be forthcoming, Aiden went back to work sucking and pumping Murphy's cock with his fist until Murphy froze, thrust his hips once, and came in Aiden's mouth. Aiden kept swallowing until Murphy put a gentle hand on his shoulder to push him away.

Feeling pretty satisfied that he'd made a good showing, Aiden maneuvered a still orgasm-drunk Murphy onto his back and draped himself halfway on top of him. He nestled his head under Murphy's chin and closed his eyes contentedly even though his own cock throbbed in lonely protest.

After a minute or two of listening to Murphy's breathing even out, Aiden reached down and wrapped his hand around his cock to get some relief. As soon as he closed his eyes, buried his face in Murphy's neck, and started pumping, Murphy's fist wrapped around the one Aiden had on his cock and took over. With a happy moan, Aiden tasted Murphy's skin and breathed in his scent while his hips thrust into Murphy's grip. When he was getting close, Aiden threw his head back and arched his spine, and Murphy took the opportunity to seal their mouths together. A couple of thrusts of Murphy's tongue in his mouth was all it took to make Aiden come. He moaned into Murphy's mouth and shot over their fists and onto Murphy's hip, bucking a few last involuntary thrusts until he was empty.

"We really do need to talk," Murphy said quietly.

Aiden was okay with that. He was okay with everything at that very moment actually. He gazed adoringly at Murphy and gave him a dopey nod, and Murphy chuckled.

"I'm going to get cleaned up and then go make us some breakfast."

It was on the tip of his tongue to offer to help Murphy with the getting cleaned up part, but he let it go unsaid. Murphy was going to set the pace. Aiden wasn't going to rush things. He wasn't going to push... no matter how much he wanted to.

So he wouldn't be tempted to break those promises, Aiden went to the guest bath in the hall for a quick wipe down, pulled on his T-shirt, and wandered into the living room while Murphy was in the shower. But the picture on the mantel of Murphy and his lost lover made him uncomfortable, so he wandered out onto the deck instead. He stretched in the chill morning air and turned his face to the rising sun. As he basked in its rays, he felt his confidence build. He could do this. He could make this work. He could be anyone Murphy needed him to be.

Murphy had seen some of the worst of him. He'd seen what happened when Aiden lost control, and he hadn't run. That gave Aiden hope. Even Adam had never known the whole truth about him, had never seen it. Adam had pushed once or twice to get Aiden to talk about it, but Aiden had been too afraid of chasing him away. In the end, he'd scared him off anyway, and worse....

He shivered as his guilt sucked away some of his joy and went to join Murphy in the kitchen.

"Anything I can do to help?"

Murphy searched his face with a frown between his eyebrows. "Are you okay?"

"Of course. I have a gorgeous man cooking me breakfast. Why wouldn't I be?"

"I'm not sure. You'll have to tell me."

"I'm fine, Murphy."

While Murphy didn't seem very convinced, he let it go and went back to fussing with his pans and pulling things out of the refrigerator. When the kettle boiled, Murphy poured them both a cup of black tea, and Aiden dumped a generous serving of half-and-half and sugar into his mug. If he wasn't going to get his coffee, he'd make the tea as close to it as he could. It tasted pretty good, not good enough to replace his coffee, but not bad either.

He assumed they'd eat at the little breakfast bar that separated the kitchen from the living room. But when the eggs, toast, and turkey bacon were ready, Murphy actually pulled out placemats and napkins, and Aiden helped him carry the whole lot into the small dining room beyond the kitchen. The room held only a plain rectangular dining table and chairs, a set of white built-ins in the back with simple white china inside, and a couple of oil-painted seascapes on the walls. Like the living room, it was understated and elegant, simple lines and soft neutral colors to offset the white. It was clean, not a speck of dust in sight, but it had a lonely, unused feel to it. At least here Aiden didn't have to feel Murphy's ex staring over his shoulder. There were no photographs in the room at all.

"I thought we might be able to talk better in here," Murphy said as he set the placemats down and started arranging the dishes. "I would've suggested the table on the deck, but it's getting a little cold for that."

"Okay."

Once seated, Aiden couldn't help fidgeting in his chair. Murphy looked so serious, Aiden was starting to lose his appetite.

"This isn't an inquisition, Aiden," Murphy said, as if he were reading Aiden's mind again, and Aiden was starting to wonder if he might just be. Maybe the reason Murphy hadn't freaked out over the whole spontaneous combustion thing was he had some secrets of his own.

More curious now than nervous, Aiden decided to go ahead and ask the question that had been bothering him since last night.

"So how come you aren't freaked out about what happened on the beach last night?"

Murphy blinked. "Get straight to the point, huh?"

Aiden shrugged and gave him a half smile. "If you haven't guessed, subtlety isn't exactly my thing."

"I'd kinda guessed. And to answer your question, I *was* a little freaked." The smile he gave Aiden was gentle as he said it, and he reached across the table and took Aiden's hand. "I mean. It's not every day you see something like that. You're amazing, truly. I've never met anyone like you. I knew it from the second I came within five feet of you. I thought then that you were the strongest projector I'd ever experienced, and I didn't even know the half of it, did I?"

Aiden frowned. "I don't understand."

Murphy sat back in his chair and lifted his eyebrows. "You really don't know, do you?"

When Aiden shook his head, Murphy sighed. "Aiden, you project what you're feeling, your emotions, like floodlights in front of a flashing neon sign. Anyone the least bit sensitive can feel you. I happen to be more than a little sensitive, so I have shields to protect myself. But even with them, I can't seem to block you out. I've tried but with little success, I'm afraid."

"You know what I'm thinking?" Aiden cringed. What had Murphy heard? Thankfully Murphy put him out of his misery before he could agonize over that question too long.

"No. Only what you're feeling, although for a lot of people it's the same thing. I'm an empath. Before I learned to shield myself, I could sense what everyone around me was feeling all the time. It got stronger as I got older and that, in part, was what led to my not-so-little drinking problem and somewhat hermitic lifestyle. Now I'm better able to cope. I have better tools to deal with it, though, I still prefer to avoid crowds if I can."

Putting aside his mortification at Murphy knowing everything he was feeling, Aiden concentrated on the last few things Murphy said, and a small burble of hope and excitement made him sit forward in his chair.

"So you learned how to control it?"

"Someone taught me, yes."

Aiden's hand clenched involuntarily.

"Do you think someone could teach me too? I've…." He took a shaky breath and turned away to stare at the oil painting on the wall instead of Murphy's earnest blue eyes. "Last night wasn't the only time I've lost control like that. It's been worse, *much* worse. If I could learn to control it, any of it, that would be so awesome. I would be so fucking grateful."

Aching with the need to have someone tell him he could be fixed, Aiden could barely breathe around the tightness in his chest.

"Will you tell me what happened?"

"Last night or before?"

"Any, all, you choose."

Aiden swallowed and took a breath. It was confession time, and he was terrified. But then Murphy ran the backs of his fingers down Aiden's cheek in a gentle caress, and some of his panic eased. He still couldn't look Murphy in the eye, but he thought he might be able to get the story out without any histrionics or singeing anything. "This thing inside me, it's dangerous. The fire is always there, pushing to get out. Maybe it's why I overreact to things, or maybe that's just me being broken. I don't know. I fight it. Every day I fight it. But sometimes it's not enough, and when I get upset, it gets loose."

"I don't think you're broken, Aiden."

"You don't know all of it though…. That guy I told you about before, Adam—"

"The one you said you might have hurt?"

"I did hurt him. At least that's what I heard from a friend at school. His mom is a nurse at the hospital, and she said she saw Adam there." Aiden grimaced, the guilt washing over him again. "Anyway, a couple months ago, I came back early from summer break to surprise him. We'd fought and broken up last fall, but we'd hooked up a few times over the winter, so I wasn't worried about us getting back together. I thought if I just gave him a little time, and I tried a little harder, we could make it work again. I think Adam's *different* too, like you a little, but not." He wasn't explaining this very well. "I felt things with him. You know, weird energy things, like I feel with you."

"You think he's gifted in some way too?"

"I guess so. I mean I didn't know it at the time, but since I met you… I think yeah, maybe. He was the first person I ever experienced that with. I thought it meant that we were soul mates or something. I got it in my stupid head that he'd always be there waiting for me, no matter how many stupid, crazy things I did or how many times we broke up, because we were *meant* to be together."

He pulled away from Murphy and stood up. He couldn't sit still and talk about this. He needed to move.

"Then I came back from summer break, and I went to go see him, to see if I'd given him enough time to cool off and start to miss me…

you know, want me back. Only I get to his shop and there's this new guy there, Jay, and I know… I don't know how, but I *know* the second I see him that he and Adam are together. I lost my shit. Something about the guy set me off, and it wasn't just that I knew Adam had moved on."

At least this part of the memory didn't hurt as much as it had before.

"Anyway, Adam and I fought, like usual. But I was still so scared of letting him go I couldn't admit to myself that it was over, and I kept going back to get my heart stomped on all over again." He took a breath and stopped pacing. "But here's where it gets even weirder. There's this crazy guy who's been following Adam's new boyfriend. I have no fucking clue why. And the next time I try to talk to Adam, the guy's there, and he has a gun, and Adam's boyfriend is all tied up on the couch. I walk in, and there's a *gun* in my face."

"Jesus! Was anyone hurt?"

"Only the crazy guy. I don't even know what happened. But all the shit I fight to keep bottled up every fucking day of my life just boiled over. The gun exploded in his hand. But what scared the ever-loving shit out of me wasn't the guy or the gun. It was that I lost complete control, even with Adam there."

"Adam helped you before?"

Aiden wrapped his arms around himself and stared out the window. "Sometimes. It was like his being there helped, but only sometimes. Other times I felt like I was suffocating with him around… which is why our relationship was probably so screwed up."

He didn't know he was shaking until Murphy's arms came around him, soothing him. Tears sprang to his eyes, but he shoved them ruthlessly back. It was bad enough Murphy knew every pathetic feeling he had, Murphy didn't need to see him blubbering for a third time in three days.

He had to take a calming breath, and then another, before he could get the rest out.

"There's more. I'm ashamed to admit it, but even after the crazy at Adam's shop, I still couldn't let go of the thought that I needed him. I needed that mystical connection we had, or I'd lose it completely and destroy everything I touched. It was all I could think about. But Adam wouldn't talk to me. I went to his house. I was so shaken up after the whole exploding gun thing, I thought if I could just talk to him, be near him, everything would be okay. But the new boyfriend, Jay, was there, and Adam kept trying to tell me it was over, but I wouldn't listen… I couldn't listen. I was desperate." He drew in a shaky breath and let it out. "I made an ass out of myself, screaming at him like an idiot."

He started shaking again, and Murphy squeezed him tighter.

"What happened, Aiden?"

"It was just supposed to be a stupid prank." His voice caught on the last word, and he had to fight back more tears. "I went to the woods with a can of spray paint. I was so mad. I wanted to hurt him, but only a little bit. I was going to paint "asshole" or something equally immature on this tree that meant a lot to him…. I didn't mean for anyone to get hurt…. But then all that anger and fear came boiling out of me again. I was in the middle of spraying… and the can exploded in my hand. Fire was everywhere. It was raining fire all around me. First the tree went up like a Roman candle. Then it spread to more trees, and I panicked. I had to get out of there because I was only making it worse. It was feeding off me, and I was feeding off it, and it was a nightmare. I should have tried to stop it. I should have done something, but I ran. And I kept running until I got here."

Murphy's sigh ruffled the hairs on the back of Aiden's neck.

"I'm sorry, Aiden. I'm so sorry you went through that."

Aiden shook his head. "I'm not the one you should be sorry for. It was my fault. My friend's mom said Adam got burned, but his boyfriend, Jay… they said he was in a coma for over a week because he fell in the woods going after Adam. I did that. How am I supposed to deal with that? How will he ever forgive me?"

Murphy sighed again and gave Aiden another squeeze before forcing him around to face him. "I'm afraid I can't answer that for you. It's something you're going to have to work out for yourself. But I'll help if I can."

"Just tell me you can teach me to control this fucking thing before I hurt anyone else."

"I can try."

Aiden buried his face in Murphy's neck and clung to him. He didn't deserve this. He didn't deserve a man like Murphy, but he'd take whatever help and tenderness Murphy had to offer and do everything in his power to *become* worthy of it.

CHAPTER 9

AFTER THE revelations of the morning, Murphy decided they needed to take a break. Aiden was an emotional wreck. His feelings were bouncing all over the place with surges of guilt, pain, anger, anxiety, and dozens of other emotions. It made Murphy's head spin. He couldn't even imagine the amount of energy it took to keep that contained even as much as Aiden was able to. But Aiden did keep the worst of it in. His skin had been hot to the touch, but his clothes hadn't caught fire and nothing around them had been damaged. Murphy would just have to take that as progress since he really didn't know what he was doing.

He sat Aiden down at the table again, and they ate their somewhat cold breakfast in comfortable silence for a while. When most of the storm had subsided in Aiden, Murphy decided now was probably a good time to work on a little meditation. Murphy found it calming and soothing and that seemed like the best place to start. He might need to enlist the aid of someone far more knowledgeable than himself to help Aiden deal with the power that raged inside him, but he figured he could handle a little basic thing like getting Aiden grounded.

After dumping their plates in the sink, he led Aiden to the living room, turned on his fountain, and put something soothing in the stereo. Then they both sat on the flokati rug in front the fireplace, facing each other.

"I usually do this at night when there's less people out on the beach so I can open the windows and hear the waves. But I think the white noise should work to get us in the mood. This is all about finding things that relax you, so if you have any suggestions, let me know."

Aiden shrugged and picked at the carpet without meeting Murphy's gaze. "I looked up a bunch of stuff online and tried some things, but I couldn't figure out what I was doing wrong."

"Okay, so you've tried some things. Did any of it help?"

"I kinda liked the incense. The smoke is cool."

Aiden still wouldn't look at him, and he radiated shame. Murphy had to address that or they wouldn't get anywhere with the meditation. He might not be an expert, but he knew that much.

"Aiden, look at me. I know what you're feeling. But you're going to have to push that to the side, let go of it for a little while, or this isn't going to accomplish anything."

When Aiden nodded, Murphy continued. "I'm going to see if I have any incense. I'll be back in a minute."

Lola had given him a meditation starter kit of sorts a long time ago. Murphy was pretty sure there was still some incense in there. He had to go into the spare bedroom—the one piled practically from floor to ceiling with boxes of Felix's stuff that he hadn't been able to get rid of—to find the carved wooden trunk he'd stashed the kit in, and by the time he shimmied out from between all of those boxes, he had a renewed resolve to go through and get rid of at least some of it… not right now, but soon. If nothing else, all those boxes were a fire hazard, and that might become a priority in the very near future.

When Murphy stepped back into the living room, Aiden jerked his gaze away from what he'd been looking at and gave Murphy a guilty smile. Peering past him to see what had him so entranced, Murphy spotted the picture of Felix and him on the mantle. Aiden didn't say a word while Murphy set the incense on the coffee table, and then went to the mantle and picked up the frame. With a small twinge of guilt, Murphy took the picture with him into his office and set it on the bookshelf by his desk.

"I'm sorry, Murphy. You didn't have to do that," Aiden said when Murphy returned.

"It's okay. You don't need any more distractions, and it's too cold to do this outside… at least for me." Murphy chuckled, and Aiden gave him the smile he'd been hoping for.

"Now let's get started and see if anything I've learned can help you."

He pulled out a stick of incense and reached for the lighter, but Aiden stopped him.

"Let me do that."

Curious, Murphy handed him the incense and watched in awe as Aiden touched his finger to the end of the stick and it immediately started smoking. A flame erupted a few seconds later, and Aiden smiled and handed the stick back to him.

"That's incredible," Murphy said, staring at it for a few seconds before blowing out the flame and placing it into its holder.

Aiden blushed and shrugged as a trail of dancing smoke rose from the bright orange coal. "I can manage that little bit without burning the house down at least… candles too, if I'm not too keyed up."

Murphy's curiosity and his libido both perked up at the same time. That small burst of energy from Aiden called to his own gifts, making Murphy a little short of breath. He longed to reach out and touch, feel, explore, but he shoved those feelings aside. He needed to focus on the moment and what Aiden needed, and that wasn't sex, at least not right this second.

"Okay. Now I want you to close your eyes and follow my voice. Slowly take a deep breath in and let it out just as slow…. With each breath I want you to clench and then relax a part of your body, starting with your toes… then your feet… and your lower legs…. Breathe in for a count of eight, hold, then out for another eight count, tense each muscle as you breathe in and then let it relax on the exhale…."

Murphy continued to speak in low tones, relaxing his own body even as he watched Aiden follow his instructions.

"Now I want you to turn your thoughts inward. Focus on your core, the deep well at the center of your being, the still, silent pool… fathomless, its surface smooth as glass like a mirror, nothing escaping, nothing coming in. It's peaceful and serene… not even a ripple."

Murphy continued to speak calmly and quietly, but he found it harder and harder as Aiden's agitation seemed to grow rather than recede. Aiden was restless, shifting and squirming, and the emotions coming off him were anything but serene. After another few minutes, Murphy sighed and gave up.

"I'm sorry, Aiden. I must be doing something wrong."

Aiden looked miserable and shook his head. "No. It's me. *I'm* sorry. I just can't get into it. I tried to visualize that pool you were talking about, but that isn't what I see when I look 'inward.' Nothing in there is calm and still… ever. But just being here with you helps. And I do feel better. The whole muscle-relaxing thing could work. I think."

Unwilling to give up quite yet, Murphy worried his lower lip until a memory of one of the first meditations Lola led him through surfaced.

"Hey, I have another idea. The reflective pool always worked best for me, so I thought it might help keep you calm and keep things from overflowing on you, but maybe this other meditation will work better. It's a really basic one for grounding, according to the person who taught me."

"I'm willing to try anything at this point."

"Okay. Good. Close your eyes again and breathe like before."

Murphy led Aiden through the basic relaxation exercise again until Aiden's agitation had faded a little.

"Now, this time I want you to imagine you're a tree. Visualize your roots extending from your trunk down your legs, from your feet down into the earth. With each breath, your roots sink deeper, and any stress and negative emotions flow out away from you, down those roots. The soil is cooling, calming. It cradles you, holds you. It nourishes you with healthy green energy that flows back up through your trunk and out to your limbs, a light that expands inside you, expanding outward with each breath you take. Breathe in with the good… and out with the bad."

Aiden seemed to be responding well to this, so Murphy kept going, speaking slowly and quietly.

"When you're filled with this cool, earthy energy, I want you to visualize your branches reaching up toward the sky, the light exiting through your limbs and your crown, taking any negativity remaining with it. In its place, warm sunlight and sky energy flows down into you, blending with the cool earth energy and—oh shit!"

Between one breath and the next, the ceiling above Aiden's head turned yellow, and the rug under him caught fire. Aiden threw out his arms, frantically beating at the rug while Murphy ran to the kitchen for the fire extinguisher he kept under the sink. By the time Murphy returned, the fire was out, and Aiden was standing in the middle of a scorched and smoking ring on Murphy's rug looking mortified. The smell of burned animal hair filled his living room.

"I'm sorry. God, I'm so sorry. I don't know what happened."

The smoke alarm went off then, and Murphy started laughing. He couldn't help it. He dropped the fire extinguisher, crossed the last few feet between them, and pulled Aiden up into his arms. He kissed him until Aiden finally stopped apologizing and laughed too. When Murphy was sure Aiden was okay, he grabbed a broom handle and beat on the smoke alarm until it stopped. He opened one of the french doors to let in a little fresh air, and he and Aiden carried the rug outside to the deck.

"I'm going to have to say, it appears my limited expertise in this area is not going to be enough," Murphy admitted with another chuckle after they returned to their spot in front of the fireplace.

Aiden gave him an apologetic, somewhat watery smile, and nodded. "I don't understand why you aren't running away screaming by now, especially after everything I told you earlier… and now this. I'm such a fuckup, you have to be a goddamned saint to want to stick around."

Having heard enough of that kind of talk to last a lifetime—from Aiden and Felix and even himself at one time—Murphy grabbed Aiden's shoulders and gave him a couple of gentle shakes.

"I'm no saint. I can understand and sympathize because I'm a fuckup too."

When Aiden gave him an incredulous look, Murphy said, "I'm serious. Maybe I'm a little more together now than I was when I was your age or even a few years ago, but I'm still an alcoholic. I'm still trying to figure out how to keep going one day at a time. I'm only better now because there were people out there willing to help me, willing to let me lean on them." Murphy sighed and cupped Aiden's cheek. "Asking for help isn't a failure, Aiden. It doesn't mean you're beyond repair. I'm only here today because of the people who helped me… helped me and Felix both, when we hit our rock bottom. You made some mistakes. Everyone on this planet has made mistakes. It's part of being human. And most of those people out there don't have to deal with even half of what you've got going on inside. Cut yourself some slack."

Aiden buried his face in Murphy's neck, and Murphy closed his eyes and wrapped his arms around him.

"We'll figure it out. I promise."

"God, I feel so much better when I'm with you. When you're touching me it's like everything doesn't seem so overwhelming anymore."

"Good, because I like touching you. I like being with you. You do me good too, you know, whether you believe it or not."

"I want to believe it. I want to give back to you as much as you give me. I want to be that person."

Murphy sighed and gave Aiden another squeeze before pulling back. "I have an idea. Obviously I don't know enough to help you with the whole meditation and shielding and grounding stuff, but I know someone who might. If you can take my word that you can trust her, I'll see if she'll meet with us."

Aiden nodded vigorously, his green eyes bright and hopeful as he sucked in a calming breath. "If you trust her, then yes, please."

"I do. She was my first sponsor in AA. If I hadn't believed in a higher power going into the program, I would have after finding her, or more accurately her finding me. She was exactly what I needed when I needed it—when I finally hit bottom hard enough to be willing to accept what she had to offer."

"I'd like to hear that story someday."

"You will. Let's just get through what's going on right now, and I'll dredge all that stuff up another time, okay?"

"Yeah."

While Aiden stretched out on the couch, Murphy took his cell out on the deck to call Lola.

"Hey sweetie, I thought I might hear from you today."

"You did?"

"Just a feeling. What's up?"

"I need to ask a favor. It's a big one so you can say no if you want to."

"My heart, when have I ever refused you anything?"

He laughed. He could remember a few times when she'd had to drag out the tough love, especially during his first year of sobriety. While she'd never actually refused him anything per se, she'd certainly kicked him in the ass enough times… verbally that is.

"You remember that projector I was telling you about?"

"Uh-huh."

"Well, let's just say he's a bit more than a projector."

"You mean like you're more than an empath?"

"Yes. That's what I mean. To be honest, I would say he's the strongest psychic talent I've ever come across." Murphy lowered his voice. "Strongest and possibly most dangerous."

She was silent for a few breaths. "Stronger than you?"

"Yes. I thought I should probably be clear on that before you agreed to help."

"Phhfft. You just said that because you knew I wouldn't be able to resist."

Murphy grinned. He'd been telling the truth. He did want to warn her, even though he was fairly certain Aiden would never do anything to hurt anyone on purpose. Still, part of him had known she'd take the bait.

"Look. I tried a couple of meditations with him, and they didn't turn out very well. I don't know what I did wrong, but I figured you'd know better than I would. Do you have time to meet?"

"Sweetie, I'm retired, living in my daughter and son-in-law's basement, fifty miles from my old coven, and I hate knitting or any other bullshit handicraft. I got nothing but time."

Murphy chuckled even as he breathed a sigh of relief. If Lola couldn't help, she might know someone who could. "Is tomorrow too soon?"

"From the sounds of it, tomorrow isn't soon enough, but it'll have to do. How about we meet at that deli you like so much?"

"I think maybe somewhere more private is in order."

"Okay. You come here, then. I have a space I created at the back of my daughter's property, plenty of privacy and well shielded."

"Thanks, Lola. We'll see you maybe around noon? That should give us plenty of time to get there after we get off the ferry."

"I'll be waiting. Just come on around back and knock on the basement door. Iris is the daughter who ended up with a stick up her butt for some reason—with a husband to match—so it's better if we don't bother them with any of this."

"Okay, Lola. See you tomorrow. And thanks. You're the best."

"Don't I know it."

They were both laughing when Murphy hung up. Lola had thirty years as a professional boardwalk psychic and twenty as the high priestess of a coven under her belt. She had to know something they could use.

Murphy didn't have the heart to send Aiden home after that. If Aiden felt better with Murphy around, then Murphy would stay around. That wasn't exactly moving slow, like he'd planned, but he thought it was for the best. And if he was honest with himself, he was as starved for human contact as Aiden was. He'd been hiding from that fact for the last five years, using his sensitivities as an excuse to stay cooped up in his and Felix's house, surrounded by dusty and faded memories. Aiden's need gave him new purpose now, and Aiden's spirit made him feel ten years younger. He liked that feeling.

They took a walk on the beach at sunset. Then Murphy cooked dinner for them. Afterward they spent the evening on the couch watching whatever channel their random button pushing landed them on. Knowing tomorrow might bring a whole new level to the weirdness between them, Murphy made sure they avoided any heavy conversation and allowed the mundane to work its own kind of magic. Aiden needed a break from beating himself up, from agonizing over what had happened and what might happen. He needed to start from a place of strength and solidity before he could move forward. It had taken Murphy a long time to learn those lessons from Lola—and everyone else in the program—but he was pretty sure Aiden would be a much quicker study. His heart was in the right place already.

That night, they made love twice. The first time, Aiden got his two out of ten after a quick dash back to his parents' house to grab condoms. Aiden might have been wounded and unsure outside of the bedroom, but in bed he took charge like he was a decade older than Murphy instead of the other way around. Murphy wasn't exactly complaining. In bed—at least in bed with Murphy—Aiden had an outlet for all that energy, all that fire inside him, and Murphy met him with equal passion, taking everything Aiden had to give… even if he collapsed into an exhausted heap afterward, boneless, with jelly for muscles.

Their second lovemaking was in the shower, where Murphy was happy to do a little showing off of his own. As the warm water cascaded over them, Murphy worshipped every inch of Aiden's gorgeous lean body with his hands, his mouth, and his gifts. Water caressed them both, traveling in whatever patterns Murphy chose as he blew Aiden's mind with another spectacular blowjob—if he did say so himself. It was Aiden's turn to collapse into a puddle of jelly legs in the tub after he shouted his release at the ceiling. And as Murphy crawled on top on him in the confined space, he grinned smugly from ear to ear.

"Holy shit, you're going to drown me," Aiden croaked.

Murphy chuckled and cuddled in as the steam and warm spray from the showerhead continued to blanket them. They couldn't stay that way for long without Murphy's legs cramping to the point where he'd need to be dragged out of the tub. But he'd enjoy it while he could.

Eventually they made it back to the bed, and the following morning Aiden drove them to the ferry to Hyannis. Once the ferry was underway, Murphy hopped out of the Jeep and dragged Aiden up on deck to enjoy the open air. Anxiety rolled off Aiden in waves, so to take his mind off the meeting to come Murphy pointed out landmarks and sea life, sharing his joy at being out on the water, his element.

"Come on, Aiden," he said playfully when Aiden still remained white-knuckled on the railing. "Lola's not that bad. Everything's going to be fine. It's beautiful out here, enjoy it."

"It's not that," Aiden answered tightly.

"Then what?"

Aiden closed his eyes and gulped in some air. Now that Murphy was looking more closely instead of being distracted by the water, he could see that Aiden was a little green around the gills.

"I can't swim," Aiden finally whispered.

"What?"

Aiden huffed out a loud breath and glared challengingly at Murphy. "I can't swim, okay? I've said it. Laugh all you want."

Murphy was more surprised than amused. "I'm not going to laugh. I'm just a little surprised."

When Aiden's grip on the rail tightened and he groaned, Murphy wrapped his arms around him from behind. "I won't let you drown. I promise."

The look Aiden gave him was half gratitude, half exasperation. "I know I'm not going to drown right this second. I'm just not too keen on large bodies of water."

Then why the hell did you come to an island?

The voice in his head only sounded a little like Felix that time, and Murphy realized he hadn't heard much from that corner recently. The thought made him a bit sad, though he knew it was probably for the best. He couldn't live in the past forever.

"So how come you never learned?"

"My folks tried when I was a little kid… or I should say they hired people to try. I know this might come as a shock to you, but I wasn't exactly an easy child to deal with."

That last was accompanied by Aiden's now familiar bitter laughter, and Murphy didn't join in. He sensed real pain there, deep and scarring, so he kept quiet and squeezed Aiden a little tighter.

"Anyway, I never really liked the water. It got in my ears and my eyes, and back then I could throw some pretty impressive tantrums… still can I guess. So the nannies and the instructors tried to throw me in the water. I pitched plenty of loud and embarrassing fits, and my parents gave up. That was before they shipped me off to the hospital and gave up on me pretty much entirely. After that they paid for one shrink after the next, until I was old enough to refuse to go, then they paid for school… as long as it was far away from wherever they were."

This wasn't exactly how Murphy had expected their conversation to go, so he had no idea what to say to that.

"Uh…."

Brilliant.

Felix's voice was a little stronger this time. It always was when Murphy was making an ass of himself or putting his foot in his mouth.

After clearing his throat, he tried again. "Do you want to talk about it?"

"Not much to say. I'm fucked-up, always have been. Even my own parents didn't want to have anything to do with me."

Murphy could feel every muscle in Aiden's body tense, one by one, as he held him.

"Why the hell am I even bothering with this? Maybe I should just slit my wrists and be done with it."

"Hey. Don't say that," Murphy snapped, giving Aiden a hard shake.

Aiden blew out a breath and slumped his shoulders. "I'm sorry. I'm sorry. I'm tense, and I'm being a drama queen again. I know." He put his hands over his face and groaned. "I'm just—"

"Nervous, stressed, overwhelmed, and tired," Murphy filled in for him.

With a laugh Aiden folded his arms over the ones Murphy had across his chest. "You know… I have to say it's a little unfair you knowing everything that I'm feeling all the time. I can't hide anything from you, not that I've ever been very good at hiding my feelings in the first place. But it would be nice to have a few secrets left."

"I'm pretty sure there's plenty I still don't know about you. Besides, after today you may be able to hide your feelings from me along with everyone else, though I hope you feel you never have to."

"I would think you'd rather not be dragged along on my crazy train *all* the time."

The words were said in jest, but Murphy knew differently.

"In all seriousness, Aiden, it helps to know what you're fighting. Maybe that's why Fate brought us together. You hide more than people realize. Someone without my gift would never know the battle you fight every day of your life. The battles I fight every day are hard enough. I can't even imagine what this must have been like for you as a child."

After a long silence, Aiden said, "The first real fire I ever started I was twelve years old. Luckily for me I wasn't strong enough before that to do more than crisp a few sheets… a few crib bumpers that were quickly replaced." His voice sounded far away as if he was talking about someone else. "But they couldn't pretend it didn't happen that time. First, my nanny flipped out, wanting to know where I'd hidden the matches. Then my folks flipped, and I was punished and told never to do it again. The second time, it was the living room drapes. The nanny quit—my fourth or fifth by that time—and I was sent to a shrink to find out why I was turning into a pyro. I got sent to the institution when I burned down a shed on the grounds of the private school they sent me to." He laughed. "I'd run in there after popping a boner in the middle of the locker room and getting pummeled by a couple of boys.

"No one ever believed me. They put me on drugs that made me a zombie, and it worked sort of. I never lost control because I never felt anything at all. After I turned eighteen, my folks stopped even the pretense of trying. And now, as long as I don't bother them, they don't bother me. We see each other sometimes for an awkward holiday abroad, but that's about it. I know they're pissed I'm not back at school right now, since they already paid tuition, but they can certainly afford it."

Murphy didn't know what to say to that either, so he stayed silent, and Aiden let out another bitter laugh.

"I know, 'poor little rich kid.' Everyone should feel sorry for me because my mommy and daddy pay for everything I could ever want but don't give me cuddles."

"Don't do that," Murphy scolded gently. "Until someone has walked in your shoes, they have no right to judge you. Just because you grew up with privileges other people can't even dream of doesn't mean you had it easy. It doesn't mean damage wasn't done to you."

Aiden turned in Murphy's arms. When they were face-to-face, Aiden gave him a hard kiss on the lips. "I don't know what I did to deserve you, but whatever it was, I hope I never stop."

Murphy was too busy blushing to respond to that one. He felt like a kid again, positively giddy with infatuation. It was a feeling he'd thought lost to him only a few short weeks ago.

Take it with both hands, my heart. You deserve it.

CHAPTER 10

By the time the ferry docked, Aiden was wrung out and jittery. He hadn't planned to dump all over Murphy like that, and now all he wanted to do was go home, curl up on Murphy's couch, and hope Murphy developed a limited case of amnesia for the last couple hours… or the last couple days, so Aiden could get a do over.

As they joined the line of disembarking cars, he cursed himself for doing everything he'd said he wasn't going to do. He wasn't going to spew drama all over Murphy. He wasn't going to be that immature, bratty, attention-craving drama queen anymore. He had to fix his own problems. Murphy was so supportive now, but he'd get tired of dealing with Aiden's shit eventually. Everyone did.

"Are you okay?" Murphy asked from the passenger seat as they pulled onto twenty-eight, following the instructions of the GPS.

No. But I'm never okay. That's the problem.

Frustrated that he couldn't hide anything from Murphy, Aiden took a calming breath and forced his body to relax.

"I'll be all right. I'm sorry for all that earlier."

"Don't be sorry." Murphy placed a hand on Aiden's thigh and gave it a gentle squeeze. "I'm honored you felt you could share that with me."

When Aiden gave him a disbelieving frown, Murphy chuckled. "Aiden, I told you, feelings are kind of my thing. It's what I do. It's who I am. My mother always said I was 'sensitive' or 'gentle'—much to my father's dismay." Murphy laughed louder this time. "I honestly never had to come out to my parents because it was blatantly obvious from a young age. I mean I didn't put on her dresses or makeup or ask to take ballet or anything, but I was always... *sensitive*."

Murphy's smile was contagious, and Aiden relaxed a little more. "Sensitive or not, I don't want to wear out my welcome in the first week. Adam had the patience of a saint, and he couldn't deal with me much past the first few months we were together. I think I should pace myself."

Murphy's smile faded, and Aiden cursed himself anew for bringing up Adam again.

Am I ever going to have some sort of filter between my brain and my mouth? God, I need to just shut up.

When Murphy withdrew his hand and settled farther into his seat, Aiden would have kicked himself too, if he hadn't been driving.

"Do you miss him?"

"Who?"

"Adam. You talked about that connection you had, about how you thought it meant forever."

For once Murphy actually sounded like he was the one that needed reassurance. Aiden had no problem stepping up there.

"No. I mean, yeah, I miss him a little, I guess. He's a really good guy. He's stable and dependable. I liked that. I *needed* that. But those things I liked most about him in the beginning were the things that drove me crazy later on. He was so stubborn, so set in his ways. It was like moving a mountain to get him to come into town just to see a movie or something, you know? Sometimes I think I fought with him just to get a rise out of him. I didn't do it on purpose, but... I don't know. Maybe that was me being crazy as usual."

Aiden pulled his Jeep into a parking lot so he could look Murphy in the eye.

"But that mystical connection I thought I had with him, it wasn't right somehow. I didn't know it then. It took meeting you for me to finally see that. Adam is on my mind because of what I did, not because of what we had. It's because I hurt people, because I know he'll hate me if he ever finds out, and I don't know how to fix that. I don't know if I can."

He had more to say. He wanted to tell Murphy how strongly he felt for him already, how different it was from anything he'd ever felt before.

But Murphy could already sense his emotions. There was no point in overwhelming him with the words too. And if Aiden said them out loud, Murphy couldn't pretend to ignore them anymore.

They were going to go at Murphy's pace.

He pulled the Jeep back onto the road, and they spent the rest of the drive to Lola's in silence. Murphy kept a reassuring hand on Aiden's thigh, and Aiden tried not to let his anxiety get out of control. The touch helped. Having Murphy near made him feel calmer.

The GPS led them to a quaint little tree-lined neighborhood street, and Aiden parked in front of one of several nearly identical two-story brick-front colonials with manicured lawns and shrubs flanking plain cement walkways. This one's only distinguishing features were the house number beside the door and the beat-up, rusted little yellow sedan, covered in pagan-themed bumper stickers, that he'd parked behind. Given the caliber of the rest of the vehicles on the street and in driveways, Aiden had a feeling the HOA was probably having a shitfit about what he assumed was Lola's eyesore of a car, parked proudly out front for everyone to see instead of in the two car garage.

The rebel in him liked her already.

Instead of going to the front door, Murphy led them around back and down a set of concrete steps to a french door. A bright purple velvet curtain with a large gold sun emblazoned on it blocked the view inside, and Aiden could smell the nag champa even before the small, round, silver-haired woman opened the door.

"Murphy!" Lola cried, pulling Murphy into a hug that bent him nearly in half to return.

When Murphy stepped back, Lola surprised Aiden by pulling him into a hug too. The thick ropes of amber around her neck dug into his collarbone, and the dozens of metal and bead bracelets on her wrists rattled and clinked as he awkwardly tried to return her embrace. Her cheek was cool against his skin when she pulled back, and a cloud of nag champa and patchouli filled his nostrils. Aiden felt his anxiety begin to ease under her welcoming smile and faded gray eyes.

"Well look what you brought me, Murphy," she said, taking a step back and eyeing Aiden from head to toe. She placed a hand to her chest and chuckled. "You didn't tell me he was gorgeous. Holy Goddess, I could feel him the second the two of you pulled up. You're lucky I took my heart meds this morning, or you might have been calling an ambulance for me."

Not sure what to make of that, Aiden glanced questioningly at Murphy, but Murphy only smiled and shrugged.

"I'd say you should come in and sit down," Lola continued, "but I think maybe outside in the circle would be better."

Murphy frowned. "So soon? I mean. Wouldn't you be more comfortable inside? I thought we might talk for a while before we jumped into anything, so Aiden could tell you a few things first."

Lola stepped out the door, pushed past them, and slowly levered herself onto the first step. "Dearheart, he's leaking all over the place. I don't need him to tell me anything. Any sensitive within a few hundred feet of him or more could feel that. I'm surprised he doesn't have a dozen psychic vampires buzzing around his head like a cloud of mosquitoes." Using the iron handrail mounted to the wall and her cane, she pulled herself up another couple steps. "Come on. I've got some fancy lawn chairs Iris bought me out in the circle now, since sitting on the ground is kind of out for me and several of my friends. They're padded and plenty comfortable." At the top of the steps she turned and grinned down at them. "Besides, he's putting off enough juice I might dance a jig out there and back and still have energy to spare for you to take me to lunch after."

Murphy hurried after her, and Aiden followed right behind him. When they caught up to her, Murphy offered her his arm, but she shook her head and reached for Aiden instead. "No offense, Murphy, but if I'm going to take a helping hand, it's going to be from the one who'll recharge my batteries. No sense wasting all that lovely warm energy he's throwing out there… and from the looks of things, I'm going to need it."

Feeling a little disgruntled by the way she kept talking about him, Aiden took her arm and helped her across the manicured backyard toward a stand of trees. Once through the trees, the land opened back up into a small circle, ringed in stones and various lawn ornaments. A couple of cushioned wrought iron chairs and a small copper fire pit sat in the middle.

"It's not the stone circle at the sanctuary, but it's the best I could manage in Iris's backyard so far. This one's just for me, though, so it doesn't have to be too fancy."

Aiden helped her to her chair, and then stood shifting nervously from foot to foot unsure of what to do next.

"Murphy, you sit there," Lola said, pointing to the other chair. "I think Aiden here needs to be on the ground to start with."

Aiden glanced at the somewhat damp moss beneath his sneakers skeptically. But when both Lola and Murphy continued to stare at him expectantly, he huffed and plopped his butt on the ground. Hopefully he'd get a chance to let the ass of his shorts dry before he had to be seen in public again.

"Okay, now we're comfortable, let's have that chat," Lola said once Aiden was seated at her feet.

His ass felt damp already, making Aiden a little peevish. "Can I ask again why we couldn't do this inside?" he grumbled.

"Because my apartment is filled with stones and crystals and charged items that would most likely go haywire with all the psychic energy you're throwing around. Hermes would probably be pissed at me for a month if I let you in there like you are now."

At a questioning look from Aiden, Murphy supplied, "Her cat."

"Uh, okaaay." Aiden shifted uncomfortably on the ground. His shorts squished a little between his butt cheeks, and he tried hard not to scowl. He was asking this woman for help. Murphy trusted her. If his road to self-improvement had to start with his ass in the mud, he could deal. One glance at Murphy's concerned expression, and Aiden's resolve strengthened. He wasn't going to fuck this up.

"Alright, then, tell me what you've tried already, because obviously it isn't working," Lola said to Murphy.

"I tried the meditations you taught me, the mirror and the pool, and that didn't work."

She nodded sagely. "Understandable."

"So then we tried the tree meditation. I thought grounding was the best thing, but, uh, that didn't work out so well."

"Didn't work out how?"

Murphy grimaced, and Aiden answered for him. "I burned a hole in his rug and melted the paint on his ceiling."

Her eyebrows shot up, and she looked back and forth between the two of them. "Literally?"

When both he and Murphy nodded, Lola frowned and worried her bottom lip. "I could tell you were a powerful projector from what I felt when you pulled up, but I didn't realize...."

She pulled her glasses off and squinted at Aiden. Her faded gray eyes were unfocused as if she were looking through him, and Aiden tensed under her scrutiny.

"Oh my," she whispered. "My, my, my, my, my."

"What?"

He was trying not to get cranky. He really was. But this whole situation was wearing on his already frazzled nerves. They kept talking about him like he wasn't there. He felt like a fucking bug under a microscope.

Can everyone see how fucked-up I am?

This was a mistake. She couldn't help him. No one could. He was going to have to spend the rest of his life in a fucking fire-proof room, *alone*, because Murphy would get tired of his bullshit and leave like everyone else and—

"Aiden?"

Murphy's voiced pulled him out of his little internal tantrum. He glanced up to find Lola leaning way back in her seat away from him and Murphy halfway out of his chair.

Shit.

He clamped down on his irritation and fear stuffed them back in the box inside his head. Then he took a couple of deep breaths. "I'm sorry. I'm good. Nothing to worry about. I got it... Sorry."

At least his shorts were dry now, even if the moss under his butt might take a while to recover.

"Is it like that all the time?" Lola asked, her voice a little breathy.

"Not all the time. It got much worse after... Adam," Aiden responded guiltily.

At Lola's questioning glance, Murphy said, "He had a little accident with a forest fire."

Aiden cringed. That was putting it mildly.

"It's why I came here, to Nantucket, I mean. But I can't seem to get control again. I'm better since Murphy's been helping, though."

"But before this little forest fire, you were doing okay?" Lola asked.

"Mostly."

"How did you manage before?"

Aiden thought back on all the years of fighting, every day and night, fighting his temper, fighting *all* of his fucking over-the-top emotions, wishing he was someone else, *anyone* else.

"I don't know. I just did. I didn't have a choice."

While Lola seemed to ponder this, Murphy got down on the ground with him and snuggled against his back. Aiden sighed in relief and dropped his head back against Murphy's shoulder, and Murphy wrapped him in his arms. That was all it took to make his world right again. He couldn't say it out loud, but this time he kind of hoped Murphy could sense the depth of his feelings.

When he glanced back at Lola a little self-consciously, she was smiling at them, her gray eyes almost disappearing behind her wrinkles.

"I have to say, I've never met anyone like either of you," she said. "Despite the shape you were in when we first met, Murphy, I felt blessed the day you walked into my life… and now it appears I'm doubly blessed. The Goddess isn't done with me yet."

He had no idea what she was talking about again, but whatever it was seemed to make her happy. Murphy tightened his arms, so Aiden was happy too.

"But, dear Goddess, we need to get you shielded somehow, or you're going to blind this old woman," Lola finished with a chuckle.

Aiden blew out a breath and straightened determinedly in Murphy's arms while Lola pursed her lips and tapped her chin.

"This isn't exactly your standard situation, but don't lose hope. Murphy was a surprise when I met him, and we muddled through, found something that worked… but we picked that particular meditation for him because not only did it speak to him, but the kind of shield he needed was the kind that keeps energy out not in. He's receptive, like me. He needed something to reflect energy—*emotions*—away from him. I don't think that's what you need."

"What do I need?"

Her wrinkled face scrunched in a grimace. "I'm not quite sure yet. I need to talk it out a little…. To put it mildly, sweetheart, you're too busy blasting outward to worry about anything coming in. I would have thought grounding would help, but I guess, as you are now, maybe the ground can't take it."

She chuckled at her own joke and tapped her cane on the circle of yellowed moss surrounding him.

Patience was a lot easier to come by when Murphy's arms were around him. The old Aiden would have been pacing the circle right about now. But new Aiden simply settled his back against Murphy's chest and waited while Lola stared off into the trees and muttered to herself.

Eventually her mumbling and muttering coalesced into actual sentences. "What you need is something to bleed that energy safely. Maybe some black tourmaline to absorb the runoff… or maybe a way to channel it somehow." She focused on him again. "The problem is most of us in this world are trying to get *more* energy, not less. I have crystals and wands and potions all for storing energy for me to use when I need it, and here you are with so much extra you don't know what to do with it. Where's the fairness in that?"

He shook his head. "Believe me. You don't want what I have. All it does is screw everything up. It's the bad kind, not the good kind. I can't tell you how many times I wished I'd never been cursed with this."

Murphy tensed a little behind him, but Lola beat him to the punch when she snapped surprisingly vehemently, "Don't you dare say that. The Goddess gave you a gift, a connection to the universe very few people could ever even dream of."

Her gray eyes fairly glowed with intensity now, but instead of reacting to her bit of temper how he normally would have, with a burst of anger, Aiden took a deep breath and allowed Murphy to leech some of the heat away from him. Lola's frown disappeared as she watched them, and she nodded approvingly.

"It's not bad, Aiden. I promise," she continued in a softer voice, "Here, Murphy, open that box over there." She pointed to a black plastic tote on the other side of the circle, next to a tree, and a moment later Murphy's comforting presence at his back was gone.

When Murphy reached the box, she said, "Bring me the brown velvet bag."

After he brought it back, she dug inside and pulled out a half-used white taper candle. "The plastic box is a bit of a mood killer, I'll admit.

But it saves me from carrying all my witchy stuff out here every time I want to do a ritual. Anyway, take this."

She handed the taper to Aiden and lifted her eyebrows expectantly. Aiden smiled. This at least he could do.

He touched the tip of his finger to the wick and let go his stranglehold on what was inside him the tiniest bit. A small flickering flame burst into life, and Lola let out a long sigh as she stared at it dreamily.

"If I were a lesser woman, I'd be jealous right down to my creaky old bones…. And if I hadn't seen it with my own eyes, I might never have believed it." She sighed again and then shook her head. "But the point is, this isn't bad, is it? It's light. It's warmth. It's beautiful. Like anything else in nature, it's neither all good nor all bad. Without that big fiery ball in the sky, none of us would be here, would we?"

"I guess not," he agreed begrudgingly.

"Good. So get that negative thought out of your head first, or we're not going to get very far."

He would try, but he wasn't sure how successful he'd be. His "gift" had done nothing but ruin his life from practically day one.

Lola settled a little lower in her chair, drawing his attention back to her. The smile she gave him was wistful. "It's not all bad. I know it may feel that way sometimes, but there's always something positive to be found. You've blessed me with a sight I never thought I'd see. To bear witness in one lifetime to two people with such strength—two who can manifest such energy on the physical plane, with such a clear, direct connection to two different universal powers—is truly a blessing. That *can't* be a bad thing."

She'd divided her attention between the both of them, and when Aiden turned a questioning glance to Murphy, Murphy crouched down in front of him. With a smile Murphy cupped his palm around the top of the candle, and between one breath and the next, the flame went out. But Murphy hadn't just blown it out, because when he took his hand away, the wick was black and smokeless, as if it hadn't been burning only a second before.

Startled, Aiden searched Murphy's eyes. "How did you…?"

He shrugged. "I haven't had a chance to tell you everything yet."

Aiden was captured by the deep, gentle blue of Murphy's eyes. He could literally stare into those eyes all day if Murphy let him.

"You can wow each other and make googly eyes later," Lola grumbled from behind Murphy. "We still have work to do, and I'm hungry."

Murphy chuckled as he stood up. "Later."

When Murphy was settled behind him again, Lola clapped her hands together and said, "Alrighty, then, I may have cut it short, but your little interlude there might have given me an idea."

If she meant the Murphy part, Aiden was all for it. Anything that kept Murphy in touching distance was good.

"You need a constructive outlet for some of that energy. When do you feel tired?"

"Not often." Then Aiden grimaced as he thought of something. "I guess I feel the most tired after I've flipped out over something… and fighting to keep it all inside is exhausting. I'm very tired of that."

"*Flipping out* expends emotional energy… as does fighting with yourself, although not in a very constructive way. You need to find something that uses energy without negative consequences. You want what's inside you to come out steady and positive, like that candle, not in spurts, burning the place down. You got me? Now you say it's been worse since the 'little forest fire.' Why do you think that is?"

"It's worse when I'm upset. I only really lose control when I'm freaking over something."

"What have you been doing about it?"

Aiden grimaced. "I went to my parents' house to get away from everything, from everyone. I thought it would be safer that way."

Lola glanced at Murphy before she said, "Well, now you know running and hiding from your problems didn't work out so well, huh?"

Aiden scowled and bit his tongue. She didn't have to make him feel stupid or like a chickenshit. He'd done what he thought was safest for everyone. Maybe he *had* run away from Adam and that whole situation, but Adam didn't want to talk to him or see him. He'd said so.

Aiden could feel a real pout coming on, but then Murphy gave him a squeeze. "Lola, we're trying to be constructive here. I don't think we need the tough love quite yet."

"Phfft. I'm too old—and hungry—to beat around the bush. It's obviously been a long time, Murphy, if you think that's my tough love. But I had a point there too. Look, I'll leave the emotional stuff to you, Murphy. That's your gig. But from an energy standpoint, Aiden, what I'm saying is, hiding out, separating yourself from people, seems to be the wrong direction. You aren't the stay at home and read a book kind of person. Am I right?"

"Not really," Aiden admitted.

"Well, then, that's what I'm saying. You have all this energy, personal energy, psychic energy. You hide out all alone, bottling it up instead of using it, and eventually your cork's gonna pop, understand? I could teach you tons of different meditations, but I don't think they'll do you much good. Meditation is too passive, at least until you've bled off a little of that juice, or age starts to slow you down. From the sounds of it, you've even turned keeping calm into a fight, and that's because it's not your nature. You need to find a way to work *with* who you are, instead of against it."

"What if I don't like who I am?" The question slipped out. He hadn't meant to say it out loud.

"Aiden—" Murphy began, but Lola chose that moment to give Aiden a none-too-gentle tap on the knee with her cane.

"Get over it. You've got work to do, so you work with what you got. None of that defeatist shit, or you won't get anywhere."

He wasn't sure what his expression looked like, but her tone softened a little as she continued. "Like I said, no one and nothing in nature is all good or all bad. You've got some good qualities in there, or Murphy here wouldn't be hovering over you like a mother hen. All I'm saying is, work with what the universe gave you. Do the best you can. If you've wronged, do what you can to make it right. If you fail, try again. You have enough drive and spirit for ten people. You don't just wield fire. You *are* fire. It's kept you going this long, just aim it in a direction that will do some good… for you and the world."

"I'm still not sure how."

"Practice. Pick a safe place and light some fires. Bleed it out before it comes out when you don't want it. Find an old folks home and dazzle them with your winning personality. Feed *them* some of that energy. Join a club. Make friends. All of these are positive outlets. Live life as a glowing ember rather than an open flame. An ember gives off heat at a controlled rate without spilling out onto everything around it." She shifted her attention to Murphy, and her smile gentled even more. "It looks like Murphy here might be more than willing to help you work through some of your emotional triggers and issues on top of the rest of it. He's good at that. Listen to him… and maybe when you're feeling a little more mellowed and stable, we can revisit more conventional energy work, grounding, and shielding etcetera."

So Lola wouldn't be waving her magic wand and making everything okay. He had to admit he was a little disappointed in that, but at this point he was willing to try anything. At least he felt cared for and accepted within that little circle of stones. He'd admitted the whole truth to two different people in the space of twenty-four hours. He was "out" for the second time in his life, and so far, the reactions had been a lot more accepting than Aiden had anticipated.

"What puzzles me is why no one in either of your families taught you any of this," Lola murmured, almost to herself, breaking in on his thoughts.

"My parents aren't exactly the esoteric, new age type," Aiden replied dryly, "even if they were interested in helping me out anymore."

"And no one else in your family is like you?"

"No."

Her puzzled frown only deepened.

"Huh. Weird. So who named you, then?"

"My parents did."

"Is it a family name?"

"I don't think so. I mean, I guess I never asked. Why?"

She just looked at him.

"What?"

"Well, in Gaelic, Aiden literally means fire."

"Really? I'm sure my folks didn't know that when they picked it."

"It baffles me how much knowledge has been lost. I mean both Murphy's parents' families come from islands, *big* islands, but still islands. And their family names… I mean *come on*."

Aiden was lost again. When he turned to Murphy, Murphy shook his head. "Let's stick with what we have for right now. I think Aiden has enough to think about without the soapbox lecture."

They quit not long after that and piled into Lola's car, since, as she said, "There ain't no way my old bones are getting up in that red monstrosity." At lunch, while Murphy and Lola talked about people they knew and got caught up, Aiden picked at his food and thought. Other than a couple of worried glances in his direction and a reassuring hand on this thigh under the table, Murphy left him alone, and Aiden was surprisingly okay with not being the center of attention. Maybe he was getting better. He certainly felt better, even if they hadn't really done anything yet.

Lola had essentially told him to do the opposite of everything he had been doing. A weight had been removed from his chest. He could go out. He *should* go out. He still had the whole guilt and penance thing to deal with. But maybe if he did what she said and volunteered somewhere that would count, karmically speaking. And if he found something to wear himself out physically every day, that might help too. He could think of a few ways Murphy might be able to help with that.

Murphy insisted on paying for lunch, and Aiden had been too distracted to put up much of a fight about it. His mind was still spinning with choices as they walked Lola back to her door. He barely noticed as Murphy and Lola hugged and said their good-byes. He only snapped back to the present when a surprisingly strong, blue-veined hand clamped down on his shoulder and dragged him down into a hug.

"You'll do fine. You have so much to offer the world, Aiden. You just need to point it in the right direction, not stifle it," she murmured in his ear before letting him go.

"Thanks, Lola."

He'd been right from the first. He liked her a lot, even if she pushed some of his buttons. He could hardly blame her for that. His buttons weren't exactly hard to find.

Murphy continued to give him space until they were back on the ferry home. Aiden was still tense on the water, but not as nervous as earlier, so when Murphy rested his forearms on the railing next to him, Aiden mirrored his move.

"You haven't said much since we left the circle," Murphy said tentatively.

"I've been thinking."

"I'm sorry she didn't have a more concrete solution, but I think what she said makes sense."

Aiden scooted a little closer and leaned his head against Murphy's shoulder. Physical contact was always better.

"It does make sense. I guess. I mean I hid out at school for a long time, avoiding conflict, avoiding stress... avoiding real life. But I had outlets there. I loved the theater. I loved the productions and being on stage and hanging with my friends. I knew I couldn't hide out forever. Obviously, real life and real stress caught up with me anyway. But I can have both, right? I can have a real life and do the things that make me happy too. I can get out there again."

Aiden felt Murphy sigh next to him, and his voice was a little sad as he said, "Yeah. You should get out there. Do things. Meet people. You aren't the kind of person who'll be happy hiding away."

Sensing more than encouragement in his words, Aiden bumped his hip to Murphy's.

"I'm not ready to run off to Broadway or anything. I can find outlets right here. I don't have to actually go anywhere, Murphy."

"You might think so now, but things on the island are pretty quiet in the winter. Summer maybe, but...." He shrugged and continued to stare out across the water. "You should go back to school too, finish your degree at least."

Aiden chuckled. He couldn't help it. "Murphy, look at me."

When Murphy turned those deep blue eyes his way, Aiden smiled. "I've had enough credits to graduate for a long time. I just kept going back because it was a safe place to hide... and because of Adam. All I have to do is talk to my advisor, and I could probably have the diploma in my hand in no time. I don't ever have to go back to Athens if I don't want to."

"But will you be happy here?"

"I'm happy here with you."

With a sigh, Murphy took Aiden's hand and turned his attention back out to the water. "I'm happy too."

Aiden resisted the urge to do a dance on deck. He was too mature for that... or he wanted to be at least.

The silence between them stretched comfortably until Murphy said, "You know, maybe the next time those kids from the beach have a party, you should go."

His tone was nonchalant, but Aiden could feel tension radiating from where they touched. He didn't have to be an empath to figure that one out.

"Maybe," he replied just as casually. "But I think I might check out the Theater Workshop. Those might be more my type of people. Even if I can't get a job there, I could try to see if they'd take me on as a volunteer or something."

The smile Murphy gave him was so relieved and approving Aiden didn't want to spoil it. But Murphy was the only one he had to talk to about these things—the only one who knew what he'd done—and he needed a little more reassurance.

"You think this is the right thing to do? I mean, after what I did to Adam. Do you think it's safe?"

"I think so. You were safe before. You never deliberately hurt anyone. And if Lola's right, this should help make it better. And I'll be here if you need me."

Aiden had to clear his throat before he said, "I'm not sure I deserve this… you."

Murphy stood up then and used their joined hands to drag Aiden to one of the benches. When they were seated facing each other, he said, "Listen. I'll tell you as many times as you need to hear it, but everyone deserves a second chance. Everyone deserves a little understanding and compassion, particularly someone with as good a heart as you. I'm not perfect. I've made plenty of mistakes in my life and hurt people I cared about. What matters is, you realize it now, and you do your best to face your past, to make amends if you can. At some point, you're going to need to face what happened. Fix what you can. Resolve what you can. Otherwise you won't be able to move forward. You need to talk to him."

"He told me not to call," he objected weakly.

Murphy sighed. "I know. But I think you need to at least try. If this keeps eating away at you, you aren't going to be able to find your balance. This thing will always be there, haunting you, shadowing your life, *because* you are a good person. If you weren't, what happened wouldn't bother you as much as it does."

"Will you help me?"

"As much as I can, but you're the one who has to make the call."

At the announcement over the PA, they went below and climbed back into his Jeep. They were both quiet while the boat docked and on the way home. Murphy hadn't said he needed to make the call tonight, but Aiden felt like he needed to get it done and over with, or he'd never start getting better. Only, the more he thought about facing the past, about making that call, the more nervous and jittery he became. He could barely keep still in the driver's seat even with Murphy's hand on his thigh. He probably should've had Murphy drive, but it was too late now.

When Murphy suggested they stop for carryout, he pulled over with a sigh of relief. He wasn't quite hungry yet. His nerves had his stomach tied in knots. But the side trip would put it off that much longer and this way he could drown his sorrows in leftovers tomorrow without having to leave the house.

While they waited for their order in the little alcove at the front of the Chinese place they picked, Aiden fidgeted until he spotted a familiar face outside. Richard waved at him, and Aiden waved back, ridiculously relieved to have some sort of distraction. He moved to the door to step outside but stopped with his hand on the handle when he saw Murphy's expression. Then the frown disappeared when Richard came through the door a moment later, and Murphy was actually smiling blandly as Aiden stepped back to give the man room.

"Aiden. How are you?" Richard said, beaming at both of them. "I haven't seen you at the coffee shop the last few days. I hope you're not still feeling sick."

Despite his polite smile, Murphy was tense next to him, and Aiden frowned in puzzlement until a thought hit him.

Murphy was jealous.

The smile Aiden threw Richard's way might give Richard the wrong idea, but Aiden couldn't help it. He took Murphy's hand in his and squeezed as he answered, "I'm okay. I've just been making do with coffee at home for a few days."

Richard took a step closer but stopped when he glanced down at their joined hands. Aiden was relieved Richard stopped because he knew even from their brief encounter before that Richard was a real hands-on kind of guy, and while Aiden liked Murphy to be a little jealous, the last thing he needed right now was more drama.

"Well, I'm glad to see you're feeling better," Richard continued without missing a beat. "I need to get going, but maybe we can talk again over coffee sometime."

He waved cheerily at both of them and then stepped back out onto the street and disappeared.

"I don't like that guy," Murphy grumbled under his breath.

Another smile split Aiden's face. He couldn't help being pleased that Murphy could get possessive. "He's not so bad, maybe a little chatty. But he seems pretty nice."

"Hmph."

"Jealous?"

"Of him?" Murphy's pout was actually kind of adorable.

Aiden was bad. He let Murphy frown all the way through picking up their food and out to the Jeep. But before he turned the key in the ignition, Aiden leaned across the seats and gave him a peck on the lips.

"I hope you know you don't have anything to worry about. I'm a one-man guy too. I mean, don't get me wrong. I'm as much of an attention slut as the next drama queen, but I'm not an actual slut, not when I'm in a relationship anyway."

At Murphy's chuckle, Aiden laughed and for a full two minutes of the drive home he forgot about what he still needed to do tonight in favor of sappy thoughts about Murphy. But when they pulled in the driveway and Aiden shut off the ignition, all his anxiety came rushing back. At least the food gave him an excuse to go directly to Murphy's without having to wait to be invited. He didn't want to go back to his own place for this.

After putting the food on the counter, Aiden sat on one of the bar stools and propped his chin on his palm while Murphy unpacked the bags and put things away. When everything was as pristine again as it had been when they'd walked through the door, Murphy gave him a gentle smile and asked, "Would you like me to make you some tea?"

"I should probably make that phone call now, before I lose my nerve."

"Do you want to go outside or me to go to another room?"

Tempting as it was to cling to Murphy or to find some other excuse to put it off, Aiden said, "I'll go out on the deck. Some tea would be nice, though. I might need it after."

"Okay."

The now-familiar and somewhat comforting clunk of the teakettle on the stove came from the kitchen area as he pulled open the french doors and stepped out onto Murphy's deck. He got his cell out of his pocket, pulled up Adam's number, and with a shaking finger hit Send.

With each ring his nerves grew, and he was finding it a little hard to breathe, but eventually the phone clicked over to voice mail. A little ashamed at how relieved he was that Adam hadn't picked up, he huffed out a breath as his shoulders relaxed. The sound of Adam's familiar, deep voice on the recording made him cringe a little, and it took him a couple of seconds for the words to come out when he heard the tone.

"Adam. I know you said not to call, but… but there's something I need to tell you. I'm not trying to make trouble. I know I was really shitty the last time we talked. But I'm not trying to do anything, I just…. Shit. Please call me back. I promise I won't flip out on you, but there's something you need to know, something I need to tell you, okay? Please. Okay. Bye."

He hit End and buried his face in his hands with a loud groan.

Could I have sounded any more like a complete asshole?

CHAPTER 11

AT THE whistle, Murphy removed the kettle from the burner and set it aside. A quick glance outside showed him Aiden was no longer on his cell, so he went ahead and poured the water into the two waiting mugs before making his way to the french doors.

"Everything okay?" he asked after cracking open the door.

Aiden bit his lower lip and shook his head. "Voice mail."

"You left a message?"

"Yeah. I sounded like a complete idiot, but I did it."

"You took the first step. That's all you could do. Ball's in his court now."

"What if he doesn't call back?"

He knew Aiden didn't need an answer to that, but he said, "We'll cross that bridge when we get there. Come on. The tea's ready. Come inside."

While Murphy went to get the tray, Aiden crossed the living room and flopped down on the couch with a loud sigh. He was still clutching his phone tightly when Murphy sat next to him, and the longer Aiden sat there silently twisting the phone in his hands, the more Murphy believed he needed to come up with a distraction. Aiden's tension was exhausting. He couldn't even imagine how tired it had to be making Aiden.

"It's been a long day. How about a bath?"

Aiden's head jerked up and his lips eased into a half smile as he cocked an eyebrow. "A bath?"

"Yeah. You know. Fill a tub with warm water. Climb in. Put some nice music on. Maybe light a few candles. I know you don't swim, but I think you'd be okay in a tub."

When Aiden's smile widened, Murphy could feel the weight of emotions ease as well.

"Will I be alone in the tub, or will I have company?"

His green eyes sparked with the question, and Murphy felt an answering warmth start in his belly. He'd mostly been thinking of ways to make Aiden relax, but this idea was good too.

"I'll go fill the tub," Murphy said with a grin, his tea forgotten. "You grab the candles."

Murphy pointed to the various white column candles scattered around the room as he said it, and Aiden hopped off the couch and started collecting them while Murphy headed for the bathroom.

When Aiden came through the door a minute later, he had a full armload of candles, and Murphy had to laugh even as he felt a tiny burble of unease. Aiden caught him looking askance at the sheer number and shrugged.

"Lola said to practice. Don't worry. It's okay."

Murphy cocked an eyebrow, and Aiden rolled his eyes. "Really. I mean obviously I'm anxious to get this thing with Adam over with, but I'm not flipping out. I'm not going to lose it, especially not with the prospect of you all wet and slippery in that tub."

"You like that idea, huh?"

Aiden dumped the candles in the sink and closed the few feet between them. He crowded close to Murphy, hooked his thumbs in Murphy's belt loops, and gazed up at him with hooded green eyes.

"I like it a lot," Aiden whispered against Murphy's lips before sealing their mouths together in a long, hot kiss.

It took a while for the sound of water splashing in the tub to register enough to remind Murphy he would need to shut it off at some point. He reluctantly withdrew from their kiss and gave Aiden a gentle shove toward the sink.

"Get busy practicing then while I finish up here."

The grin Aiden gave him was pure sin, and not for the first time Murphy counted his lucky stars Aiden had come crashing into his life.

Anything less than a full-blown crash might not have dislodged Murphy from the lonely but safe little nest he'd built for himself, and look what he might've missed out on.

While Aiden set the candles on every available surface, Murphy dug out some scented bath salts to add to the water. He had the full complement of bath accessories: salts, oils, bath cushions. The large jetted tub was one of the first things he and Felix had added to the house, and Murphy had spent many, many hours lolling away his evenings in here, particularly in the winter when the ocean was out of bounds.

Even though he didn't fill it as much as usual, the water from the tap had already started to cool a bit by the time he shut it off. He had a feeling Aiden wouldn't mind, though. The air in the room was already warm and buzzing with his energy, and when Aiden turned off the overhead lamp, it glowed with the soft flickering light of a dozen candles.

"It's beautiful," Murphy murmured, and Aiden's answering smile was all the reward he needed.

Murphy stood and kicked off his shoes. He started to unbutton his shirt, but Aiden rushed over and stopped him.

"Let me. Please."

As Aiden picked up where Murphy left off, Murphy let his hands fall to his sides and watched Aiden's nimble fingers work.

"I realized something, and I feel bad because I've only just realized it," Aiden murmured. He didn't lift his head, his gaze stayed firmly fixed on his task. "Today was all about me."

"That was the point wasn't it… to help you?" Murphy asked breathily as Aiden shoved his shirt off his shoulders and let it fall to the floor.

"Yeah. I guess. But it can't always be about me. I know that. I want you to be happy too. I want to do something for you."

Aiden tugged Murphy's undershirt free from his trousers and his warm fingers stole beneath the hem, caressing Murphy's sensitive belly. After a shaky inhale, Murphy chuckled. "Don't you worry about that. I'm happy. Believe me."

Aiden's fingers stopped moving and he glanced up with sober green eyes. "Are you?"

Struggling to think beyond how close Aiden was, Murphy pulled enough brain cells together to cup Aiden's cheek and hold his gaze as he said, "Yes. I am. Happier than I've been in a long time."

The smile Aiden gave him was dazzling as was the emotion pouring off him. Then Aiden fisted a hand in Murphy's hair and kissed him hard. He laid claim to Murphy's mouth, and Murphy was more than happy to let him. All that passion, all that fire was addicting, and Murphy drank it all in. Before he even realized what was happening, Aiden was helping him step out of his pants and his boxers. And while Murphy slid into the warm heaven of the tub, Aiden made a show of removing his polo, shorts, and boxers.

Murphy wrapped a fist around his cock and stroked himself beneath the water to gain a little relief as he watched. He'd intended their bath to be a relaxing experience, but he should've known better. Maybe that would be possible a few months down the road but not this soon. He wasn't exactly complaining though as Aiden sauntered over to the tub, naked, hard, and beautiful. Murphy held out his arms, but Aiden chose to slide in behind him and pull him against his chest.

Content to be pampered, Murphy relaxed against him and let Aiden's hands wander wherever they wanted. They were breeching new levels of intimacy at a rather accelerated pace, but Murphy couldn't dredge up any angst over it. He needed this. He needed the heat and admiration in Aiden's eyes. He needed the tenderness and the passion, all of it. He just hadn't realized how much until now.

With confident hands Aiden stroked the length of Murphy's body. He caressed, massaged, lathered, and teased until Murphy was a puddle of happiness and aching need in his arms. Submerged in his element and being pampered by Aiden was as close to heaven as Murphy thought he could come, and he let Aiden take his time though he ached for more with every touch.

"God, you're good at this," Murphy moaned as Aiden nibbled on his neck and gave his cock a few lazy pumps. "You can make it all about me any time you want."

Aiden chuckled against his skin. "I have my moments."

He shifted his hips, pressing his cock into Murphy's lower back, and Murphy sat up a little, pushing back against him. Thanks to Aiden's constant warmth, their bath hadn't gotten even a degree colder, but even if the bath wasn't getting cold, Murphy's need was fast approaching desperate levels. Judging by the hardness at his back, Aiden couldn't be faring much better. To move things along, Murphy wrapped his fist around the one Aiden had on his cock and tightened his grip. If he'd been able to think past his own aching need he might have taken advantage of the fact that they were submerged in his element to take care of Aiden at the same time. But he was beyond concentrating on anything but how good Aiden's hands felt on him and the pressure building in his balls.

He let his head fall back to rest on Aiden's shoulder and arched into their fists. He pumped his hips, moaning between ragged breaths, while Aiden rubbed his cock against Murphy's lower back and ass, his breaths quick and uneven in Murphy's ear. When Aiden's free arm tightened around Murphy's chest and he placed a gentle, lingering kiss on Murphy's temple and moaned, Murphy lost it. With one final thrust he shot over their fists and into the soapy water surrounding them, shuddering out a few final drops before collapsing against Aiden.

As he stared dreamily up at the flickering light on the ceiling above the tub, Aiden tightened both arms around his chest and thrust against his ass.

"That was so hot," Aiden whispered. Then he nuzzled Murphy's neck and ground his cock against Murphy some more.

Murphy could have happily fallen asleep right where they were, but Aiden was obviously in need of a little reciprocation, and Murphy prided himself on being a considerate lover.

Fighting post-orgasmic lethargy, Murphy maneuvered himself around in the water until they were face-to-face. He kissed Aiden with languid passion, able to enjoy the taste and feel of his lips now that his cock wasn't screaming for his attention. He pulled back and before Aiden's glazed green eyes could focus on him, he slid down Aiden's body, closed his eyes, and dipped below the surface of the water. His gift didn't exactly allow him to breathe underwater. He still needed oxygen. But with all the hours he spent in his element he could certainly hold his breath for a long time, and he could make enough of a vacuum by pushing the water away from his nose and mouth to create a decent pocket of air beneath the surface—not that he'd need it now, given how close Aiden was to coming already. But it might come in handy for future exploration.

Aiden's fists clenched and unclenched fitfully on Murphy's shoulders, but he didn't put any pressure or try to hold Murphy down in any way. At one point, as he swallowed around Aiden's cock, Murphy swore he heard Aiden's head thump against the edge of the tub but he didn't surface to look. By the way Aiden kept trembling and arching his spine, Murphy was pretty sure Aiden was still conscious and wouldn't appreciate Murphy stopping to check on his welfare.

Long before Murphy began to run out of breath, Aiden's hands tightened on Murphy's shoulders in warning, and a moment later Aiden shot down Murphy's throat. Murphy held him in his mouth until the last of Aiden's shudders subsided. Then he lifted his head above the water, pushed his sopping hair out of his eyes and grinned down into Aiden's pleasure-glazed green eyes.

"Have I told you already you're really good at that?" Aiden murmured breathlessly.

"Doesn't hurt to hear it again."

"You're *really* good at that."

"Why thank you, kind sir."

While Murphy crouched with his ass on Aiden's thighs, Aiden regarded him with sleepy sated eyes as he bit his lower lip. "Murphy, would you show me?"

"I thought I just did."

"No, I mean, show me what you can do, how you did that with the candle earlier."

"Oh. That. Okay."

Since he was already starting to get goose bumps with his torso out of the water, Murphy decided to start there. He closed his eyes and melded with the water in the tub. Water was drawn to water. The water within his body drew the water without, and it moved up his torso until a thin layer of quickly cooling liquid encased him up to the neck.

"Holy shit, that's cool."

Murphy smiled down into Aiden's wide green eyes and allowed the water to sluice off him back into the tub. He cupped his hand in the water and used his gift to form the liquid into a sphere in his palm that he held out to Aiden. Aiden poked a finger at it and watched raptly as the water clung to his finger and then snapped back into the sphere as he withdrew. With a smile, Aiden held out his palm, and Murphy placed the sphere in his hand. When the water began to boil, Murphy let go of it. Most splashed back into the tub, but the part that remained in Aiden's palm was converted to steam almost immediately.

"Can you do this with other stuff?" Aiden asked.

"No. Like I suspect it is with you and fire, water is my element. It's me."

"But we weren't in water earlier in Lola's circle. I mean my ass was wet, but that was about it."

Murphy chuckled. "There's always a certain amount of water in the air, but that wasn't all I used. The human body is more than fifty percent water, and I suspect maybe more than that in my case."

When Aiden gave him an odd look, Murphy frowned. "What?"

Aiden scrunched up his nose. "I don't know. I guess that maybe sounds a little creepy. Like an episode from *Star Trek* or something where the aliens sucked their victims dry. Could you do that?"

"Ew. I don't know. Why would you even go there?"

When Aiden laughed, Murphy put his hand down, and with an extra push from his gift, sent a wall of water over Aiden, drenching him and splashing onto the tile on the bathroom floor.

"Hey!" Aiden sputtered and wiped water off his face then made a grab for Murphy. They wrestled a bit, but the tub really wasn't conducive to much roughhousing. Murphy surrendered pretty quickly and decided it was probably time to get out.

After a quick but thorough toweling off, they stumbled to his bedroom and collapsed on the mattress together. As before, Aiden curled around him, and Murphy passed out cocooned in the warmth of physical contact, overjoyed Aiden seemed to enjoy cuddling as much as he did. He slept so much better with someone next to him.

Cuddlers unite.

"We should do that again," Aiden mumbled before his breathing slowed, and Murphy smiled.

He slept soundly until sometime in the middle of the night when he felt Aiden climb back into bed.

"Everything okay?" he asked groggily as he struggled to sit up.

"It's fine. I just left my phone in the other room."

"Miss any calls?"

"No. Nothing yet."

Aiden's anxiety prickled against Murphy's consciousness. He scooted across the mattress and drew Aiden into his arms.

"I'm here if you need me," Murphy whispered as he rubbed his face into Aiden's soft copper hair.

Aiden drew in a long breath and sighed. "I know. And I'm so grateful for that, even though sometimes I wonder why you put up with all this. I mean you only met me a few days ago and look at the bullshit I'm making you deal with."

"We've been over this already."

"I know. But I'm still afraid any minute now you're going to realize I'm not worth it."

Murphy growled, rolled across the mattress and turned on his bedside lamp. When Aiden didn't sit up or even turn to look at him, Murphy grabbed his pillow and bopped Aiden on the head with it.

"You need to stop that," Murphy said sharply. "You need to stop putting yourself down. It's not doing anyone any good."

Aiden sat across from him on the mattress, watching him warily with the pillow clutched in his lap.

"I know all about guilt and self-loathing. I know how they feel, how they drain you. They're supposed to be horrible so you learn, so you do something about it. But if all you do is wallow in it and do nothing but wallow, you haven't learned anything. You haven't solved anything. You took the first step toward solving the problem today. You should feel good about that… at least a little."

Aiden's cheeks flushed, and Murphy could feel the increase in his emotional intensity like a wave. "It isn't just that, though. I know I'm trying. I'm just terrified I won't change fast enough, and in a couple of weeks—maybe months if I'm lucky—you'll get fed up with me, like everyone else."

Getting mad obviously wasn't helping, so Murphy sighed and lowered his voice. "Aiden, we've only just started. Give me a chance before you lump me in with everyone else."

Aiden closed his eyes and nodded. "I'm sorry. I don't want to put this all on you. That's the last thing I want to do." He blew out a breath and chuckled. "If you didn't feel everything I'm feeling all the time, it would be a lot easier to hide my neuroses from you, you know."

At Aiden's wry smile, Murphy chuckled too. "I know. We'll work on that. But in the meantime it does cut through some of the bullshit. Our conversations are open and honest at least. I don't have to drag it out of you."

"Except it doesn't go both ways. I only know what you tell me, and my overactive imagination can come up with all kinds of things to worry about."

Murphy crawled across the space that separated them, drew the pillow aside, and pushed Aiden down onto his back. "All I can do is promise to be honest with you," he said as he propped himself on his elbows and looked down at him. "I'm thirty-seven years old, Aiden—much as it pains me to admit that to you. I haven't spent all those years hiding under a rock. Well, maybe the last five, but before that I had my fair share of relationships. I've been around long enough to know the importance of communication, the importance of honesty. I write columns about it every month. And while I may not be able to talk about everything I'm feeling, right when I'm feeling it, I won't hide anything from you. I'm too old to play games."

Aiden wrapped his arms around Murphy's back and pulled him down. He buried his face in Murphy's neck and squeezed him tight. "I'm so glad I met you, Murphy. I'm so glad you're here. I don't know what I would have done if you weren't." Aiden paused for a breath and then chuckled. "But no pressure or anything."

"I can handle it," he murmured back, and he meant it.

CHAPTER 12

AIDEN'S RINGTONE woke him from a dead sleep. Struggling to untangle himself from Murphy, he nearly ended up on the floor as he scrambled for the phone. When he spotted Adam's name on the screen his stomach twisted, and he was suddenly short of breath. He hurried out of the room while a still mostly asleep Murphy mumbled and squinted at him.

"Hello?"

"Aiden?"

"Yeah, it's me. Thanks for calling me back."

Standing naked out on Murphy's back deck wasn't exactly how he'd pictured this conversation. At least it was cloudy and gloomy out so he doubted too many people would be on the beach.

"I just got your message this morning. Where are you? Your parents called me like a month and a half ago wondering where you were. They said you weren't answering your cell. They were worried about you. Some PI they hired came by here asking questions not long after that, and with all that stuff that happened with Bob, I started to get worried too."

Not enough to actually call me yourself, though.

Aiden pushed that uncharitable thought aside. He didn't deserve Adam's concern. "I'm sorry. I kind of needed to disappear for a while. But I've talked to my folks. They know where I am now. I'm sorry if you were worried."

Adam did that big sigh on the other end of the phone, the one that Aiden had heard way too many times, the one that said he was praying for patience. "Well, I'm glad you're okay."

Aiden got a little choked up then, and he had to clear his throat. "Look, Adam, I know you told me not to call you anymore, but there's something I need to tell you. I should have told you sooner… I should have done a lot of things. But I was scared you'd hate me if you knew, and I didn't think I could handle that."

"I don't hate you, Aiden. I just needed you to let go. I needed you to realize we can't ever be what you wanted us to be."

The words still hurt even now. Knowing Murphy was only a few dozen feet away, naked and beautiful in bed, helped immensely, but the rejection still stung. He took a steadying breath.

"I know. I know it, Adam. I knew it the minute I saw you with Jay. A couple of seconds and I knew you guys were a better match than we could ever be. I only freaked because I was scared to let go, scared I'd never meet anyone else who'd connect with me the way you did, who'd put up with me."

"Aiden—"

Adam's voice sounded pained, and Aiden shook himself out of the past.

"Look, Adam. This isn't why I called, and I hate doing this over the phone, but I'm not likely to be going back to Athens any time soon, and I need to tell you something." He gulped in a breath. "It's my fault. What happened, the fire… Gaia. It's all my fault. I'm so, so sorry. Drew called me. His mom said she saw you and Jay in the hospital… that Jay got really hurt. God, I'm so so sorry. I didn't do it on purpose. Please believe me—"

"Wait. Stop. I don't understand. What do you mean it was your fault?"

"I didn't mean for it to happen. We had that stupid fight, and I flipped out. I just went up there to do some stupid prank, but I lost it… and then everything happened so fast I panicked. I couldn't control it. I had to get out of there, or it might have been even worse. I didn't know anyone would get hurt… I—"

Aiden stopped there to catch his breath around the boulder that was sitting on his chest. The silence on the other end of the line was deafening.

"Adam?"

Another long silence, then Adam said, "I don't know what to say."

"I know. I'm sorry. I'm so sorry. I never would have done something like that on purpose. I swear. I never meant to hurt anyone. I never meant to do that to your special place. Please tell me you don't hate me."

"I still don't understand. I mean the fire investigator found no trace of accelerant beyond bits of a can of spray paint. And even with the drought, he said that shouldn't have been enough to destroy an old-growth tree like Gaia. He said the fire would have had to have started small and built over time. How is that possible if, as you say, it got out of control too fast? That doesn't make any sense."

He heard the beginnings of suspicion and anger in Adam's voice, and his first reaction was to get defensive. He was reacting to Adam's anger. Part of him wanted to scream something stupid and hang up in a huff, but it would only come back to haunt him later. Adam might even call the cops, and his history of arson and mysterious fires would come up, and that whole nightmare with his parents and cops and psych wards might start all over again.

"Talk to me, Aiden. Make me understand." The warning in his tone was clear, and Aiden fought his first reactions, fought for control. Thankfully, Murphy must have sensed something because he was suddenly there with Aiden, reaching for his hand and watching him with concerned eyes.

As soothing energy pulsed from where they touched, Aiden swallowed and tried to explain. "Do you remember what happened in your shop with that crazy guy, Bob?"

Adam grunted.

"You remember what happened with his gun? How it just exploded? It was like that only much worse."

Adam was quiet as he seemed to digest that. Aiden knew he was still being vague, but he was afraid to say too much, afraid to get into it over the phone, especially since he and Adam had never really talked about this before.

After a few more seconds of agonizing silence in which Aiden clutched desperately at Murphy's hand, Adam said, "We need to talk. But not like this. We need to do this face-to-face."

Aiden had assumed Adam would never want to see him again, so it took him a while to wrap his brain around that.

"You want to see me?"

"I think we should, yes. But I need to talk this out with Jay first. I'll send you a message after that. Okay?"

Now Adam was being cryptic, but he wasn't yelling or talking about going to the police, so that was better than Aiden expected.

"Uh, okay… Adam? I'm sorry."

Adam grunted distractedly. "We'll talk about it later."

And with that less than encouraging statement, Adam hung up.

Aiden stood with the phone dangling uselessly in his hand until Murphy gave his other one a squeeze.

"Hey. What happened? What did he say?"

"He said we needed to talk in person."

"That's a good thing, isn't it? I mean he wouldn't have bothered if he hated you, right?"

With a grimace, Aiden shrugged. "Unless he wants me there in person so he can punch me in the face."

Murphy frowned at him. "Is he that kind of person? Did he hit you before?"

An abstract corner of Aiden's mind found Murphy's narrowed eyes and the angry tightness of his jaw pretty damned sexy, but he wouldn't lie to keep it there. He wasn't that much of an attention whore.

"No. Adam wouldn't hurt a fly. Not unless they were trying to hurt someone he loved… and even then I think he'd have a problem with it… or at least be wracked with guilt after. I just don't know why he wants to talk in person. I was expecting him to hang up on me after telling me he never wanted to hear from me again. I mean, he didn't even yell at me…. I almost wish he had."

"Why?"

"I don't know. I guess if he'd yelled, it would've meant he still cared enough to get pissed…. I mean I deserve it too. I was all ready to get reamed. It's fucked-up, but it would have felt, I don't know—"

"Cathartic?"

"Yeah. I guess."

Despite the fact that Murphy had thought to put on a robe before coming outside, Aiden saw him shiver as he said, "Come on. The water should be hot by now. Let's go inside. I'll make you some tea and we can talk."

Still a bit jittery and on edge, Aiden didn't trust himself in a confined—and flammable—space. "Would you mind if we had our tea out on the beach? I think I need to be out there for a little while."

Murphy studied his face for a few beats before nodding. "But only if you promise to get a fire started out there so I don't freeze my balls off."

"I can do that."

Aiden turned to step off the deck, but Murphy stopped him. "Uh, Aiden? I'm enjoying the view immensely but maybe you should put some clothes on too."

He looked down at himself and flushed. "Oh, yeah, right. Probably a good idea."

While Murphy puttered with the tea, Aiden threw on his shorts and a T-shirt and hurried back to the beach for a little alone time. He didn't really think he'd lose control, but he wasn't in the mood to be confined indoors right now either.

CHAPTER 13

THE ICY breeze hit Murphy like a smack in the face the moment he stepped outside again. It was better now that he was dressed and had a jacket on but still not exactly the kind of day he'd be inclined to spend sitting on the beach. An unbroken blanket of thick gray clouds rolled overhead. There wouldn't even be a ray of sunlight to cut the chill, and the air was heavy with the threat of rain.

He hunched lower in his jacket as he juggled the two travel mugs into one hand and pulled his door closed with the other.

I should have grabbed a scarf too.

Winter was definitely on its way. And if the recent weather reports were to be believed, it would arrive sooner rather than later. At least this hermit season, he would have someone to share his cave with. Aiden had said he wasn't in a hurry to leave, and though, every once in a while, he felt a twinge of unease that once Aiden didn't need him anymore, he might find Murphy's life a little too dull to keep his interest, Murphy would continue to hope he was wrong.

Pushing that aside, Murphy slogged through the cool damp sand until he found Aiden crouched near the small circle of black that marked what remained of the bonfire from the party.

"Hey. Where's that fire you promised me?"

Aiden looked up at him with a grimace as Murphy handed over a mug and dropped to the sand next to him. "Sorry. There isn't anything to burn. I don't know if my gift is strong enough to make sand burn… but I'm pretty sure neither of us want me to find that out."

Murphy glanced at the pile of unburned wood left over from the party in confusion until he remembered where that wood had come from. Warmth bloomed in his chest for Aiden's consideration even as guilt threatened to overwhelm it. He'd managed to spend the last couple of days without grieving, *really* grieving, for Felix even once. He hadn't exactly forgotten about him. That was impossible in their house, surrounded by the things they'd bought together. But he hadn't felt that heart-wrenching emptiness either. He'd been too distracted.

With a long sigh, Murphy shook off the guilt and took Aiden's hand. He couldn't cling to a memory forever. Felix wouldn't have wanted him to tear himself up over actually choosing to live his life instead of just going through the motions. Felix probably would have been appalled at the five years Murphy had already wasted.

He squeezed Aiden's hand to get his attention and pointed to the pile of broken boards flecked with the remnants of white paint.

"There's a whole pile right there."

Aiden's slender dark auburn eyebrows drew down. "Are you sure?"

"Yes. It's just going to rot out here until someone uses it. The bench is gone, and I'm okay with that… at least I am now."

The sad smile Aiden gave him was very sweet, and Murphy tugged him over for a kiss before letting him go so he could build the fire. Without Aiden's warmth, Murphy huddled in his jacket and clutched his mug to his chest against the bitter wind that seemed determined to find every gap in his clothes.

Once Aiden had the wood in a pile, the fire came to life with breathtaking speed. It burst forth in a great whoosh, sucking in all the air around it for a fraction of a second before the wind rushed back in.

Watching Aiden truly let go and release the energy inside him was a rather awe-inspiring experience. Murphy knew from sensing the battle inside Aiden, how hard he fought every day, but the sheer almost orgasmic relief on Aiden's face as he set that fire ablaze sent a knife of pity into Murphy's heart. No one should have to fight that hard, though Murphy knew so many people in this world did. Behind the façade people showed to the world, battles raged against depression, addiction, dementia, as well as physical illnesses, battles that most people never realized, but Murphy felt all too keenly without his shields. But maybe, with Lola's help, he and Aiden could win this together.

When Aiden dropped onto the sand behind him, Murphy settled back into the circle of his arms with a contented sigh. Aiden was a warm shield at his back, still radiating a bit of anxiety, sadness, and guilt but happiness as well. They sipped at their tea in silence, while Murphy gazed thoughtfully into the wildly dancing flames, chased in all directions by the wind off the sea.

"We make a pair, don't we?" he said thoughtfully.

Aiden's arms tightened around him in response. "I'd like to think so."

The note of hesitation in his voice might have been lost to the wind if Murphy hadn't been pressed up against him.

"You don't have to think, Aiden. You can know. If I haven't said it before it was only because I thought it might be too soon. But we've covered a lot of depth in a very short period of time, so I guess that's kind of a moot point now." He wrapped a hand around the arms circling his chest and squeezed. "I'm not going anywhere, Aiden. I like you. I like you, a lot. And I fully intend to stick it out and see where this thing leads, as long as you do."

He felt some of the tension leave Aiden's body as he buried his face in Murphy's hair. "I like you a lot too. More than like," Aiden whispered, his lips grazing the back of Murphy's ear in a way that sent tingles down Murphy's spine.

One day at time.

His days had been pretty good lately. He was looking forward to them now, instead of just counting them off. Although Alexa, his editor, was probably going to have a fit if he kept skipping out on his work to spend time with his new lover. He smiled into the fire and sipped his tea until he felt Aiden's anxiety begin to spike again.

"Do you want to talk about it?" Murphy asked.

"I was hoping the phone call would bring some kind of closure. That's all. I thought, even if he yelled at me, at least that would release some of the pressure, and I could figure out what to do next. Now I have to wait, and I have no idea why he wants to talk in person… and not knowing is killing me."

Murphy wasn't exactly sure how he felt about Aiden getting together with his ex, but he wasn't going to upset Aiden with that right now. All he could do was trust and hope for the best, like Aiden. He might fret a little in private, though. Hopefully he'd be invited to this little get together, and he could get a read on this Adam for himself. It wouldn't exactly be ethical or fair of him to pry like that, but Murphy wasn't above bending his ethics every once in a while.

He never said he was perfect.

"I know it's hard. But we can hope that if he's willing to meet you in person, you might expect a better outcome than him writing you off permanently. That would be a good thing, right?"

When Aiden grunted an affirmative in his ear, Murphy twisted in his arms until they were face-to-face.

"I'm going to hope for the best for you… but you're right, sometimes it doesn't work out that way. Sometimes the best way to make it up to the people we've hurt is to let them get on with their lives without our interference, whether good intentioned or not. After Felix and I climbed out of the pit we'd created for ourselves with the drinking, I had a lot of burned bridges to mend. It was hard. And there were a couple of people we hurt that didn't want to have anything to do with our apologies or our attempts to make amends. I lucked out that most of our true friends were willing to forgive a great deal. But Felix's brother still wasn't talking to him up until the day he died."

Murphy searched Aiden's face in the glow of the fading firelight and forced a smile. "Adam *wants* to see you. I think that means he's willing to give you a chance to explain yourself. And you know I'll be there for you, no matter what."

Aiden's sculpted lips curved up at the corners as he nodded. "Thanks, Murphy. I can't tell you how much that means to me."

"We're a pair, right?"

"Yeah."

Murphy kissed him, the warmth of Aiden's lips drawing Murphy's attention to how cold his ass was now that Aiden wasn't pressed up against it.

With an exaggerated shiver he said, "Look. The fire's almost out and even with you as living electric blanket my toes are starting to ache. Do you think we're okay to go inside now?"

"I think so."

"Come on. You can do your part and warm me up inside."

By the time they made it to Murphy's bedroom a line of clothes littered the living room and the hall. As he lay comfortably warm and sated, watching Aiden sleep, Murphy felt nothing but peace. There would be hurdles… plenty of hurdles. Aiden wasn't the sort to live a quiet life. But Murphy had been quiet too long. He might be closing in on forty, but he wasn't dead. In fact, he felt more alive than he had in a very long time.

OVER THE course of the following week, as Aiden spent time exploring the local theater groups and volunteer organizations for more mundane ways to bleed off some of his energy, Murphy was able to settle back into his routine. He went on his morning run every day. He made breakfast for the two of them. While Aiden cleaned up, he did his meditation exercises and then set to work on his mail and preparations for his next column. In fact, instead of distracting him from his work, spending most of his nights with Aiden actually left him feeling invigorated, inspired. He even plucked up the nerve to dig through the piles of notes for that follow-up novel he hadn't touched in years. He wasn't quite ready to make it a priority yet, but he thought he might be in time.

He was moving forward again, and it felt good.

As Aiden connected with other people on the island, particularly at the theater, Murphy saw less and less of the anxious and distraught young man he'd first met. If he'd thought Aiden glowed before, it was nothing to the energy he radiated after spending a day with "his people," behind the curtain.

"I'd forgotten how much I loved that part of school," Aiden practically gushed around a mouthful of Murphy's pasta at dinner, near the end of the week.

"I'm glad you were able to find something here on the island."

"Oh yeah. And I'm guessing things will pick up closer to Christmas, and of course during the tourist season. They don't really have any job openings right now, at least nothing I'm looking for, but some of the people I talked to said audition dates will be posted soon for a show starting next year. I'm cool with that, and I don't mind volunteering for a while. I did lots of behind the scenes stuff in school, even if that wasn't exactly my favorite part."

He practically vibrated in his seat as he took another bite, and Murphy couldn't help but drink it in.

Aiden lifted his eyebrows and gave Murphy a self-conscious smile. "What?"

Realizing he must have been staring, Murphy blushed and he shook his head. "Nothing. It's just good to see you so happy."

Aiden set his fork down and leaned back in his chair with an almost hesitant smile. "I *am* happy. I mean. I know I still have a lot to deal with. Adam hasn't called back yet, and I probably shouldn't be this happy because of everything that happened…. But I am. I'm afraid to say it out loud in case I jinx it. But you, and now this thing with the theater… and everyone's so nice there, and Lola saying it's not only okay but necessary that I be who I am. I just feel really good, so much better than I have in a long time. I feel like maybe I'm not crazy… or I'm only as crazy as a lot of other people. You know? Some people are neurotic, some people are depressed, some people are hyperactive, and some people, like me, just have a little harder time controlling their feelings." He shrugged. "I can use it for good or I can use it for evil, and as long as I choose good, as long as I'm trying, I'm on the right track… nobody's perfect, right?"

"Right. Nobody's perfect."

After dinner, while Aiden finished washing the dishes, Murphy tidied up the in the living room. Aiden wasn't a slob, but he wasn't the slightly neurotic neat freak Murphy was either, so he tended to leave things lying around when he was distracted. Murphy didn't mind. It was probably the mother hen in him that kind of enjoyed having someone to look after again.

When he picked up Aiden's coat to hang it in the hall closet, he found a book he didn't recognize on the table underneath.

"*Heath Ledger: Hollywood's Dark Star*," Murphy read the title aloud. "Did you pick this up today when you were out?"

Aiden looked over his shoulder at the book Murphy held and grimaced. "No. I stopped by the coffee shop to talk to Crystal, and that guy, Richard, was there. He said he'd just finished it and thought I'd like it. I couldn't figure out a way to say no, and it looked interesting, so I went ahead and took it."

Now it was Murphy's turn to frown. He dropped the book back on the table, and at the sound Aiden raised his eyebrows. The longer Murphy remained silent the wider Aiden's smile got until Aiden finally dried his hands on a dishtowel and sauntered over to him.

"You're cute when you're jealous," Aiden murmured with that cocky little smile Murphy had seen more and more lately.

Usually Murphy liked that smile.

"I'm not jealous."

When Aiden continued to grin at him, Murphy harrumphed. "Okay, maybe a little. But I don't like that guy. I don't know why. I just don't."

"Did you read him?"

"No. I try not to read people most of the time. He just bothers me. It seems like he's always somewhere close by when we go out. And now this book."

Aiden crowded close to Murphy and slid his arms around his waist. "It's just a book."

"No, it's not. It's a conversation starter and a way for him to ensure you come back to return the book. And doesn't it seem a little odd that you just started looking into the theater, and he shows up with a biography of an actor only a few days later?"

At least Aiden seemed to think about that instead of rejecting Murphy's worries out of hand. And maybe Murphy was being a little overprotective… but he still didn't like the guy.

Aiden laughed and kissed him again. "I thought you said you saw him at one of your meetings. What happened to standing up for one of your peeps, solidarity, and all that?"

"Just because he's in the program, doesn't mean I have to like him. We're all still people. There are still assholes in AA, just like anywhere else."

"You know I'm not interested in him or anyone else but you, right?" Aiden asked. His gaze had sobered a little but his lips still twitched with a smile.

"Yeah."

"It's not like I'm going to get in a car with him or follow him back to his place or anything. But I promise to only talk to him in public places if it makes you feel better. And you know I can take care of myself."

Murphy was a mollified enough to let Aiden guide him to the couch and away from the book with no objections. Aiden stretched sideways across the cushions and opened his arms in invitation, and Murphy gratefully dropped into them. He'd never met anyone in his entire life that liked to cuddle and show physical affection as much as Aiden did. And he was thankful for that fact every single minute they were together.

As had become their routine over the past week, Murphy clicked on the TV for a little post dinner relaxation on the couch, but the first thing that came on the screen pushed his hopes for a carb-coma nap on Aiden's chest right out of his mind.

"The storm system we've been following across the upper Midwest seems to be gaining momentum, and the low pressure system forming off the mid-Atlantic is creating favorable conditions for our first nor'easter of the season. We'll be keeping a close eye on this one over the next few days. It's hard to say right now, but if these conditions continue, the New England coastline could be looking at another Athena, folks. Stay tuned, and we'll update you as the storm develops."

"Athena?" Aiden asked when a commercial came on.

"You remember hurricane Sandy and the disaster it left in New York and New Jersey?"

"Yeah. I heard about it on the news."

"Well Sandy didn't do too much to us here on the island. We got out of that one pretty lucky. But only like a week later, we got hit hard by a nor'easter, Athena. It plowed right through us. The ferries and airport were closed for a couple of days. It was bad. Your Jeep could probably handle the flooding, but we should probably think about going out for supplies if they keep saying it's going to be that bad, just in case. I was holed up here for several days last time, while the downed trees and power lines and general mayhem was cleaned up."

Murphy's mind raced with all the things he might need to get and cringed over how packed the grocery stores were probably going to be tomorrow, until Aiden tightened his arms around Murphy's chest and began nibbling on the back of his neck.

"Oh no," Aiden whispered in mock terror. "You mean we might get stuck indoors for a couple of days. Whatever would we do to pass the time?"

With a chuckle Murphy gave in and let Aiden pull him farther into the couch cushions. "Don't joke. These storms can do some pretty good damage."

"I would think you'd be pretty safe from a storm surge, wouldn't you? I mean with what you can do, do you really need to worry about flooding?"

"Gift or no, if the ocean wants to be in my living room, I'm not sure I'd have much say in the matter honestly."

"Maybe," Aiden murmured.

He obviously had an exaggerated opinion of what Murphy could manage, but maybe Murphy underestimated himself as well. He'd never actually tried to push the limits of his gifts. Aiden might be the one to make him explore that part of himself more fully.

Then Aiden bit harder on his neck and fondled Murphy through his lounge pants, and Murphy forgot about anything other than getting them both naked for a while.

CHAPTER 14

THE FORECAST on the morning news the next day was even more ominous than the one from the night before, and by the following evening, the weather reporters were definitely calling it a nor'easter. Aiden was excited. He couldn't help it. He'd never been in any kind of big storm, and he was looking forward to it, except for the fact that Murphy was freaking out.

They followed the newscasts all that day as the sky darkened, but so far, other than it being a little windier and the mercury dropping, Aiden didn't see what the big deal was, so he spent most of the day finding ways to distract an anxious Murphy. That part was pretty fun actually, and Murphy didn't seem to mind. Though he did grumble every now and again that they should be doing more to prepare.

On the morning the storm was due to hit Nantucket, Aiden stood out on Murphy's deck and watched the sky with ever-increasing giddiness. He was pelted with stinging little raindrops and grains of sand that seemed to come from one direction and then another while Murphy's shell wind chime tinkled like crazy as the wind made it whip and dance. They'd already packed away Murphy's deck furniture first thing. Murphy had dragged them out of bed at the ass crack of dawn, telling Aiden it was his fault that they hadn't done any of this yesterday. Now Murphy was off somewhere else in the house executing his storm preparedness plan... or whatever.

Murphy knew better than him, though. But he was kind of being a grumpy jerk, so Aiden was giving him a wide berth. After about the third time Murphy stomped through the living room and gave Aiden the stink eye through the french doors, Aiden decided he needed to get out for a while, before the bad part of the storm hit, and they were possibly trapped inside for days.

"Hey Murph, why don't I go get the rest of the groceries and supplies you think we'll need, while you batten down the hatches here? You can show me what to do for my folks' place when I get back, okay?"

For the first time that morning, Murphy actually smiled, his relief and gratitude at not having to fight possible crowds pretty obvious. Aiden really liked Murphy's smile, so before it could disappear again, he kissed Murphy good-bye, grabbed his keys, and headed for his Jeep.

He could get used to this playing house and relationship stuff. It wasn't so hard if he paid attention. Yeah, he'd fucked up royally with Adam—and pretty much every boyfriend before Adam—but maybe he was finally getting the hang of it. All he had to do was try not to be an asshole or a brat, do nice things for other people, and they'd do nice things for him too. It was all pretty simple when he thought about it.

The wind whipping at his soft top as he drove into town made him think he should probably put his Jeep in the garage once he got back, or he might lose it during the storm. Most of the little shops near their houses were already closed up, so he had to go farther away than he wanted, but he was okay with that. He actually kind of enjoyed splashing his Jeep through the puddles and feeling the wind pulling and pushing at it.

Since there were still plenty of cars out on the road with him, he figured he shouldn't be too concerned yet. One of the benefits of modern storm tracking technology was everyone could wait until the last minute… like him apparently. The list of supplies Murphy gave him was almost two pages long, so Aiden probably wouldn't have been able to find everything at the local market anyway, and the Stop & Shop wasn't that far away. They were on an island, nothing was that far away.

People were crazy in the store, but he did his best to dodge between the carts and bodies to get what he needed. By the time he returned to his Jeep and piled everything inside, the rain was steadily coming down, but still not heavy. The misty drops stung, though, so Aiden was pretty wet as he dived into the driver's seat and slammed the door on it with a sigh of relief. The cold never bothered him, but unless he was naked in a shower with Murphy, he hated being wet.

His hair had grown out a bit since the last time he'd had it cut, and it always went a little crazy and wiry in the damp. All that time he'd spent styling it that morning had been wasted the second he'd stepped outside. He fussed with it a little in the rearview mirror now but gave up pretty quickly. Murphy didn't care if his hair was perfect. Murphy wanted him for who he was, and that was all that counted. He silently told his vanity to put a sock in it and started the engine.

Conditions were quite a bit worse on his way back through the little strip of stores closest to their houses, and Aiden slowed to a crawl as he passed by the coffee shop. The lights were still on as he peered through the fogged up windows of his Jeep, and he could just make out Crystal behind the counter.

They were making her work on a day like today?

He pulled into a spot and hopped out. After lifting the hood on the jacket Murphy had lent him, he made a mad dash for the door.

"Hey, sweetie, I knew you couldn't go without me for more than a couple of days, even if you had to brave the weather to reach me."

She put her hand on her forehead and swooned over the counter, and Aiden laughed as he dripped all over the mat by the doors.

"What are you doing here? They can't seriously expect you to keep this place open during the storm?"

She shrugged. "Naw. My place is only a couple blocks from here. I'll close up as soon as it gets really bad or if I lose power, whichever comes first. Don't worry. I'm not gonna risk life and limb for minimum wage and tips…. Speaking of which, you want some coffee?"

Since he was already there, Aiden ordered himself a latte and a chai for Murphy and grabbed a couple of muffins to help make it a little more worth her while for coming to work that day. His credit card was still working so he'd continue to help his parents boost the local economy. They probably didn't even notice what little he'd spent so far anyway. Their accountant may have called their attention to it by now, but obviously they didn't care.

No one else came in the shop while he chatted Crystal up for a few minutes, and once his order was ready, he decided he really needed to get home. The wind was howling between the buildings now and he had a fantastic set of plans for him and Murphy to ride out the storm… and he should probably do something with his parents' house too.

"Bye, Crystal. Be safe and don't wait until the last minute," he said before tucking the carton with his drinks and the bag beneath his jacket and jogging to his Jeep.

His windows had steamed up even more with all the wet, so after climbing inside and stowing the drinks and the bag on the passenger seat, he grabbed a stray T-shirt out of the back and wiped the worst of it away. He'd almost finished with the passenger side window when movement outside caught his attention, and he glanced across the street.

In the yellow glow from the coffee shop windows, Aiden caught a glimpse of a short, balding man hurrying along the sidewalk. It was hard to see him clearly through the mist and rain, and Aiden almost dismissed the guy, but something nagged at him and he kept watching until the man stepped in front of the shop windows next door. The lights were still on there as well, and Aiden froze as he got a good look at the man's profile. He knew that face.

Holy shit, it's Bob.

The crazy freak with the gun who'd tried to kidnap Adam's boyfriend and almost shot Adam in the process was scurrying down the street not five miles from where Aiden was staying.

Aiden blinked, and the man moved out of the light, his features now obscured by the gray and the rain.

It can't be. I was just seeing things.

He tried to rationalize, but his mind kept insisting it knew what it saw.

With his heart racing, Aiden jumped out of his Jeep and hurried across the road. By the time he reached the other side, the man was almost to the corner, and despite his misgivings, Aiden hurried after him. He had no intentions of actually catching up to the guy. But he had to know. He wasn't even going to try to fathom why Bob would be on Nantucket of all places, hundreds of miles from Ohio, but he needed to make sure before he called the police.

Aiden wrapped his hand around his phone in his pocket as he followed the small figure in the flapping trench coat, but he was behind the guy, so he couldn't get a good look.

Come on you bastard, turn around!

As if the guy heard him, he turned, and in the light from a gift shop, Aiden got his close up.

Shit! It is Bob.

Unfortunately, that meant Bob saw him too, and Bob didn't seem as surprised to see Aiden as Aiden was to see Bob.

Uh, oh.

Aiden pulled his phone out of his pocket as he turned and ran for his Jeep. He didn't want to find out if Bob had managed to replace the gun Aiden had destroyed. By the time he reached the alley next to the coffee shop he'd punched in 911, but he could hear Bob's footsteps thudding behind him. He had his finger poised over Send when an arm shot out from the darkness between the buildings and yanked him off his feet.

With a surprised yelp, he landed in a sprawl on the wet ground and his phone flew from his hand and skidded across the pavement. Without bothering to look for it, he surged to his feet and opened his mouth to shout for help, but an icy fist wrapped around his throat and suddenly his world spun. He tried to claw at the hand. Heat surged out of him along with burgeoning terror, but suddenly he had no strength, and his hands fell uselessly to his sides. His vision blurred, and the last thing he remembered seeing was a hazy white face and black eyes as a voice shouted, "You *idiot!*"

CHAPTER 15

MURPHY WAS good. He didn't go into full on mother hen panic mode until Aiden had been gone at least an hour and a half. He did begin questioning the wisdom of sending Aiden out on his own into the rain and wind after perhaps an hour, but he didn't start to freak until at least a half hour after that. He was pretty proud of himself for making it that long. Then the hour and forty-five minute mark came and went, and Murphy couldn't take it anymore. He had to dial Aiden's cell. Aiden could make fun of him for it later, *after* he was sure everything was okay.

"Hey, you've reached my voice mail. You know what to do."

Murphy took a calming breath and tried to steady his voice so Aiden wouldn't know how worried he was. "I was just checking in, making sure everything was okay. Call me back as soon as you get this."

He hit End and immediately started pacing his kitchen. Maybe Aiden had left his phone in the car while he went into shop. Maybe he'd let his battery die. Maybe the signal was screwed up because of the approaching storm. Maybe….

The television in the living room spouted the same information it had ten minutes ago as Murphy tried to stay calm. But the storm was getting closer by the minute, conditions were going to get bad in only an hour or two according to the satellite tracking, and Aiden should have been back by now. Even if he'd had to go farther away to get something on the list, the island wasn't that big.

After a few more minutes, Murphy tried Aiden's cell again, and it went straight to voice mail like it had before. He paced and fretted. He checked the signal on his phone and fretted. He peered out into the darkening skies and mounting waves crashing into the shore and fretted, until he couldn't take it anymore. He had to do something.

Forgetting about any other preparations he probably should have been doing, he grabbed his windbreaker and his keys and headed for his car. He'd go as far as the coffee shop in the village and ask that girl, Crystal, if she'd seen him. Aiden's cherry red Jeep was hard to miss, and Aiden would have to pass him if he was already on his way back. There was really only one road from there to the house, so it was unlikely they would miss each other.

And if Aiden isn't there and she hasn't seen him?

He didn't have an answer for that.

His hands white-knuckled on the wheel, Murphy drove through the ever-increasing wind and rain. His shields were cracking around the edges because his anxiety and the angry seas around the island were wrecking his control, but he ignored the brief bursts of emotions from passing cars and focused all his attention on the wet road ahead of him.

His hands ached by the time his short drive to the village was done, but the moment he spotted Aiden's red Jeep across the street from the coffee shop, his relief was so keen all of his aches faded to the background. Most of the shops had closed for the day, so Murphy was able to pull in right beside Aiden's Jeep. Aiden wasn't inside, but that probably just meant he was over at the coffee shop. They would have to have a conversation about calling in and giving him a heads up next time a situation like this arose, but that could wait until after Murphy hugged the life out of him.

Though the lights were still on in the shop, the door was locked when Murphy tried it. He wiped at the rain-splattered glass and peered inside, but he couldn't see anyone. Feeling that tightness begin in his chest again, Murphy banged on the doors. When he didn't see any movement inside, he pounded a few more times and called out, "Hello? Anyone there?"

As the rain pelted him from behind, he huddled a little farther under the protection of the awning, dropped his shields, and extended his ring of awareness outward, unwilling to admit the fact that he already knew Aiden wasn't there. Crystal appeared almost as soon as he felt her combination of curiosity, mild annoyance, coupled with a hint of anxiety. Murphy pulled back the hood on his windbreaker and waved and her anxiety fled even as her curiosity grew.

Ignoring his mounting panic, Murphy snapped his brittle shields back in place so he could concentrate on getting answers.

Crystal cracked open one of the glass doors and poked her head out. "Hey, Murphy. I'm sorry we're closed for the day. I've already shut everything down except the lights."

"Have you seen Aiden?"

"Oh, yeah. He stopped by less than an hour ago to check on me."

"An hour? He hasn't come home yet. His Jeep's still in the parking lot, and he's not answering his cell," Murphy blurted as he fought the waver in his voice and the urge to hyperventilate.

She glanced over his shoulder and frowned. "He was just here. He came in, said hi, and left." She stepped back and waved him in. "Come inside before we both drown."

"Thanks." Murphy drew in a shaky breath and blew it out again. He would not panic yet. There could be a reasonable explanation for why Aiden hadn't returned to his Jeep or called… while a potentially dangerous storm was approaching, the Jeep was full of groceries, and he knew Murphy would be worrying.

He felt sick.

Crystal's concerned brown eyes searched his face. "Hey, do you need to sit down?"

He swallowed and swallowed again before he said, "No. I just really want to know he's okay."

"Let me try his cell, see if I have better luck. Maybe the storm is doing something hinky with the signal or something."

She worried her lip as she dialed and then held her phone to her ear, but her face fell and she shook her head.

Unable to sit still, he climbed back to his feet and headed for the door.

"I'm going to take a look around, see if anyone else remembers seeing him," he said as he pulled his hood back up and stepped out into the rain and wind.

"I'll keep trying his cell." She pulled a slip of paper from her apron and a pen. "What's your number? I'll call if I hear anything."

Anxious to get moving, Murphy rattled it off and set off down the street with only a quick "bye and thanks."

The coffee shop was close to the end of the street, so after peering in a couple of alleys and darkened empty shops, Murphy turned around and headed back up the street in the other direction. As he was passing the coffee shop this time, he heard a ring tone coming from the side of the shop, Aiden's ring tone. With mounting panic he followed the sound until he snagged Aiden's phone from underneath a large, wheeled dumpster. The display read Crystal's name. He clenched the phone in his fist and closed his eyes.

This doesn't mean anything. He might have dropped it by accident. That's why he hasn't called yet.

But the words rang hollowly in his head. Something was terribly wrong, and he knew it. He stumbled to his feet and rushed to the door of the coffee shop. Crystal came hurrying back to the front and let him in. He held out the phone as he said, "It was under the dumpster outside. I need to call the police."

But the sheriff's department already had their hands full with the storm. Calls were already coming in faster than they had manpower to answer according to the woman he spoke to. Aiden hadn't been gone more than a few hours, and while the circumstances might be suspicious, the woman still couldn't tell him when they'd be able to get a car out there to help. Murphy barely stayed on the phone long enough for her to finish. He understood. He really did. But that didn't make hearing it any easier.

"They can't tell when someone will come. There's too much going on out there already."

Crystal could probably have figured that out from the look on his face, but saying it goaded him into action. He couldn't just sit there and wait.

"Do you live close by?" he asked her.

"Yeah. A couple of blocks away."

"Can you keep an eye out in case they do send someone?"

"I can do that. But where are you going? You probably shouldn't be out in this either."

He shook his head and pulled the hood on his windbreaker back up. "I need to find to him. Something's wrong. It has to be. Otherwise he would've shown up by now. I'm going to swing by my house and his to make sure he didn't walk back for some reason. But then I'll search the whole island if I have to."

"Murphy, I don't know. How can you possibly think you can find him in all this? I mean really. It's a mess out there and only going to get worse."

"I'll find him."

Aiden blazed like a fucking rescue flare in a sea of birthday candles. If Murphy could get close enough, he'd be able to sense him. He'd just have to drive around with his shields down until he did. He wasn't even going to think about any other reason why he might not be able to feel him. Fate wouldn't be so cruel as to take a second lover from him when he'd only just found him. He had to believe that.

A gust of wind nearly knocked him off his feet and took the door out of his hands as he stepped outside. Murphy wrestled the door closed, spared only a quick reassuring smile for Crystal as she peered worriedly at him through the glass, and charged through the stinging rain and wind to his car.

Once inside, he took a deep breath, sent up a prayer to whoever would listen, started the car, and let his shields fall.

CHAPTER 16

"HOW MUCH of a fool could you possibly be? I told you not to go out there, not to be seen!"

"I'm sorry, Father. But we needed supplies."

"You needed more cigarettes, you mean."

The coldness and disgust in the second voice sent a chill through Aiden as he tried to swim up out the pool of darkness. Both voices grated on his ears. But that one, more familiar than the other, that voice scared him.

"We needed food too. I had to get out before all the shops closed for the storm," the second man whined. "Most of them were already closed."

"And now you've ruined my carefully constructed plan. You've forced me to take action in the middle of a storm, with no way off the island, and that deviant *friend* of his sure to call the police when his little boy toy doesn't come home… all so I could save your miserable hide when I should have let him turn you in. You have failed the church, Bob, and you have failed *me*."

That voice belonged to Richard, but Aiden had never heard him like this. He tried to lift his head to get his bearings, but he was weak as a baby.

What the hell happened?

Struggling not to panic, Aiden took a couple of breaths to fight the weakness and exhaustion. He shivered with an unfamiliar chill as he assessed his current situation. His ankles and wrists were bound with thick plastic zip ties that cut painfully into his skin, and they'd duct taped his mouth. He was inside somewhere, but he could hear the rain battering against the windows and the howl of wind gusts around the building, so he hadn't been out that long.

"No, Father. I can make it right. I can be a good soldier. I'll think of something. Please!"

Bob's wail sliced through Aiden's skull, and he cringed. After a couple of tries, he was able to get his eyes open, and when his vision cleared, he spotted Bob and Richard facing off in the center of a large empty room. Well not actually facing off, since Bob cowered in front of Richard, shivering in the dripping, ratty trench coat Aiden had spotted him in, while Richard stood tall and stripped to the waist. Richard was dripping with either rain or sweat, and the skin on his face, neck, and chest was flushed a deep red.

"I knew I never should have trusted you. I knew I should have sent you away and dealt with this myself."

Richard's volume increased with each word, and he began pacing the empty floor like a caged animal. Every hint of the suave, friendly man Aiden had talked to had vanished, replaced by something much scarier.

"But, Father, *please*. Give me another chance. I know I ruined your plan, but maybe this way is better. Maybe we don't have to bring him back with us. I only wanted to bring him and the others to show *you*. But you've seen the demons for yourself now. You can tell the others. They know yours is the word of God. They will believe if you say it. We could kill him here. We could even video it so the others could see. Then we could hide him and leave the island as soon as the storm passes. We wouldn't have to worry about the cops finding him or anyone seeing him when we take the ferry."

"No."

Luckily Aiden didn't have the strength to do anything other than shudder when the phrase "we could kill him here" left Bob's mouth. Otherwise he probably would have flopped around on the floor in a panic and alerted them to the fact that he was awake.

"But that makes the most sense. We finish the demon, send him back to hell. We rid God's earth of his evil like you said. The evil must be vanquished so we can live in the light. It's better this way, and we can go back for the others I found, the ones who aren't as dangerous as this one.

We can take one of them back for the flock to see if you really think we need to."

The backhand Richard landed on Bob's cheek sent the smaller man flying back to crumple in a heap against the wall behind him.

"I said no. He comes with us."

Those words should have given Aiden a measure of relief. Except for the fear in Bob's eyes as Richard strode across the space that separated them and lifted Bob to his feet with one hand fisted in the front of his jacket.

"You will find a way off this cursed island for all of us, *now*. Do you understand?"

The fist twisted in his coat kept Bob balanced on his tiptoes as the ugly little man nodded his head emphatically. Richard unceremoniously dropped him back on his feet, and Bob crumpled to the floor again while Aiden shivered with more than just the cold that had seeped into his bones.

"Go. And don't come back until you've found something."

Too late, Aiden realized Bob was looking straight at him. Nothing close to sanity still resided in the man's face, but the worst part was when Richard turned to follow his gaze. Aiden's stomach twisted, and he struggled uselessly as Richard came toward him.

"Don't worry, Aiden. I won't let him hurt you," Richard crooned. He glanced briefly over his shoulder at the sound of the door closing behind Bob. When he turned back his face softened into that bland, harmless smile he'd sported every other time Aiden had seen him, as if they were still in the coffee shop having a chat over a latte. The look should have been comforting, but the flat black of Richard's fully dilated pupils made Aiden shiver. "Bob's a good, obedient dog. He'll do as he's told until we don't need him anymore. Everything's under control."

Aiden shook his head frantically, his pleas and denials muffled by the tape. Whatever Richard had planned, Aiden didn't want any part of it.

"Don't get yourself worked up." Aiden cringed away from the gentle hand Richard placed on his shoulder. "I know you're scared now, and you don't understand, but you'll see. Once we get off this goddamned island, the world is our oyster." He laughed suddenly, maniacally, his veneer of reason and sanity slipping. "Holy shit! I'd forgotten how good it felt. Months, *years* wasted on a few piddling talents in an entire congregation of addicts and losers, cosseting them, grooming them, spouting all that God and Light and forgiveness bullshit to maintain my little flock of sheeple… and five seconds with you blows all that out of the water. The power in you, it's incredible. And what have you done with it? Nothing. But I'll change that. You and I are going to do great things together. I'd forgotten the rush! I feel like a god."

You've got to be fucking kidding me.

Something of Aiden's disbelief and scorn must have shown on his face, because Richard's eyes narrowed as some of his terrifying glee faded.

"You'll see. I'll make you see."

Richard's hand on his throat was the last thing Aiden felt before the room spun and darkness swallowed him again.

When he woke for the second time, he felt like he was going to throw up the breakfast Murphy had made him that morning. His world no longer spun, but it rocked in great heaving surges. His mind wasn't working well enough to understand what that meant until the smell of mildew and sea spray smacked him in the face, and the bright orange blobs at the edge of his vision resolved themselves into life jackets.

Oh God. Not a boat.

He couldn't swim, so boats ranked right up there with root canals, snakes, and spiders on his not-fun-o-meter.

Fuck!

Don't panic. Don't panic.

Fuck!

He had to get out. He couldn't let them take him out on the water.

Are they out of their minds? It's the middle of a fucking storm. The weather guy said hurricane force winds… so not the time for boats, assholes!

Oh yeah, they are *out of their minds.*

Fuck!

Aiden flopped around uselessly in the tiny cabin, dislodging the life jackets, ropes, and various other items from the curved walls, but he was too weak to do much more than that. All he managed to accomplish was to make the bands on his wrists and ankles cut deeper into his flesh and exhaust himself even more. Eventually what little strength his panic gave him fled, and he ended up panting through his nose, flat on his back, staring up through the small rectangular hatch at the roiling black clouds charging across the sky.

A wave of dizziness hit him. He closed his eyes against it as well as the spray carried on the violent wind gusts that reached him through the hatch. As he fought his panic, the cool droplets of water on his cheeks made him think of Murphy, and some of his panic ebbed.

What would Murphy do? What would he say if he were here?

He'd say Aiden needed to calm down or he'd end up dead.

Murphy was probably out looking for him right now. Aiden had been gone long enough he had to be freaking by now. He clung to that hope. Someone out there knew he was missing and would call the police.

The image of Murphy's face, even etched with worry, helped. He held on to it as he took a long breath and then another, trying to slow his frantic heartbeat. Murphy would be his still pool, his deep well with the mirror surface. He had to think, not just react. The situation wasn't good, but he wasn't helpless… or he shouldn't have been.

He'd spent so long fighting what he was, it rarely occurred to him it could be useful at times. But unfortunately, now that he needed it, he realized the fire was gone. With all the terror bubbling inside him, he should have ignited everything within touching distance long before now. Instead he was freezing cold and could barely move a muscle.

What had Richard done to him?

As another surge of panic threatened to overwhelm him, he fought it down with what little strength he had left. With shaking breaths, he drew his focus inward, like Murphy had tried to teach him, but he had no idea what he was looking for. The fire had always been right there at the surface, screaming to get out. He'd never had to look for it. It just *was…* and now, nothing.

After all the times he'd wished for it to go away, to leave him alone and let him live a normal life, now it was gone, and all he felt was despair and an aching, cold, empty loss. He shivered in his damp clothes. The saltwater stung his eyes and his abraded wrists, and his own muffled whimper reached his ears. His worst childhood fear was about to come true. He was going to drown. This wasn't histrionics. This wasn't the drama queen talking. He was actually going to be swallowed up by the cold and the wet and the black from his nightmares. The two crazy bastards out there were going to get him killed, and it didn't even matter why.

Aiden teetered on the edge of despair. The empty place where the fire used to be mocked him even as the lunatics outside shouted at each other over the wind.

"Get it started, you fool!"

"I'm trying! But Father, please, please, we don't have to do this. The flock will believe. We just have to show them the others."

"My decision is made."

"But why? Why do we have to bring him back? You said the earth needs to be cleansed of their evil. We can do that here."

"Are you questioning The Word?"

"No! No. But—"

"If you are too weak, if you doubt God's will, then you can stay behind once you've gotten the engines started. I will continue his mission without you."

"No. I'll do it. I'll do it."

Aiden heard the footsteps on the stairs just before he received a sharp kick to the ribs.

"God's will is plain. He said so. He said you must perish. The earth must be cleansed… I don't understand. I don't—but Father knows. He always knows. If he says it's true, it must be. But he's different now. What do I do? What do I do? Think. Think."

Bob continued to rant like that as he crawled over Aiden and tossed things around in the tiny cabin. Aiden curled into a ball after the third or fourth time he was hit with flying debris or another kick, too weak to do more. Then at last, Bob seemed to find what he was looking for. He slammed what might have been some kind of toolbox into Aiden's shoulder on his way out the hatch.

Still reeling from the burst of pain that radiated from his arm, Aiden's seesaw of despair and hope that Murphy would find him in time swung heavily to the side of despair, but with it came a bleak sort of calm. An abstract corner of his mind, rarely heard from in the past, wondered if normal people had this blackness, this void inside them all the time, if this was what it meant to *be* normal. Without his fire, the darkness yawned wide. He could think more clearly now, but what was the point? Is this what threatened to swallow people up when their light went out?

Oh sure, now that I'm about to be sent to my watery grave, my head clears my ass enough for me to experience some sort of epiphany.

Great timing guys.

Thanks bunches.

Aiden was gearing up for a good wallow in misery and helplessness when he felt a spark ignite in the darkness. A moment later he heard an engine roar to life, and the spark became a flame. His breath quickened with the tiniest bit of hope, and when he felt the boat's second engine ignite, he actually smiled as much as he could within the confines of the tape.

This he could work with.

CHAPTER 17

BY THE time Murphy made it to the boat basin, he could barely contain his panic. He had to count out each breath to keep from hyperventilating, and his hands felt like they'd been permanently fused into claws around the steering wheel. The combination of the downpour from the sky, the waves surging only a short distance away, and the general level of anxiety every human being on the island was emitting probably would have landed him in the emergency room begging for sedation if he didn't know Aiden was out there somewhere needing him. Of course, if Aiden weren't in trouble, Murphy would have been curled up on his couch with his shields fully up, probably enjoying a little high from the storm surge behind his house, instead of inviting the whole of Nantucket to share their feelings with him. But that wasn't going to happen, so he just had to suck it up and deal.

Murphy giggled a little hysterically and stepped on the gas, but a second later he slammed on the brakes as a familiar flicker of hope and fear caught his attention.

Oh gods, thank you!

He whipped his car into the first spot he could find and leaped out, uncaring if he got towed. Aiden was close. Aiden was alive.

The sensation was weak. If Murphy hadn't had his shields down, he never would have felt it, but at least he had a direction to go in now. He wasn't wandering blind.

He targeted that signal and ran, but a second dark aura of emotion soon overshadowed Aiden's, and Murphy's stomach twisted even as he pounded down the slippery boards to the boat moorings. That darkness was sickeningly familiar. Once while completely hammered at one of the fashionable parties he and Felix used to attend when their book first hit the big time, Murphy had stumbled into a room full of partiers jacked up on coke… a *lot* of coke. That twisted, almost maniacal joy of an addict on his high wasn't something he could forget, and Murphy put on another burst of speed in sheer dread.

The roar of two outboard engines soon eclipsed the howl of the wind, and Murphy's feet slid out from under him as he tried to stop his headlong sprint. From his ass on the slippery dock, Murphy cried out in more than pain as he watched the boat pull away from its moorings and head out into the crashing waves.

The shock only lasted a few seconds before Murphy was scrambling for his phone.

"Nine-one-one what is your emergency?" the harried voice on the other end didn't give Murphy hope that the police would be any more helpful this time, but he had to try.

"My friend's been kidnapped! He's on a cruiser called the *Aspen*, headed out into the bay right now."

In the agonizing seconds it took to give her his own information plus all the details he had about the boat and the kidnappers, Murphy pulled himself to his feet and sprinted to the slip where his own boat was docked for the summer.

"Sir, we're receiving other reports confirming that a boat left the docks and the state police and Coast Guard have been notified. We urge you to seek shelter until the storm has passed and let the officers do their jobs."

"I can't do that," Murphy panted as he clawed the ropes loose and tossed them onto the deck of his wildly bouncing boat. When the last one was free, he leaped on board and scrambled for his keys.

"Sir, I urge you to—"

"My cruiser is the *Errant Desire*. As soon as I catch up to them, I'll call back with our location, heading, and speed on the radio."

"Sir, don't—"

Murphy hung up on her and cranked the engine. For the first time since they'd bought the boat, Murphy was grateful Felix had had such a need for speed. If they'd done what Murphy wanted and gotten a pretty little sailboat, he never would have had a chance in hell of catching up to the other boat. He gave the ridiculously large engine full throttle once he cleared the dock and focused what mental energy he could on clearing a path through the crashing waves ahead of him. Water surged over the sides in great gouts as he steered around the waves and squinted through the downpour, searching the chaos.

Eventually he had to give up using his eyes and reached out with his gifts instead. Ignoring the voices attempting to contact both boats over the radio, Murphy centered himself as best he could under the circumstances and searched with his gift. Aiden's emotional signal was getting stronger, and with a cry of relief, Murphy turned his wheel and headed northwest.

With his head pounding from the strain and his body a block of ice, aching with the effort it took to stand upright while his deck surged and rocked beneath him, Murphy followed that spark and prayed. He had to use every bit of skill and talent he possessed to dodge the dangerous swells and gain on them. His boat was in the air almost more than in the water, and his bones rattled each time his *Errant* crashed back into the waves.

Stay together, sweetheart. Just a little longer.

For a while he was afraid the monstrous motors on the back of the other boat would be too much for his *Errant*, but luckily the other captain didn't seem to know what he was doing, and Murphy finally caught sight of them not long after. With his heart in his throat, he watched as the other boat surged and tipped perilously, but to his vast relief, it appeared to be slowing down.

He snatched the microphone off the hook by the wheel. "Mayday, Mayday, Mayday. This is the cruiser *Errant Desire*, the cruiser *Errant Desire*. I'm still in pursuit of the cruiser *Aspen*, the cruiser *Aspen*. I have them in sight. We're—" Murphy glanced down at the GPS, but it was useless in the storm.

Shit!

He scanned the area but couldn't see any buoys or landmarks. Water fell from the sky in thick sheets obscuring everything the waves didn't block. He knew this sea like the back of his hand, but not like this. His compass was all he had. He couldn't give them any real numbers.

"Say again, *Errant Desire*."

"Shit! We left Nantucket harbor bearing west, northwest. Speed 30 knots. I need help. Please!"

"*Errant Desire* we have been advised of the situation. Please confirm report of a possible kidnapping in progress."

"Yes! My partner, Aiden Flanagan, was kidnapped by two men. They're all on the *Aspen*."

"*Errant Desire*, can you confirm whether the men are armed?"

"No… I don't know. I only saw them ride off."

Murphy almost lost his footing as a huge wave hit the side of his boat, and for a few panicked seconds, he lost sight of the *Aspen*. When he spotted it again, the cruiser had slowed to a crawl.

"This is the *Errant Desire*. The *Aspen* seems to be in distress. It's slowing down."

"*Errant Desire*, can you see any obvious signs of distress? Is the *Aspen* taking on water?"

"I can't tell from here. But I think it's stopped now, dead in the water."

"*Errant Desire*, be advised Massachusetts State Police and the Coast Guard have been informed of your situation, but conditions are too dangerous for air support at this time. If you can get us a better idea of your location, we will send assistance as soon as conditions permit."

Murphy cut the engine a little, but he sure as hell wasn't going to wait until the police could get there. He didn't come all the way out here to watch both of their boats capsize in the storm while he stood around with his thumb up his ass. He could feel Aiden's fear from here, and the storm wasn't getting any weaker.

"I understand. I'll do what I can."

Fighting the waves to keep his boat on course, he strained to get a sense of what was happening on the other boat. Aiden radiated mostly fear, but the other two men pummeled his senses with a chaotic mess of rage, confusion, frustration, fear, and that sickening joy. Murphy's chest squeezed painfully at the sheer insanity in the conflagration. The source of the blazing energy flared almost as brightly as Aiden had the few times he'd come close to losing control, and Murphy couldn't understand why he hadn't felt the man before.

As he got closer, the sheer size of one of the men compared to the other struck a chord in Murphy, and his stomach did another twist.

Richard.

Murphy sensed the change the moment the men on deck spotted him. The closer he got, the higher the tension mounted. While the storm raged on around them, another erupted on the boat, and Murphy cut his engines back to idle in panicked indecision. What if they were armed? What if they hurt Aiden because of him?

"*Errant Desire*, what's your status? *Errant Desire*, repeat, what's your status?"

The call came over the radio after repeated attempts to hale and caution the *Aspen* went unanswered. Something was happening on the other boat. Richard stood in the pouring rain and wind in nothing but a T-shirt while the shorter man's coat flapped wildly beneath an orange life jacket. Even without his gift, Murphy would have been able to tell they were arguing by their posture and flailing arms, but he was more concerned that he hadn't actually seen Aiden yet. Why were his feelings so weak? Why hadn't he used his own gift?

Gods, what do I do?

CHAPTER 18

"WHAT THE hell is happening?" Richard roared.

"I don't know!" Bob whimpered back. "The engines just died."

Aiden could hear the two men scrambling around the deck now that the engine noise was gone. He knew what had happened. Despite being tossed around like a ragdoll inside the cabin, he'd drawn power from the engines in a slow steady stream. The engines in turn had had to work extra hard to keep up with the demands both Aiden and Richard had put on them, and in the end, they'd used up every drop of gas in the tanks. Aiden had never realized he could do such a thing before now… but desperate times and all that.

"It's a sign!" Bob wailed.

Aiden could hear the panic in his voice even over the howl of the wind and the thundering waves. "God is punishing us. We never should have let the demon leave the island. The other boat is getting closer. He has to have called the cops on us. What are we going to do? They'll be waiting for us at the docks, even if God lets us make it that far. What do we do?"

There's another boat?

Aiden was strong enough to sit up now. Bracing against the hull, he peered out through the open hatch to where Bob and Richard faced off on the wildly rocking deck.

"Oh for God's sake, shut up, you idiot! You were barely more than useless before. Why did I ever think you could possibly accomplish anything without royally screwing it up? You're a goddamned loser, Bob. A fucking gambler and a drunk and a loser, crazy as fuck, and about as useful."

"Father, no! Don't say that. I can be a good soldier. I just need another chance. We just should have taken care of him on the island. That's all. I don't understand why we had to do it this way. I don't understand why we had to bring the demon. We could have been safe on land if we'd just stayed and taken care of it there."

"There are no demons, you fucktard!" Richard howled at him. "There never were. Or maybe they are demons. I don't know. But if they are, then so are we!"

"No! No, we've been given gifts to better serve God. You said so. You said—"

Richard spun away from Bob and threw up his hands.

"I needed you to do one thing, *one goddamned thing*. Find them for me. Score me a few good ones to keep me going, and what do you do? For years you find me the weakest, most pathetic talents out there, and before I know it, I'm surrounded by a whole flock of 'em whining and begging for attention and a shoulder to cry on. Then, when you finally find me a real source, a fucking nuclear power plant of good times, you have to fuck it all to hell with your incompetence and give the whole fucking game away. Goddamnit, why didn't I just kick your ass out of the boat the second we hit deep water?"

The fear, hurt, and confusion on Bob's face was almost painful to watch. If the guy hadn't been completely insane and threatening to kill him, Aiden might have almost felt sorry for him. Aiden's growing dread at the rapidly deteriorating situation between the two men reached a fever pitch when Bob's face suddenly hardened and he reached into his coat and pulled out a gun.

"You've been taken over," Bob declared shakily. "The demons have found a foothold in you."

Richard spun back and leveled a finger at him.

"Don't you dare use my own words, you little fool. It was a line of bullshit even when I said it. Put that thing away."

Aiden could see the gun waver in Bob's hand.

"I said put it down. Now!"

Richard's voice cracked like a whip and a blast of energy washed over Aiden. The touch of it made him shiver in revulsion. He had to get the hell out of here. He didn't know what that was, but he hoped he never found out.

In desperation he blocked out the freak show outside the cabin and reached for the flickering flame inside him. Murphy was out there. He had to be on the other boat they were talking about. All Aiden had to do was get off this boat and away from the gun and everything would be fine.

A slightly hysterical giggle bubbled up inside at that thought.

I'm in the fucking ocean, in the middle of a huge storm, and I can't swim. Oh yeah, all I have to do is get away from these two and life will be just peachy.

But another thought spoke louder than the panic. The crazy men had a gun. Aiden couldn't let Murphy get close enough that he might be shot. He'd never forgive himself if Murphy got hurt because of him. And even after only so short a time with him, Aiden didn't even want to think about a life without Murphy in it.

A little codependent?

Probably.

But he'd worry about that *after* he managed to survive this goddamned catastrophe.

He focused his attention inward and breathed. He tried to remember all the visualizations that had made things worse when he'd tried to meditate before, and as he concentrated, the flame in his mind's eye grew brighter. He no longer felt the cold. The empty dark space within him shrank back as his energy and confidence grew. The despair melted away, replaced by resolve and determination to do something, *anything* but cower in the cramped little space they'd tossed him.

When the anger flooded his system, Aiden welcomed it like never before. This once he was free to let it build. He didn't have to fight it. He let the rage suffuse him and relished the heat that kindled within every cell in his body.

A loud cry split the air as the zip ties binding his hands and feet softened and snapped, and Aiden opened his eyes in time to see Bob flying over the side of the boat.

"Help! Someone help!"

Bob's pleas rang out from somewhere beyond the rocking boat, but Aiden couldn't see him. With awkward stumbling steps, Richard paced the small deck like a caged animal, his chest heaving and the gun dangling from his hand seemingly forgotten.

Aiden pulled the dampened tape from his mouth, snagged a life jacket, and fumbled with the buckles as fast as he could manage. The thought that he might end up in the water made his hands shake, but he didn't think he had any other options. Rage told him to charge Richard and wrestle the gun away, but he retained enough of his senses to know he couldn't let Richard close enough to touch him. Richard had done something to him with his touch, and even though Aiden had no idea what it was, he wasn't stupid enough to want a repeat.

Trying to be as unobtrusive as possible, Aiden crept out the hatch and searched the waves for the other boat.

Even at a distance and through the stinging rain, he recognized Murphy the instant he spotted him. But his heart fell when he realized Murphy was alone. If help was on its way, it hadn't arrived yet. A stab of renewed panic went through him—this time not for himself—when he heard the other boat's engine rev. Murphy was coming.

Richard must have heard it too, because he quit his pacing and swung to face both Aiden and the approaching boat.

"Get down," Richard barked, waving the gun at Aiden.

Because he would've been tossed around like a ragdoll if he let go of the hull, Aiden raised only one hand and moved off his perch above the cabin. Richard's brown hair flew wildly about his head as he clutched at the seat in front of him and tried to keep the gun leveled at Aiden.

Cursing inwardly at his weakness, Aiden froze. Even if he knew how he'd made Bob's gun explode in Ohio, he still didn't have the strength to manage it now.

With a sinking feeling he tried to stall.

"Richard, you can't be serious. Come on, man. What are you going to do, shoot me? You're in the middle of the fucking ocean. The cops have to be waiting for us on the mainland, even if they aren't on their way here. The boat is dead. Give it up."

"Shut up! You think I give a shit about the cops? No one can stop me. I'm a fucking god."

You're a fucking lunatic, is what you are.

When Richard's smile only grew as Murphy's boat came closer, Aiden realized Richard had a perfect way out.

Murphy.

Aiden's stomach twisted, and his heart felt like it would beat out of his chest. Every part of his lizard brain was screaming at him to stay where he was. His panic over the whole prospect of drowning threatened to overwhelm everything else, but he couldn't let the panic win. He *loved* Murphy. They were connected soul deep. He couldn't go on if he lost part of his soul, could he?

He turned and looked out at the raging sea all around them and whimpered in resignation. Murphy would be close enough to get shot in a matter of seconds. Aiden was out of time.

Stuffing his blinding terror of the water down deep, Aiden edged closer to the side of the boat, squeezed his eyes shut, fisted both hands in the fabric of his life jacket, sent up a silent prayer, and jumped.

"No!"

Richard's shout followed him as he hit the water hard, but thankfully he bobbed right back to the surface like a cork before abject terror could set in. He gasped in relief the second he cleared the water, but just when he thought this wouldn't be so bad, a giant fist of water slammed him back under. When he popped up again, he thrashed wildly, squinting his eyes against the stinging rain and seawater and desperately searching for Murphy's boat, but he couldn't see anything but gray and more gray. The icy water was leeching what heat he'd managed to build, and he was tired, so very tired. He closed his eyes against another wave and curled in on himself as much as possible, clutching the life jacket desperately.

Murphy, please, please, please tell me you're coming, and I didn't just leap to my watery death.

CHAPTER 19

MURPHY'S HEART lodged in his throat as he watched Aiden's red hair disappear beneath the waves.

God, Aiden, no! I'm not close enough yet!

The wind ripped away the string of curses that flew from his mouth as he cranked the engine and headed for the spot where Aiden went in.

"Mayday, Mayday, Mayday. This is the *Errant Desire*. This is the *Errant Desire*. Man overboard on the *Aspen*. Repeat, man overboard. At least one, possibly two, men in the water now."

When Aiden popped back to the surface, Murphy's heart surged, but his relief was short-lived, because the bright orange life vest disappeared again almost as soon as Murphy caught sight of him. Everything inside Murphy cried out to be in the water. If he was in the water, he could keep Aiden safe. He knew he could. He just had to get a little closer.

"Copy that, *Errant Desire*. One possibly two men in the water. Be advised Coast Guard has been notified for search and rescue. Can you give any more information on your location?"

Murphy couldn't think. Aiden was in the water. Aiden couldn't swim. Aiden's panic clawed at his senses.

"No. I don't know. I can't see anything."

"*Errant Desire*, are you in a position to offer assistance?"

Way ahead of you.

"I'm going to get him. Just please hurry."

He didn't bother to listen to the response. As soon as he was close enough, he dove over the side and started swimming. Tamping down on both his fear and Aiden's terror, Murphy focused his energy, dove beneath the surface, and propelled himself in a straight line to Aiden's thrashing body.

The closer he came to Aiden, the harder it was to block out Aiden's panic. Murphy couldn't maintain his concentration and lost what control he had over on the water around them. The currents pulled at him as Murphy's head spun with Aiden's near incoherent terror.

"Aiden!"

He got too close and got whacked in the jaw by a flailing arm as a wave swamped both of them.

When he breached the surface, he tried again. "Aiden! It's me. Aiden!"

Murphy was afraid Aiden might be too far gone, but the crack of a gunshot a second later seemed to snap him out of it, and he swung to face him. Now Murphy wanted to panic because someone was actually shooting at them, but he swallowed it, and the split second Aiden stopped thrashing, he snaked around behind him and wrapped an arm across his chest.

"I got you. I got you."

He could hear Richard shouting from the other boat, but he couldn't make out what he was saying. It didn't matter anyway. The only thing that mattered was getting Aiden out of there.

"Murphy?" Aiden croaked in between hacking coughs.

"Yeah. I got you," he panted. "Just close your eyes and trust me, okay?"

Aiden took a few hiccupping breaths. "Okay."

In desperation, Murphy focused his energy and used the water to propel them as he swam. He couldn't duck beneath the surface where it would be easier, not with Aiden and his life jacket, so he did the best he could to force the waves back and away from them. He paddled with the one arm and kicked with every ounce of strength left in him, terrified that any second he'd hear another gunshot, but none came. The wind carried snatches of angry shouting from the other boat, but that was it. Then they were at the small platform on the back of the *Errant Desire*, and Murphy nearly cried with relief.

"Aiden, we're at the boat. Can you pull yourself up?"

He took Aiden's hand and wrapped it around the wildly jumping edge of the platform, but Aiden lost his grip almost immediately.

"Come on. Try again. We need to get you out of the water. It's too cold to stay in, and I can't do it by myself."

Murphy was tiring quickly. He'd stretched his gift farther than ever before, and he was beginning to pay for it now. He could have tried to climb out and grabbed for Aiden, but he was stronger in the water, and he couldn't leave Aiden alone again, not even for a few seconds.

After another failed attempt to get Aiden onto the platform, Murphy began to reconsider. The Coast Guard or the police might be on their way. The water in the sound was actually fairly warm this year, despite the icy rain falling from the sky. If he had the strength to manage it, they could probably last a couple hours in the water before they had to worry about serious hypothermia. They didn't have to get out right away. He could keep Aiden calm and keep the boat between them and the crazy asshole with the gun.

But as soon as he had the thought, he felt Richard hit the water. Even in the raging seas and confusion, Murphy could feel the man. The barely controlled rage and energy rolling off him poisoned the sea around him. In dread, Murphy swung around and searched the water. The other boat had drifted farther from them. Richard must have decided he couldn't let them get away.

"Shit! Aiden, love, you need to get in the boat."

If worst came to worst, he could probably use his gift to get the gun away from Richard, without getting close enough for the man to use it. But he couldn't do that and take care of Aiden too.

"Try again, baby. Come on," he yelled over the howl of the wind.

When Aiden grabbed the edge of the platform again, Murphy closed his eyes and pushed with his gift as well as his arms. This time, Aiden was able to get his upper body onto it, and as Aiden slowly dragged the rest of his body up, Murphy searched the sea.

He could feel Richard coming. Whatever Richard was, he fairly glowed to Murphy's senses now, a malevolent presence that the already angry seas wanted rid of. As Aiden finally tumbled into the relative safety inside the boat, Murphy struggled with a wave of rage that wasn't completely his.

Richard had kidnapped Aiden. Hurt him. Richard could drown before he ever reached their boat. He could be swallowed by the sea, and no one would ever believe it was anything other than an accident of nature... or an act of God.

The thought of using his gift to harm sickened him, but the temptation was there. Richard's rage, Murphy's element's rejection of this thing polluting it, and his own anger at what had been done to Aiden threatened to overwhelm him as he closed his eyes and took calming breaths.

"Murphy?"

Aiden's voice cut through his thoughts. When he looked up, Aiden held a hand out to him. Aiden coughed several times and moaned, but the hand remained as steady as the surging boat allowed, offering him salvation and a world of hope in that one simple gesture.

With a rush of relief, Murphy let the blackness in him go and reached for that hand. Using it and his grip on the platform, Murphy scrambled up the back of the boat and flung himself onto the deck. Without even stopping to catch his breath, he lunged for the helm and hit the throttle. He still didn't quite know where they were. Being submerged in the water hadn't helped when the seas were this rough. But it didn't matter. They just needed to get out of there. If they headed north, they'd hit land eventually.

Requests for information still clamored over the static on the radio, so the second he had a free hand, Murphy snagged it.

"This is the *Errant Desire*. This is the *Errant Desire*. I've picked up Aiden Flanagan, the victim, and we're headed north, hopefully toward Hyannis for medical attention... exhaustion and hypothermia possible but no visible injuries. The other two men, the kidnappers, were armed. I repeat they are armed and fired on us. I don't know what condition they're in, but we're not staying to find out."

"Understood, *Errant Desire*. Thank you for the warning. Authorities will be notified. Be advised shore and harbor conditions are extremely dangerous. The harbor master has closed Hyannis. Repeat, Hyannis is closed due to dangerous conditions, large swells, downed boats, and high on-shore winds."

Shit.

Murphy's hands shook as he grasped the helm and the radio. Now that the imminent threat had passed, he was starting to feel a little lightheaded. At full strength he might have tried for the harbor anyway. He didn't care if his boat got a little beat up, as long as he got Aiden somewhere warm and safe. But as he was, he wasn't sure he could manage the effort it would take to get to shore without serious injury. He might be able to ground her on a beach somewhere, but getting Aiden ashore and getting help after that might be more than he could manage. Pushing those worries to the side for a moment, he concentrated on what he had to work with. The least he could do was get Aiden as safe and warm as possible right now.

His little boat didn't have much of a cabin, more of a cubby under the forward deck for storage, but he thought maybe he could squeeze Aiden in there for a little protection against the elements. His own teeth were chattering pretty hard, now that he was out in the icy wind, but he had to take care of Aiden first.

"Copy that. Will attempt to find a safer landing."

Glancing over his shoulder, Murphy spied Aiden huddled in the fetal position on the deck. He couldn't feel Richard anymore, so he decided he could risk slowing down.

"Aiden, are you okay?"

"Uh-huh."

Murphy could barely hear him over the wind, but at least he'd responded.

"Do you think you can crawl into the cubby down there? It'll get you out of the rain."

"What about you?" Aiden asked as he slowly got to his feet and stumbled across the heaving deck. Aiden's lips were as blue as Murphy's felt when he collided with Murphy's chair.

"I'll be okay. Just get inside."

"But you're f-f-freezing. I c-c-can help."

Even with all the craziness, Murphy couldn't help but bark out a laugh. "You're a block of ice. Get inside."

"D-d-do we have p-p-plenty of gas?"

"I've got us covered. We're going to be fine."

"But how much gas?"

Aiden was starting to sound a little loopy. Frowning in concern, Murphy pointed to the gauge. "See, we're fine. Now will you go inside?"

He had to grit his jaw to keep his teeth from chattering, but a moment later Aiden's arms wrapped around his waist and warmth began seeping through the back of Murphy's sodden jacket. He groaned in pleasure even as he tried to pull away.

"Aiden you need to get yourself warm first. Don't worry about me."

"I can do both, just tell me when we start to run low on gas, and I'll stop."

Surprised and a little confused, Murphy looked over his shoulder, but Aiden's eyes were closed and his eyebrows were drawn down in concentration. A wave crashed over the side of the boat, and Murphy swung his attention back to what he was doing. His hands squeezed the wheel hard as he negotiated the worst of the swells, while Aiden radiated heavenly warmth at his back. He let the heat soothe him, drawing strength from the knowledge that Aiden was safe and didn't seem to be hurt or as exhausted as he'd feared.

When he spotted the number seven buoy at Horseshoe shoal, he nearly cried. He knew where he was now. Hyannis was closed, and the forecasters had said the storm was moving up the coast, so heading south again was probably their best bet for getting out of it. All he had to do was make sure they didn't sink before he could get them back to Nantucket.

With renewed hope, he relayed his location and course over the radio, sent up a tired prayer for their continued good luck, and headed for home.

CHAPTER 20

AIDEN CLUNG for dear life to the back of Murphy's chair as they bounced over waves and the wind whipped icy fingers through his soaked clothes. His legs shook with exhaustion, and his head pounded. All he wanted was for this nightmare to end, but he wouldn't be useless. Murphy had come all the way out here for him. He had to do something in return, so he continued to draw heat from the engine, and he prayed silently to anything and anyone who might be listening for their safe return.

Ironically, after a while he settled into a kind of trance. After all his attempts in the quiet of his parents' house and Murphy's, now, in the water, during a huge storm and one of the most traumatic experiences of his life, *now* he could meditate.

Friggin' hilarious.

He was actually far enough gone into his own head that he barely even registered when the boat stopped rocking as wildly as it had been and Murphy was talking into the radio again. It took Murphy squeezing the arms Aiden had locked around his chest for him to fully realize they'd stopped altogether.

"Come on, Aiden. Come back, love. You can let go now. We're beached."

"Huh?"

Aiden opened his eyes. His world was no longer jerking wildly, only rocking occasionally as a stronger wave hit the side of the boat. After a couple of failed attempts, he was finally able to unlock his muscles enough to let Murphy go and straighten from the hunch he felt like he'd been in forever. He had a feeling every inch of his body was going to ache once his extremities thawed out enough to feel it.

"Let's get you to dry land," Murphy said gently as he stood up and turned to face him. He laid a hand on Aiden's shoulder and chuckled. "Well maybe not dry."

In a haze of exhaustion, Aiden couldn't quite get his limbs to work. He kind of flopped over the side when Murphy helped him out of the boat. Murphy didn't seem to be in much better shape, though, so they clung to each other as they slogged through the knee-high water that Aiden was pretty sure used to be a beach.

They were still trudging through water when they finally reached pavement. The street actually had a river running down it. Aiden glanced blearily about, but there was a distinct absence of lights of any kind on the street or in the buildings.

"I wonder if the power's out all over the island," Murphy mumbled tiredly.

Aiden didn't care. He just wanted to be somewhere out of the wind and rain, somewhere warm.

"Let's just go home," he said.

"I'm going to get you to the hospital first," Murphy replied, his voice gaining a little more strength.

"No. I don't need a hospital. I'm just cold and tired. Let's go home."

"Aiden—"

But then a police car pulled up and stopped on a side street that wasn't as flooded, and whatever Murphy was going to say was pretty much moot. They were bundled in blankets and stuffed into the car. Then they were taken to the police station. At least he was out of the rain, and they'd given him a blessedly hot mug of coffee to sip on while they pummeled him with questions, first to ascertain if he needed any kind of medical attention—which he didn't—and then to try and make sense of what had happened. He wished them luck on that one, since he had no idea.

They took Murphy off to another room, Aiden assumed to do the same thing to him, but he really wished they hadn't. He didn't want Murphy more than five feet away from him… ever again, though he was pretty sure that was probably the shock talking… probably.

"Mr. Flanagan, you're sure you don't know why these men pursued you."

Aiden tried not to roll his eyes. He'd already answered this, and every other question they could come up with, twice. His admittedly limited patience was wearing very thin.

They're trying to help, Aiden's conscience, sounding suspiciously like Murphy, tried to remind him.

He sighed and rubbed his throbbing head. "No. I don't know. Like I told you, the little crazy guy, Bob, was spouting off about demons, and God, and all kinds of craziness. He did that back in Ohio too. They were just insane."

"But your parents have money, right? It's possible they could have been seeking a ransom of some kind."

Aiden gave up. If the cops needed an explanation they could understand, he wasn't going to stand in their way of drawing the wrong conclusions.

"Yeah. My folks have money."

Not that they'd pay a kidnapper too much to get me back, unless it was to avoid bad press for Dad's company.

Stopping before that whiney pity party could start, he shifted uncomfortably in his seat. Just because his folks hadn't had much but criticism for him in the last several years didn't mean they wouldn't come through for something like that. He was just feeling cranky because he was exhausted, and he hadn't seen Murphy in over an hour.

"Mr. Flanagan—"

Aiden held up a hand to stop him.

"Look. I'm exhausted. Murphy has to be too. Can we please go home now? I'm sure we've told you everything we know by now, and we'll come back and go over all this again tomorrow when I can keep my eyes open and things aren't so crazy outside. I mean it's not like they're coming back to get me tonight. You said search and rescue couldn't even go out to look for them until a little while ago."

"We can hold off on the questions, but we advise you to stay here for the time being. The storm has moved off a bit, but it's still not very safe out there. It would be better if you waited," the officer replied.

There was no way he was going to sit huddled and dripping in a hard office chair when Murphy's warm bed was only a few miles away. Things had looked a little rough on the way to the station but not that bad.

"I need to sleep, and I can't do that here. I'm sure Murphy's exhausted too. Please."

The officer sighed and went to the door they'd taken Murphy through.

"You think we can let them go for now?" he asked after knocking and poking his head through the door.

Aiden didn't hear the reply because he kind of zoned out for a second, but then Murphy was coming toward him and all was right with his world.

"Can we go home now?" he whined. Something about being dead on his feet made him revert back to his five-year-old self, but he didn't have the energy to give a damn.

"You're sure you don't want to go to the hospital?" Murphy asked, concern etched deeply into his face as his tired blue eyes raked Aiden from head to toe.

"No. Really, Murphy, I'm okay. Please. Besides, the power is probably out at the hospital and things are probably crazy there too. Let's just try to get home. We'll use that fireplace of yours, you can make me some tea, and then we can pass out and deal with all this in the morning, okay?"

Murphy sighed heavily and after a nod from the two officers, his shoulders slumped. "Okay." He turned to the two officers behind them. "Do you think you can give us a ride back to my car? It's not far from the water so hopefully it isn't damaged."

THANKFULLY, THE floodwaters hadn't reached the engine in Murphy's Mini Cooper, and it started right up as soon as Murphy turned the key. Aiden sighed in relief. They were one step closer.

"Getting home may be a bit of a challenge, but I'll do what I can," Murphy mumbled tiredly.

He had to weave in and around a lot of downed tree branches and deep puddles, and the trip seemed to take forever, but eventually they pulled into Murphy's driveway. Aiden blew out a relieved breath, fumbled with the latch until the door opened, and practically fell out of the car. Once he righted himself, he stumbled after Murphy and up the front steps.

As a testament to how exhausted Murphy had to be, he didn't even try to clean up the pile of wet clothes they left on his bedroom floor. He just handed Aiden a pair of sweatpants and a sweatshirt and grabbed a set for himself, and then they collapsed onto his bed and passed out.

Sometime in the middle of the night, Aiden woke with a jolt, frantically searching the darkness and sweating against Murphy's chest. Tendrils of his nightmare clung to him like spider webs, and he shivered and buried his face into Murphy's neck.

"Are you okay?" Murphy croaked groggily.

"Yeah. Just a nightmare. Water, wind, guns, crazy guys… you know, the usual."

The joke might have been funnier if his voice hadn't cracked at the end. Murphy didn't laugh. He pulled Aiden closer and kissed the top of his head.

"We didn't have much time to talk, but we can now if you want to."

Safe and dry in the warmth of Murphy's bed, even though they were both a little crusty with sea salt, Aiden relaxed and pressed his lips to Murphy's throat.

"Not much to say really. I was out of it, most of the time." He shivered again, warm but still not quite warm enough. "Whatever Richard did to me knocked me out for a while. When I was awake—yeah, I'm not gonna lie—I was scared shitless. I mean, talk about having my worst nightmare come true. But then Richard had Bob's gun, and he was going on and on about how he was a god or something… and you were getting close enough to get shot, and I realized there were worse things in this world."

"That's why you dove in, to protect me? Oh, Aiden."

Aiden tightened his arms around Murphy and nodded against his neck, too choked up to answer in words. They were both quiet until the tightness in his throat eased enough for him to speak again.

"I knew you wouldn't let me drown. Between you and the lifejacket, my brain knew I'd be okay, even if the rest of me was freaking."

Murphy huffed a breath into his hair and clutched him tighter. "You scared me half to death when you jumped in… but thank you for trying to protect me."

"I couldn't let Richard get anywhere near you, whether he had the gun or not. God, he was such a crazy freak, and I didn't have a clue."

Murphy kissed the top of his head again and began stroking his back.

"Neither one of us sensed it. Of the two of us, I should have been the one to feel something, but I didn't. It's not your fault."

"I know. It's not like I asked to be kidnapped off the street. I mean, I could've been more careful, paid more attention, but really, I don't know of anyone who would've seen that level of crazy coming." He paused there and worried his lip. "Do you think they'll find them?"

Murphy shifted, drew in a deep breath and let it out on a long sigh. "I don't know. I hope so."

Aiden's stomach chose that moment to growl, and Murphy chuckled. "You haven't eaten since this morning have you?"

"No."

"You want me to make something?"

Despite a strong desire to stay curled up in the warmth of Murphy's bed, Aiden was suddenly starving.

He nodded as he eased his death grip on Murphy's chest. "Yeah, I'll help you. I think I can manage a walk to the kitchen, now that we've had a couple hours sleep. Maybe we can have some of your famous tea too, and I can make that fire I've been fantasizing about since before all this shit started. I think I'm gonna need it to chase the last of the chill away. I don't know what he did to me, but I've never been this cold in my life. How do normal people not spend all day everyday blue and shivering?"

"We manage," Murphy replied wryly.

Aiden snorted. "You can't talk. You are so not normal. I hate to break it to you."

They both laughed on their way down the hall, and Aiden thought he just might be okay. He was too tired for a full-on freak out session right now, but even if he had one later, he wasn't worried about it like he might've been if Murphy wasn't there.

When they were standing in the kitchen, with the kettle heating, Murphy moved in close and cupped Aiden's chin in his palms. He searched Aiden's face with concerned eyes. "Maybe we should call Lola tomorrow and see if she knows what he did. I'd feel better if she could tell us something at least."

With a shrug, Aiden said, "Sure. Couldn't hurt. It would be great if she could tell me how to make sure it never happens again. I mean, I've prayed to be rid of it most of my life, but if that's what it feels like, I don't want that anymore. It was like a whole chunk of me was missing. I don't want to be normal that bad."

With a sigh, Murphy dropped his forehead to Aiden's. "I don't want you to be anything but what you are."

Murphy said it with such sincerity, such feeling, Aiden didn't have the heart to rattle off the flip response on the tip of his tongue. Instead he drew in a shuddering breath and closed his eyes.

"You're sure about that?" he whispered into the intimate space between them.

Murphy didn't even pause. "Yes."

"You haven't known me that long."

"But I think I know you in a way very few people can, and I like what I know very much."

Aiden fisted his hands in the loose sweatshirt at Murphy's waist and buried his face in Murphy's neck.

"I'm going to get better. I'm going to work hard to be a better person. I promise."

"You can if you want to, but do it for yourself, not me," Murphy murmured, holding him gently. "I'm happy with who you are now and whoever you want to be later… as long as you don't change too much."

Blinking so he wouldn't cry, he pulled back and gave Murphy a wavering smile. "God, I love you, Murphy… I know it's soon, and I should've probably waited to tell you, but—you saved me… more than just today. I mean today was fucking fantastic. You rode right in there to my rescue like a fucking white knight, but you saved me even before that. I love you so much."

Afraid he might have gone and gushed a bit too far, he held his breath and waited for Murphy to say something… anything. But Murphy did something better. He cupped Aiden's face again and pulled him into a kiss. It started as a tender brush of lips, but deepened into an extended sensual exploration of each other's mouths until Aiden had to pull back and gasp for breath.

"I love you too," Murphy whispered against Aiden's temple before he kissed that too.

Now he really was going to cry. Thank goodness the kettle started whistling, giving him an excuse to step back and compose himself. While Murphy made their tea, he walked on wobbly legs over to Murphy's fireplace. Behind the white plaster vase filled with dried ornamental grasses Murphy had placed on the hearth in front of it, Aiden found a stack of neatly arranged logs that looked like they were more for show than actual burning.

"Can I light these?" Aiden asked over his shoulder.

"That's what they're there for."

"Yeah, but they look too pretty to burn."

Murphy chuckled. "Are you making fun of me?"

"Nope."

"I can still feel you, you know. I know when you're lying."

"Shit."

Murphy laughed again. "Just light the damned fire."

Aiden grabbed some paper and kindling from the neat little cubby in the hearth, shoved it under the grate, and opened the flue. Any other day he wouldn't have bothered with the kindling, but he wasn't sure he was up to lighting the logs without it yet. He put his hand into the paper, but instead of just letting go, he had to actually pull some of the fire inside him, and he shuddered, remembering the emptiness that had been there only a few hours ago. To his relief, the fire came when he called it, and the paper burst into flame. As the kindling caught and then the pretty dry logs above, Aiden sat and soaked in the heat, staring into the dancing flames.

"Try not to melt my sweatshirt," Murphy murmured as he handed Aiden a steaming mug and a plate with a sandwich, and dropped onto the floor beside him.

Aiden set them down on the hearth and pulled the sweatshirt off. This close to the flames he was feeling more like himself. The ice inside was finally thawing, and the heat on his bare skin felt like heaven.

"Better?" Aiden asked with a smirk.

"Much," Murphy said with an appreciative smile.

They sat quietly for a while, the only sounds the crackle and snap of the fire. Murphy sipped his tea, seeming content to simply keep him company while Aiden recharged and inhaled the sandwich. At some point, Aiden reached out a hand, and Murphy took it. Aiden threaded their fingers together, enjoying the hum of connection between them, now that he could almost match Murphy's energy again.

"So what happens now?" Aiden asked quietly.

"We rest a bit more, take it easy. We live. We love. We take each day as it comes."

"The cops probably aren't done with us."

"No. I would say not. And I need to get my boat towed back to the dock and checked out. We'll have to check both houses for damage at some point too, though it looks like we probably lucked out there—oh, shit! I need to call Crystal and let her know you're okay. She's probably worried sick."

"Why would Crystal be worried?"

"I went to see her, looking for you. It's how I found your phone… which, by the way, is currently on my boat. Hopefully it fared better in the drawer I tossed it in than *my* phone did in my pocket. I haven't checked yet, but mine is probably toast after taking a swim with me. Do you have her number written down somewhere?"

"No. It's in my contacts on my phone, but that's it."

"I guess it'll have to wait until tomorrow. We can stop by the coffee shop on our way, see if she's in."

Some of Aiden's happy faded as he realized how much trouble he'd caused.

"I'm sorry, Murphy."

"For what?"

"Everything that happened I guess, your phone, your boat."

"I thought we already established that it wasn't your fault."

"I still feel bad."

Murphy scooted closer and kissed him gently. "Don't worry about it. It's nothing that can't be fixed." He drew in a shaky breath and for the first time that day Aiden could see how shaken he was. His eyes were bright and his face drawn and pale as he said, "I'm just glad you're safe and nothing was broken that *couldn't* be fixed."

Aiden slid behind Murphy and wrapped his arms around him. He propped his chin on Murphy's shoulder as he whispered, "We're okay. Thanks to you."

Murphy shuddered in his embrace and rested his head against Aiden's. "Yeah."

They'd done enough talking for one night. Murphy still looked tired, and Aiden decided he could use a few more hours in Murphy's bed.

"Come on. Let's go back to bed. Everything else can wait until tomorrow."

At Murphy's sleepy nod, Aiden unwound himself and stood up. He went to the fireplace and placed his hand in the flames, drawing all the heat he could from it until it went out.

"I don't think I'll ever get tired of watching you do that," Murphy murmured sleepily.

"Oh yeah?"

Aiden couldn't help the cocky little grin that spread across his face. "Yeah."

Aiden closed the flue and then the glass doors on the fireplace to keep what smoke remained contained. Then he sauntered over to Murphy and hooked his fingers in the waistband of Murphy's sweatpants.

"You can watch me anytime you want."

They kissed, but despite the teasing, neither one of them was in any shape to do anything about it. Aiden felt reenergized by the fire, but he still needed more than a few hours' sleep to recuperate after what happened. He'd drained, or been drained of, every resource he had, emotionally, physically, and psychically. Murphy still had to remind him that they'd have plenty of time to enjoy each other from now on, but Aiden only pouted a little over that fact before he passed out cold.

CHAPTER 21

THE FOLLOWING morning the world came calling all too early, literally. Murphy's house phone rang not long after the sun came up. Apparently the owner of the beach his boat was stranded on wanted Murphy's boat removed from it. Go figure.

They had an appointment with the police before either one of them even stirred out from under the covers, and Murphy was on the phone to a towing company and left a message at the coffee shop for Crystal before he even started his first cup of tea.

The sky that morning was still a bit cloudy and gray as he looked out through his french doors while he sipped at his mug, but thankfully nothing appeared to be coming out of the sky, and the wind didn't seem to be blowing any stronger than any other day on the island. Apart from the debris all over the beach and what waited for them in town, it looked like any other day, and Murphy tried to take comfort from that. Even now, many hours after the worst of their ordeal was over, he was still shaken and jittery. He'd almost lost someone he loved for the second time in his life, and when that hit him fully, he was probably going to lose it for a day or two, maybe more.

You're going to be fine. You're stronger than you think. You didn't lose anything because *of that.*

Felix's voice was comforting this time, an old and trusted friend in his head, and he tried to let the truth of it settle in his gut. He needed his morning run more than ever, but his body wasn't up to it. He'd probably end up sick if he ran in the damp and the cold today. He'd try a little meditation later, after they took care of their obligations, and maybe he'd be up for a run tomorrow.

"Good morning," Aiden mumbled around a yawn as he reached for the teakettle and poured water into the mug Murphy left for him. They'd run out of the coffee Aiden had brought over, and Murphy assumed its replacement was still in the back of Aiden's Jeep, but Aiden hadn't complained about it yet. Perhaps Murphy had converted him.

"Morning."

Aiden shuffled over to where he stood and snuggled up behind him. His hair was wet from his shower, but he was still wearing the clothes Murphy had given him the night before.

"I gotta run to my parents' place to get some clothes before we head out."

"You heard me on the phone?"

"Yeah," Aiden grumbled. "They couldn't have waited 'til a decent hour to call? I mean, really. Don't they know what we went through?"

Murphy chuckled even as he nodded in agreement. "No rest for the wicked."

"We didn't even get a chance to be wicked yet," Aiden whined, but he was smiling slightly when Murphy turned to see his face.

"You get your things and drink your tea, and I'll hop in the shower and get dressed. The sooner we get this over with, the sooner we can hibernate for a few days."

Aiden nodded, gave him a peck on the lips, and gulped down half of his cup of probably scalding tea before he went out Murphy's front door.

After a stop at the coffee shop where Crystal hugged the life out of Aiden while another employee scowled at them, they climbed back into Murphy's Mini and headed to the police station where they got some news.

Working in cooperation, the state police and the Coast Guard had eventually found the stolen boat and Bob in the water, but no sign of Richard. The officer at the station had Aiden confirm again that Richard hadn't been wearing a life vest the last time anyone saw him, and Murphy repeat that he'd "seen" Richard in the water.

"The search will continue, on the water and along the coast, but...."

The officer shrugged, and Murphy had a pretty clear sense that they didn't expect to find Richard alive.

"So what happens with Bob?" Aiden asked.

"He was taken to a hospital in Hyannis. I think they plan to keep him there a couple of days before he's arraigned. He'll have a guard on him, though. He's not going anywhere. You'll most likely have to testify at some point, provided he's found fit to stand trial, but after what you've said about his state of mental health, he might never get that far."

Murphy didn't want either of them to have to worry about that now, so he shook the man's hand and said, "Thank you officer," effectively ending the conversation.

Aiden was quiet and pensive as they pulled out of the parking lot and headed for the marina.

"They've probably called Adam by now and the cops who were working the original case," Aiden said after a few minutes.

"Probably."

"I wonder what he's going to say."

Murphy didn't bother to answer that. He must have been grumpy because he was tired, otherwise Aiden talking about his ex wouldn't have rankled as much as it did.

Luckily his boat seemed none the worse for their adventure. He'd have it checked out thoroughly when they pulled it out of the water for winter storage, but it seemed to have made it through the storm okay. The marina was a mess, but apparently the guy he'd paid to pick the boat up hadn't had much trouble getting it back to the slip once they'd towed it from where Murphy beached it. Murphy was actually smiling a bit as he climbed out of the boat and handed Aiden's cell back to him.

"Come on. Let's go get your Jeep and go home. Hopefully most of the food in the back didn't spoil, and we can hide out from the world for a few days like we'd originally planned."

Aiden's answering smile was distracted as he fiddled with his phone.

"Shit. Adam's called like ten times since yesterday. Weird. Half of them were before we even talked to the police. He left messages."

Small pulses of surprise and anxiety trembled through the air as Aiden held his phone to his ear, and Murphy waited with rising concern.

"He's in Cambridge with his boyfriend's family. He called because he was worried about the storm, and something about Jay having a bad feeling—whatever that means," Aiden supplied distractedly before he tapped the screen on his phone and put it back to his ear. A pulse of chagrin, then concern, and another round of anxiety followed soon after, but before Murphy needed to shake it out of him, Aiden started relating the new message. "The police called Jay and told them what happened, and now Adam wants to come down and meet us. He seems really upset."

As Aiden's emotions started to spike, Murphy decided that probably wasn't the best idea. They'd both been through a lot, and Aiden didn't need the added stress right now. But when he related his feelings, Aiden shook his head.

"They're here *now*, in Massachusetts, and he said he really needed to talk to me."

"It can wait. We can even take a trip out to Ohio if we have to. This doesn't have to happen now."

Aiden's stubborn chin jutted out as a hint of anger added to the mix. "I can handle it."

Murphy pressed his lips together. He was making Aiden more upset by arguing with him. If he were honest with himself, no matter how much he longed to help, the decision wasn't actually his to make. Aiden wasn't a child, and he wouldn't appreciate Murphy treating him like one.

"I know you can, but you shouldn't have to." He sighed and rubbed his temple. "Look, if you want to do it, I'll be there. But if you don't want to, we can do it another time."

Aiden's posture relaxed, and after blowing out a long breath, he stuffed his phone in his pocket and stepped in close. "I know you're just trying to look out for me. You know I love you, right?"

Soothed by his words and the drop in intensity of the emotions he was radiating, Murphy hugged him. "I love you too."

"I don't *want* to do this, but I think I need to. He's only a few hours away, and maybe it's better this way… if I get it all over at the same time, like ripping off a bandage."

"I just don't want you to overdo it. You went through something terrifying yesterday… so did I. It wouldn't be wrong of you to need a little time to recover before you deal with something else traumatic."

Aiden worried his lower lip as a deep V formed between his eyebrows. "You don't have to be there if it's too much, Murphy. I know you're tired, and God knows you've done enough for me already."

"That's not what I'm saying."

"I know. I just think I really should get this over with, but if it's too much for you right now, I want you to know I'll understand."

Murphy shook his head and pulled him into his arms. "I'm not going anywhere… and if you think I'm going to let you meet with your ex-boyfriend without me there, you're crazy."

Aiden laughed and kissed him. They hugged a little more before he gave Aiden one last squeeze, and then led the way back up the dock to his car.

On the way home, they picked up Aiden's Jeep, using a spare key since Aiden's set had disappeared during his ordeal. The cold front brought in by the storm had kept the groceries in the back of the Jeep fairly well preserved, so they didn't have to throw anything away when they got home.

While Murphy made some dinner, Aiden went out on the back deck to make arrangements with his ex.

"They're coming down tomorrow," Aiden said when he came back inside.

"You okay?"

"Yeah. I think so. I probably won't sleep tonight, but I guess we'll see."

"Well, at least with them coming here, I can kick them out if you get too upset," he said.

He was only half joking.

"Oh yeah?" Aiden smirked as he sauntered over to him. "You gonna go all butch on me and toss them out on their ears?"

"Maybe."

"That's hot."

Murphy rolled his eyes as he removed his apron and set two plates of sausage marinara and penne on the breakfast bar.

Aiden's grin faded a little as he plunked down on one of the bar stools. "It should be fine. I didn't get the impression on the phone that Adam's coming down here to yell at me. Though the guilty part of me kind of wishes he would… but that isn't really Adam's style. I suppose that would be another reason why we weren't good for each other."

Murphy frowned as he took the seat next to him. "I'm not a yeller either, you know."

"Yeah. But that's different," Aiden replied around a mouth full of penne. "You're a talker. You talk stuff out. You know what I'm feeling almost before I do, and you're okay with dealing with emotions. Adam's more the stoic, silent, broody type, hard to make mad, but when he is, he doesn't know what to do with it, and he stays mad for a long time… unlike me. I get mad at the drop of a hat, but it goes away pretty fast… as long as I don't, you know, lose it."

Murphy put a hand on his arm and squeezed. "You'll get there, especially now that you know bottling it up is the wrong answer. Getting mad isn't a bad thing, as long as you work through it as it comes and nobody gets hurt."

"Yeah. I hope so. They're going to be here at noon tomorrow, so I guess I'll find out if I've made any progress, won't I?"

Murphy gave him an encouraging smile. "We can always go out to the beach if you think we need to."

Aiden laughed as his cheeks reddened. "I'm not worried so much about losing my cool, so to speak, with Adam. I think I feel enough guilt that I doubt I could get mad at him at this point. Jay might be another issue, though. Something about the guy set me off, and I'm not sure it was only because of Adam. It was weird."

"Well I still have the fire extinguisher under the sink, and we always have the beach as a backup plan, so we should be okay."

Aiden set his fork down and turned his seat to face Murphy. His expression was so serious Murphy put his fork down and gave him his full attention.

"I don't know if I've said it enough, but I can't tell you how grateful I am to have you. I mean it, Murphy. You're the first person I've ever met who gets me, who doesn't judge me or tell me to be someone else."

"I told you. I happen to like who you are. Aiden, you have a right to be who you are, the same as everyone else in this world. As long as you're not hurting anyone, you have every right to feel whatever it is you feel."

"I have hurt people."

"I know, so have I. Most people don't make it through life without hurting someone. What matters is you're trying not to, and you do the best you can to fix what you broke."

"Tomorrow?"

"Tomorrow," Murphy agreed.

CHAPTER 22

AIDEN WOKE from a fitful sleep a little after dawn. His prediction had been pretty spot on. He tossed and turned most of the night, until Murphy pinned him down and blew the top of his head off with one of his stellar blowjobs. Murphy had jerked himself while he'd done it, looking so fucking hot, Aiden hadn't lasted long at all, and he'd finally passed out for a while after that.

Turning his head, he watched Murphy sleep in the weak morning light. It looked like the sun was actually going to shine today, and Aiden was looking forward to soaking in as much of it as he could. Today was going to be hard enough without the sky being gray and gloomy.

When he couldn't sit still anymore, Aiden slipped out of bed and padded to the kitchen. With a sense of profound relief, he set the kettle on the stove and opened the bag of coffee he'd bought what felt like a lifetime ago. As the rich smell filled his nose, he moaned in anticipation. Murphy's tea wasn't bad, but nothing beat that first cup of smoky, dark, heavenly goodness. Before the whistle on the kettle could wake Murphy up, Aiden pulled it off the burner and poured water in the coffee press he'd brought over from his parents'.

He stepped out on the back deck with his steaming mug and carefully closed the doors behind him. Basking in the early morning sunshine, he sipped from his mug and tried to let go of some of the tension that had been building since he'd listened to those voice mail messages. Adam had cared enough to be worried about him. That was a good sign.

But it only made the guilt worse. Adam was such a good guy, and Aiden had hurt him, like *physically* hurt him and his boyfriend, but that wasn't all. He'd destroyed something sacred to Adam. He hadn't meant to, but that didn't change the fact that it was gone forever because of him. Why would Adam even give a shit about him now that he knew?

Aiden hugged himself and stared out at the waves. He hadn't drowned. Maybe that meant something… beyond the fact that Murphy was wonderful and incredible. Maybe it meant there was something he needed to do with his life, maybe more than just learning to live with what he could do, learning to control it so he didn't hurt anyone else.

"You okay?" Murphy asked from behind him.

Aiden looked over his shoulder and smiled. Murphy was in his robe. He hadn't even gotten his tea yet, and he was poking his head out to check on him.

"Mostly. I'll come in so you don't freeze."

Seeming content with Aiden's answer for now, Murphy shuffled to the stove and started some more water boiling. Aiden set his mug down and snuggled him from behind, content not to talk about anything. He'd be doing enough talking in a few hours.

The rest of the morning was fairly quiet. Murphy cooked them breakfast after he'd woken up a little. They each took a shower and got dressed. Though Aiden was sure Murphy could feel his anxiety, he didn't press conversation. They'd pretty much said all that needed to be said before.

They were sitting together on the couch when Aiden felt Murphy tense beside him.

"They're here," Murphy said.

Aiden hadn't heard anything, but maybe Murphy's spidey senses were tingling or something. They both got up and moved to the door, but it wasn't until Aiden had his hand on the handle that he felt the pulse of agitation along his skin. That same weirdness he'd felt that horrible day in Adam's yard. When he felt Murphy's hand on his shoulder, he took a deep breath and let it out. The strange feeling eased as their connection hummed though his body.

I can handle this.

He opened the door, and Adam and Jay stood looking uncomfortable on Murphy's front porch steps.

"Hey," Aiden said stupidly.

"Hey," Adam replied.

Now that Aiden had a little distance—and now that he had Murphy—he was able to look at them as a couple a little more objectively. They were a study in contrasts. Adam was broad and barrel-chested with thick legs and arms, while Jay was tall and rangy. Adam had dark hair and eyes and tanned skin, and Jay was pale pretty much all over, pale hair, pale blue eyes, pale skin. But Aiden had that same sense he'd had before, that they somehow fit together perfectly. It had driven him crazy less than two months ago, but now he found he was happy for Adam.

That's progress isn't it?

Murphy squeezed his shoulder, reading Aiden and offering his silent support as he'd done so many times before, and Aiden melted in gratitude.

"Adam, Jay, this is Murphy. This is his house."

Adam reached out a hand for Murphy to shake first. "It's nice to meet you, Murphy."

"Likewise," Jay said.

The energy flowing from Murphy's hand on him shifted as he shook hands with each man and all of them started in surprise, like they'd been shocked.

Murphy was the first to recover. "Uh, maybe we should all go inside."

"Sounds like a good idea," Adam replied.

Aiden tried to sit in the living room with the other three men, but found he was too agitated to stay still. He wasn't exactly feeling angry, like he had before when he was near Jay, but he wasn't calm either.

"Can I get either of you something to drink?" Murphy asked into the thick silence in the room.

"No, thank you. We stopped for breakfast on the way down, and I think Adam's still a little green from the ferry ride," Jay said with a chuckle.

"Seasick?" Murphy asked.

"I like to keep my feet on solid ground," Adam said with a wry smile, and Aiden felt himself smiling despite the tension in the room.

"Well, if I can't offer you refreshment, I guess that just leaves us with getting down to the reason you're here," Murphy said. He glanced at Aiden and gave him an encouraging smile.

"Yeah. I guess it does," Adam replied. "First, will you tell us what happened with Bob? The police said you were kidnapped? And he took you out on the water in that storm?"

Aiden stepped closer and took a breath before he started. "Yeah, but it wasn't just Bob. There was this guy, Richard. He's been on the island for a couple weeks, I guess. He talked to me in the coffee shop I like to go to."

"He showed up at a meeting I went to as well," Murphy added as he came to stand beside Aiden and took his hand.

Adam's gaze dropped to their joined hands and his eyebrows rose a little, but he kept silent and motioned for them to go on.

"Anyway," Aiden continued. "I don't know what happened, but they jumped me, and the next thing I know I'm tied up and they're arguing about what to do with me. I passed out again after that, and I woke up on a boat, and they were crazy enough to head out into the storm."

Aiden's chest started to feel tight as the memories surfaced, and Murphy took over telling the story from his end. Both Adam and Jay listened intently, their mouths hanging open and their eyes wide by the time Murphy finished. Aiden was impressed he and Murphy had managed to tell the tale without revealing anything about their gifts or their suspicions about Richard's. He wasn't sure why he'd left that part out, particularly since it would probably come up later, but Murphy in his usual perceptive way had caught on and had continued in the same vein.

"So Bob followed you all the way from Ohio?"

"I don't know. I mean, I guess he must have. But Bob wasn't the one in charge, not really. Richard was. It was all kind of confusing, but I think Richard was using Bob to get to me… actually to get to you guys too."

"How do you mean?" Jay asked.

When Murphy squeezed his hand in reassurance again, Aiden finally noticed Jay hadn't let go of Adam's hand since they'd been there, and it started him thinking maybe they had more in common than he thought.

"You remember in the shop Bob was spouting off all kinds of craziness?" At their nods, he continued. "Well, I wasn't exactly paying much attention then because—hello, gun—but when they had me tied up in that house, I got an earful of the crazy. Bob kept going on about how they should just kill me and go back for one of you two to take back to show "the others" as proof."

Murphy stepped in front of him, his faced deeply etched with concern. "You didn't tell me that part."

Aiden squeezed his hand and shrugged. "We didn't really get into details yet. I figured you were upset enough already."

Apparently not caring that they had an audience, Murphy pulled him into a hug. "I guess it's better I didn't know that out on the water, otherwise I might've drowned the little bastard."

Murphy's growl sent a shiver down Aiden's spine—the good kind—and despite the fact that sweet, calm, together Murphy was talking homicide, Aiden felt kind of gushy and warm inside. But they needed to finish this conversation before he could have Murphy alone, so he kissed Murphy on the cheek and withdrew.

Adam was watching them with a sort of bemused smile on his face, and Aiden could feel his cheeks heat. He cleared his throat and said, "Anyway, Richard wouldn't let him kill me, and he ended up throwing Bob overboard when we were out on the water."

"But if he didn't want to 'rid the world of the demon spawn' or whatever, why did this Richard guy take you?" Jay asked.

Now came the part where Aiden had to make a decision. How much did he tell? How much did Adam and Jay already know? Aiden knew Adam had to be special in some way. He'd felt it when they were together. Aiden had never wanted to talk about it, but Adam had tried a few times. That had to mean he knew something.

Instead of answering, he asked, "Why do you think Bob targeted you in the first place, Jay? Why did he call you a demon?"

Adam and Jay exchanged glances, and Adam shrugged.

"I could say he thought I was one of them there ho-mo-sexual-types," Jay said with a heavy faux-country accent. "But that wouldn't exactly be the truth. There's no way he would've known I was gay when he first tried to kidnap me, we hadn't exactly shared a lot of personal information."

Jay grimaced, and they exchanged another look while Adam patted his knee. The room fell silent, and this time Murphy was the one to step in.

"Let me make this easier on all of us. We all appear to be dancing around something that I have a feeling we don't need to. I may not be sensitive in the same way Lola is. I may not be able to tell exactly what the nature is of what I'm feeling, but Adam, Jay, I can sense your energy from here, and if either of you are sensitive, you should most likely be able to feel ours too. I think this Bob guy might be like Lola. He might be able to sense it too."

After a stunned silence, Aiden leaned close to Murphy and asked, "You can feel something from them?"

Murphy smiled wryly, "Let's just say, if Lola were here, she'd probably be weeping with joy and dancing a jig around us. There's power here, and it's not just ours. I feel… I don't know, a sense of flux, like water sloshing in a bowl, testing the limits of its confinement. If it could settle… who knows?"

"Bob did sense something," Jay said from behind them. "The things he said, he couldn't have known otherwise."

Murphy nodded. "He sensed you because you're a projector of some kind, like Aiden… only *not* like Aiden, different."

Jay's eyes widened as he looked between the two of them. "You can sense that?"

Both Adam and Jay sat forward in their seats a little, looking tense, but Murphy was already moving into soothing mode.

"A little. Like I said, I can't tell the nature of what I feel. I'm receptive but mostly for emotions. I'm empathic. I don't always understand some of the energy I perceive, especially if it's not emotional energy. All I know is, Aiden was hard to miss." He threw Aiden a gentle smile before turning back to them. "You, Jay, project a kind of buzzing energy, but it isn't heavily flavored with emotion. Adam, if I were to take a guess, is receptive like me, since I feel more a pull than a push from him… if that makes any sense. To help me come to terms with and control what I am, the friend I mentioned earlier, Lola, taught me a little about this stuff, but obviously not enough."

Aiden had the distinct feeling Murphy and Jay were about to geek out on esoterica and psychic chitchat. Adam looked a bit like his eyes were about to glaze over. Before they went off on a tangent, and before Aiden could lose his nerve, he moved closer to Adam. "Bob felt something in me too, something Richard wanted… something I might've been glad to give up under different circumstances, especially after what happened to you and Jay."

He worried his lower lip and wrapped his arms around himself while he waited for Adam to respond.

"Are you going to tell me what happened?" Adam asked while Jay and Murphy watched.

"I told you. It was my fault. I lost control and started the fire. I'm sorry. I know it's not enough, but I am sorry." His palms were sweating, and he felt like he was going to vibrate out of his skin. He wished Murphy was still holding his hand, but he needed to face up to this part on his own.

"You haven't told me how you started the fire and how it got out of control," Adam said, much more gently than Aiden deserved.

With a quick glance at Murphy, Aiden reached into the box of kindling on the hearth and pulled out a small twig. Snapping off a piece that would fit in the palm of his hand, he held it out and released a spark of the energy that was almost back to full strength. The tiny bit of wood burst into flame, and Adam and Jay's jaws dropped.

"Obviously what happened in the woods was much bigger," he said with a forced chuckle. "I went up there to do something stupid and childish, but I never thought anyone would get hurt… only I lost control. I was so mad and hurt and afraid, the spray can blew up, like Bob's gun did in the shop, only worse, *much* worse."

"Jesus," Jay said as he and Adam exchanged another look.

"And then you ran?" Adam asked, some of his disappointment and anger finally showing through in his voice.

Aiden hung his head. "Yes."

Murphy got up then and moved to stand next to him. Aiden drew in a shaky breath and continued, "I tried to take it back in, tried to put it out, but I was only making it worse. By the time I got back to where I'd parked my Jeep, I could already hear sirens, so I just took off."

He hazarded a glance at Adam, but the heavy knit brows and frown on Adam's face weren't exactly encouraging. After an interminable silence, Adam finally sighed and sat back against the couch cushions. "Do you have control of it now?"

Aiden glanced at Murphy before answering. "I'm getting there. Murphy's helping me… along with his friend Lola. I've been staying here, away from people—and, you know, large stretches of forest—trying to figure it out." He drew in another shaky breath and faced Adam squarely. "Do you hate me?"

To his relief Adam shook his head. "I don't hate you, Aiden. I may not completely understand how you could lose control like that and just run away after, but I don't hate you either. I'm going to need some time to absorb all this."

"I'm sorry," Aiden repeated, feeling like he had a lifetime of apologies to make.

"I almost lost Jay to that fire. He got hurt trying to help put it out. You should apologize to him too."

Well, no one said this was going to be easy.

Aiden turned to look at Jay. "I'm sorry, Jay. I heard you were in a coma, but I didn't know what happened."

Jay's lips twisted wryly as he took Adam's hand. "It's complicated. But I accept your apology for myself. It might take a while for me to forgive what you did to Adam, though."

Aiden nodded. "Fair enough."

"We've done some work up there already, but we'll be doing some planting in the spring," Adam said. "You should come and help out."

That sounded like sheer torture, but Aiden nodded. He owed them at least that much. "Okay. Let me know."

"Okay."

Murphy blessedly broke the awkward silence that followed. "Would you like to stay for lunch?"

Adam shook his head. "Jay wants to show me the island before we head back to his parents' house."

"I'm sorry you have to see it in such a mess," Murphy said lightly.

Oddly, Jay actually started blushing. "We, uh, didn't get out much yesterday or the day before, because of the, uh, storm. We need to spend some more time visiting with my parents as well. It only rained here, but it snowed in Cambridge, so we'll enjoy the island while we're here, despite the mess."

Adam was blushing too, under his tan, and Aiden looked back and forth between the two of them in confusion until Adam cleared his throat and stood up.

"We should probably get going."

Murphy stepped over to shake Jay's hand, leaving Aiden to say good-bye to Adam.

"I'm sorry, Adam," Aiden said again. "I'm sorry we never talked about this stuff before. I'm sorry for what happened, for what a spazz I was… I'm sorry for a lot of things. But, I'm glad you're happy now."

"Do you mind if we go outside for a minute?"

Murphy's face was unreadable when Aiden glanced over to him, so Aiden nodded and led the way to the back porch. Once there, Adam paused for a second seeming to collect his thoughts.

"Murphy seems like a nice guy."

"He is."

"I guess you and he are…."

Adam left the sentence hanging, and Aiden smiled and nodded. "Yeah, we are."

"And he obviously knows all about what happened and what you can do."

"He does."

"We should have talked long before this. This thing you can do, it's incredible. If I had known, maybe I could have helped."

"I know, and I'm sorry for that too. It's not exactly something I let get around, and Richard and Bob have only added another reason for me not to. But I knew there was something special about you too. I just didn't want to think about it. This thing I have, it's screwed up most of my life."

"But you can with Murphy?"

"Yeah. Well, you heard him in there. He knows what I'm feeling before I do. I *can't* hide anything from him."

Adam chuckled. "I could see where that might be a blessing and a curse."

Aiden relaxed enough to return the laugh. "Yeah. It takes some getting used to."

"It was nice to be able to talk face-to-face. I knew there was more to the story than what you said on the phone. And I do understand that it wasn't on purpose. It's just going to take a while for my heart to catch up to my head. Gaia meant a lot to me, and you're the reason she's gone. It may take some time for me to make peace with that and forgive."

The brief moment of levity gone, Aiden's smile fell away.

"I understand."

Adam nodded. "Are you sure this won't happen again?"

"Not a hundred percent, no. But I'm working on it. Murphy helps, a lot."

Adam's concerned expression turned skeptical as he glanced through the glass doors to where Jay and Murphy waited in the living room.

"He's quiet, but he's stronger than he looks," Aiden defended feeling a slight flare of temper. "He braved fucking hurricane-force winds to save me. Believe me. He's more than a match for me."

Adam lifted his hands in surrender and smiled. "Okay, okay. I'll take your word for it. I'm glad he was there for you, and you weren't hurt. I never wanted you to be hurt… not by me or anyone else."

"I know. It was my fault. I know that now…. I actually knew it then too, I just didn't want to admit it to myself."

"Give me a little time, and I'll give you some time, and then we'll see what happens."

"Yeah. Okay."

Aiden didn't exactly feel the sense of closure he was hoping for, but he was a hell of a lot closer than he had been. And when Adam lifted his arms, Aiden accepted the hug with a profound sense of relief. He could feel both Murphy and Jay watching him though so he didn't hold on as long as he might've wanted, and they stepped back inside only a few short moments later.

"Thank you for having us," Adam said to Murphy. "Because of the two of you, Bob is finally in custody. Even if that guy, Richard, was the real mastermind or whatever, I still feel better knowing Bob isn't out there anymore and can't hurt Jay. I'll sleep better, anyway."

"Yeah. Me too," Aiden replied when Murphy remained strangely silent.

Murphy moved closer to Aiden before reaching out to shake Adam's hand. "And perhaps, sometime down the road, we can all talk more about this thing we seem to have in common. The woman I mentioned, Lola, might have some insight for us, if you're willing to talk to her."

Jay perked up at that and nodded enthusiastically. "I'd like to meet her. Maybe the next time we come up to visit with my parents."

Murphy's smile warmed as he nodded at Jay. "I'm sure she'd be overjoyed."

Aiden hung back by the fireplace while Murphy saw their guests out. When he heard the door close, he let out a long, relieved breath.

It was over. He'd done it.

He'd faced Adam and confessed, and he hadn't lost his cool or broken down. He hadn't burned anything, and he'd actually managed to hold an adult conversation. He was getting better.

"Are you okay?" Murphy asked as soon as he came back.

"Yeah."

"You're sure?"

Something in Murphy's voice made him look up. "Yeah?"

"Good."

Murphy grabbed his hand and dragged him toward the hallway that led to the bedrooms. When they reached his bedroom, Murphy tore off his own sweater and T-shirt before dragging Aiden's polo over his head. After tossing it somewhere over his shoulder, Murphy pressed his thigh between Aiden's legs and pushed him back against the closed door. He stopped with his lips less than an inch away from Aiden's and said, "If you're really sure...."

Aiden swallowed, suddenly short of breath.

This is new.

"I'm really sure," he panted.

The grin Murphy gave him was pure sin. "Then I want my ten out of ten now. I don't want to wait."

Aiden's breath hitched. "You mean you want to—"

"Be inside you? Make love to you? Yes. That's what I want."

As Murphy yanked Aiden's belt free and pushed his jeans and underwear down his legs, he said, "I know he's just your ex. I know you had some things to work through with him on your own. But you're mine now, and I didn't like him that close to you."

Apparently Aiden had missed a few things while he was wrapped up in his own issues. Throughout their entire conversation, he'd had no idea Murphy was even a little uncomfortable, let alone jealous. He really needed to pay more attention. Though this growly, possessive and demanding side of Murphy was something he definitely wouldn't mind seeing again.

When Aiden was naked, Murphy manhandled him over to the bed and shoved him onto the mattress. With just that little bit Aiden was rock hard and ready for anything Murphy wanted. He felt like he could come just from the hot and possessive way Murphy's eyes raked over him.

"Don't move," Murphy ordered and Aiden's cock pulsed and jumped against his belly.

Oh, hell yeah.

After being tense and jittery all morning Aiden was definitely ready for someone else to take charge. He dropped a hand to stroke his aching cock while Murphy undid his own belt, but Murphy stopped with his pants half unbuttoned and shook his head. "No. No touching yourself. That's mine."

Aiden grinned and locked his fingers behind his head. As long as Murphy hurried, he was happy to take orders.

When Murphy was gloriously naked, he crawled onto the bed and draped himself on top of him. Aiden's cock was pressed into the groove of Murphy's hip, and Aiden took advantage of it and pumped his hips as Murphy laid claim to his mouth. Aiden moaned into the harshness of Murphy's kiss, his body's reaction to it surprisingly strong. Precome leaked from his cock as he panted and writhed, painting Murphy's skin with it.

He was lost in the heat of Murphy's body and the strength of the hands holding him down until Murphy suddenly drew back and manhandled him onto his stomach. Aiden buried his face in the pillows and arched his ass in the air when he heard the click of the cap to the lube. He spread his thighs and arched again as a slick thumb circled his entrance. When the first finger slid inside, he pushed back, wanting it to go deeper. He hadn't lied when he'd said he preferred to top most of the time, but he had a feeling Murphy was going to make him reconsider before the night was over.

He fisted the pillows as a second finger breached him and curved to hit his prostate. His cock throbbed and another drop of precome dribbled onto the sheets.

"Are you ready?" Murphy asked.

"God, yes."

Murphy withdrew his fingers and the bed dipped as he positioned himself behind Aiden. Aiden heard the crinkle of the condom wrapper. Then a few moments later, Murphy's smooth, elegant hands traced his back from his shoulders to his ass in one long, sensuous glide before spreading Aiden's cheeks. Aiden was shaking with want as he felt Murphy's crown circle his entrance before pressing forward.

With a long moan, Aiden forced himself to relax, and Murphy slid all the way home in one deep stroke. Aiden panted through the stretch and then pushed back signaling for Murphy to move.

Despite his earlier roughness, Murphy fucked gently at first. The hand locked on the back of his neck and the other on his hip left no doubt as to who was running this particular show, and Aiden reveled in it.

"Let go."

Murphy's order mirrored his own need so perfectly Aiden thought he might have imagined it until Murphy spoke again.

"I've got you. Let go."

Aiden moaned as heat pulsed and writhed inside him. He wasn't back to full strength yet, but he was close. He wanted to let go so bad, but he was afraid.

The hand on the back of his neck released, and a moment later Murphy's arm circled his chest. Murphy pulled, and Aiden allowed Murphy to lift him until he was crouched with his ass on Murphy's lap, Murphy's cock still buried deep inside him.

"I've got you," Murphy repeated as he flexed his hips. His other arm circled Aiden's waist and held him close as the hum of energy between them increased. Aiden felt a surge of cool moist air against his skin, and he nearly cried as he let loose some of the energy inside him.

"Yes," Murphy hissed a moment before he pushed Aiden forward again and began fucking him harder.

Aiden fisted the sheets and held on as Murphy pegged his gland and the room filled with the ebb and flow of their energies. His orgasm hit out of the blue. He cried out in surprise and white-hot pleasure and shot over Murphy's sheets. Murphy fucked him through several aftershocks before succumbing to his own climax. He shouted his own release, and then collapsed onto the mattress next to Aiden while they both fought to catch their breath.

"Wow," Aiden said appreciatively, and Murphy laughed.

"Uh-huh."

Aiden rolled toward him and propped himself up on an elbow. Murphy's black and silver hair was plastered to his head, and his entire body glistened with moisture. Aiden grinned and traced a finger across Murphy's chest, watching steam rise in its wake.

"You know, if this is what happens, you're not exactly discouraging me from making you jealous."

Murphy grumbled something unintelligible, took Aiden's hand, and drew Aiden with him as he rolled onto his side. His breathing evened out almost at once, and Aiden smiled, pressed a tender kiss to the back of Murphy's neck and closed his eyes.

After today, Aiden hoped he'd had his fill of drama for a while—at least the off-stage kind anyway. He had a lot of work to do and still some fences to mend, but Murphy had given him hope that it was at least possible.

I don't know who up there loved me enough to send me Murphy, but thank you. I'll take care of him, as long as he'll let me. I promise.

How the story started:

Air and Earth

By Rowan McAllister

When absentminded video game developer Jay Thurson impulsively follows his intuition westward, he never expects his rideshare to turn out to be a gun-toting madman. In an act of desperation, Jay turns for help to the gift he's long neglected and feared, and leaps from the moving car on a dark and deserted back country road.

Running for his life leads him to the doorstep of Adam Grauwacke, a roadside nursery owner and sometime vegetable farmer, whose affinity for the earth goes far beyond having a green thumb. Adam's world is ordered and predictable, dependable and safe, but despite having his dream farm and business, he's always felt something is missing. When he welcomes Jay into his home, life seems to click for both men, and together they explore their gifts and their attraction.

But harmony has no value if it is easily won, and a crazed gunman and a volatile ex might be their end if Jay and Adam can't learn to trust the strength of their bond.

http://www.dreamspinnerpress.com

ROWAN MCALLISTER is a woman who doesn't so much create as recreate, taking things ignored and overlooked and hopefully making them into something magical and mortal. She believes it's all in how you look at it. In addition to a continuing love affair with words, she creates art out of fabric, metal, wood, stone, and any other interesting scraps of life she can get her hands on. Everything is simply one perspective change and a little bit of effort away from becoming a work of art that is both beautiful and functional. She lives in the woods, on the very edge of suburbia—where civilization drops off and nature takes over—sharing her home with her patient, loving, and grounded husband, her super sweet hairball of cat, and a mythological beast masquerading as a dog. Her chosen family is made up of a madcap collection of people from many different walks of life, all of whom act as her muses in so many ways, and she would be lost without them.

E-mail: rowanmcallister10@gmail.com
Facebook: https://www.facebook.com/rowanmcallister10
Twitter: https://twitter.com/RowanMcallister

Don't miss

Lost in the Outcome

By Rowan McAllister

When Nathan Seward wakes up in a cheap hotel with a stranger, unable to remember the night before, unscrupulous plots and clandestine schemes are the furthest thing from his mind. True, he's in Houston to bid on his biggest contract yet, one that will put his software development company on the map, but he's the underdog at the table, not one of the big players. Unfortunately someone out there sees him as a threat and isn't above drugging and blackmailing him to put him out of the running. Luckily for Nathan, the man in bed next to him couldn't be further removed from the corporate world.

Tim Conrad is scraping the bottom of the barrel. He left college during his freshman year to take care of his dying mother, and life and lack of money prevented him going back. Now twenty-seven, his dreams are long buried, and he's scraping by with dead-end jobs and couch surfing because he can't afford a place of his own.

As Nathan tries to run damage control and figure out what the hell happened to him, he and Tim discover a connection neither was looking for, as well as dreams they've both forgotten.

http://www.dreamspinnerpress.com

Don't miss

My Only Sunshine

By Rowan McAllister

Tanner Wallis is nearly at the end of his rope the night Mason Seidel finds him lying next to the mangled body of a cow on the back pastures of the Seidel family's Wyoming ranch. Recently out of the hospital after he and his boyfriend were brutally beaten, Tanner is jobless, homeless, and almost penniless. His desperate hope is that Mason will believe he's innocent of the senseless crime and give him a place to heal, both physically and emotionally, until he can get on his feet again.

But Mason already has enough on his plate. He's only been back on the ranch a few months, ten years after his father kicked him out for being gay, and only because his sister begged him to come help after the man's disabling stroke. With all his responsibilities—running the struggling ranch and keeping his sister and father off his back—Mason can't really afford the distraction Tanner represents. But he can't just abandon the attractive young man either. There's trouble in spades on the ranch, but if they face it together, Mason and Tanner might find a future with a little sunshine.

http://www.dreamspinnerpress.com

http://www.dreamspinnerpress.com

http://www.dreamspinnerpress.com

FOR MORE
OF THE
BEST
GAY
ROMANCE

DREAMSPINNER
PRESS
dreamspinnerpress.com